The Magician's Ruins
By Alexa Padgett

This is a work of fiction. The events and characters described herein are imaginary and are not intended to refer to specific places or living persons. The opinions expressed in this manuscript are solely the opinions of thoughts of the author. The author has represented and warranted full ownership and/or legal right to publish all the material in this book.

Edited by Nancy Cassidy and Nicole Pomeroy
Cover design: Clarissa Yeo

For Mom and Dad. Mom, your enthusiasm is infectious.

CHAPTER ONE

I killed my mother last night.

A bit of an exaggeration, but not much. She asked me to let her die so I could inherit her magic. The lesson I learned? I hated martyrdom. Too many good people died being martyrs.

My mom was one of them, but her death meant more than saving me. All her life, she strived to find a lasting peace, a way to save her world, my world, from the whims of gods like Coyote and even Shakola, from demons like Jaguar and his Kachina brethren. Her life's work wouldn't be destroyed like her body I'd left in Waldo Canyon. I intended to balance the Elements, find that peace even if it meant kicking additional godly ass in the process. And I planned to find my best friend Layla. *Rápido.* No matter how many more gods, Kachina, demons, or other scary and as-yet-unknown obstacles I faced along the way.

I huddled closer to Zeke's back as we sped over the unforgiving asphalt, drawing ever-closer to our people's ancient lands. This was the best place to start our search for Layla, and if we were lucky, the fourth Halfling. We needed all four of the Four to fulfill the prophecy and rebalance the world.

I snorted. Luck didn't smile on us—not with the gods all but blotting out our continued existence through their cloud of demon-spawn minions.

We intended to check Coyote's den, a short distance from Zeke's house. Or, what used to be Zeke's house. Yep. Destroyed it, too, along with my mom's house, my car, and just about every tenet I'd believed in.

Busy didn't come close to describing these last few days.

"Incoming," Zeke yelled.

"You have got to be kidding," I muttered. I'd liked my world a whole lot more when I couldn't see these creatures…and when they didn't want me dead.

A cross between Jabba the Hutt and a horned lizard, this new demon, one I hadn't seen before, scuttled across the juniper-strewn landscape faster than a

1

train. The distance between us closed rapidly. Too rapidly.

Zeke skidded his motorcycle to a halt and leapt from the seat. "Stay back."

As if. Just a few days ago, I wasn't prepared to take on demons and otherworldly *coñazos*. Thankfully, that Echo María Ruiz was dead and buried under thousands of pounds of demonic ash and a few hefty regrets.

There had been big changes in my life, sure. None was so big as learning I was a spirit seducer. Correction, *the* spirit seducer. As in the only one. My role in the Prophecy of the Four, and especially the fact I was more god than not, had angered someone of importance. Someone other than Coyote. While the trickster god created many problems, not least of which was losing the two people closest to me in the world, he was now banished to Tokpella, the first and most hellish of Hisatsinom worlds. Now, some unknown god was targeting me, sending demons to kill me.

The approaching beast oozed evil. His body *dripped* goo. And it stood taller than most of the buildings in Santa Fe. Zeke raced across the grayish dirt, meeting the demon with both his spear and sword before I managed to climb off the bike, mindful of my hurt knee, and adjusted my sling. The spear entered the beast's belly while Zeke kept running up its body, yanking out his spear and slamming it and his sword into the thick hide.

"Don't let the glop touch you," Zeke yelled.

"You okay?" I called back.

He didn't answer. Concern at Zeke's grunted curse propelled me forward.

Holy *frijoles*. The beast possessed a whip-fast tail and five-foot long front legs tipped with foot-long claws.

"Yeah," Zeke called back.

The monster whipped back toward Zeke, hissing. It slammed its spiked, mace-like tail into the ground, reared, and slashed at Zeke with its front claws.

A large blob slid off the lizard's back and hit the ground a few inches from my bare feet. The ground sizzled and began to smoke. I immediately regretted the loss of my flip-flops in the last battle, although they probably wouldn't have been much help. Three of the demon's eyes locked onto me.

Zeke disappeared from my line of sight as soon as the beast tried to disembowel him. He ended up on the demon's other side, where the other three of its six eyes were located.

"*So* not how I intended this year to go," I muttered. Rent an apartment, maybe date a guy. Those were my simple, normal plans until I learned my father was the Hisatsinom creator god. My parentage wasn't helping with my desire to be normal. Within hours of the revelation, I'd been attacked, mauled, and nearly raped. And that was all before Coyote used my mom's magic to power the largest dust storm to ever cross the New Mexican desert, killing her, losing Layla, and destroying thousands of acres of land in an already-delicate ecosystem.

I might have overcompensated—hey, it was my first time fighting a god—when I flooded Waldo Canyon. On a positive note, all the water washed Coyote into a lower plane of existence. Unfortunately, the god disappeared down the whirlpool before I asked him where he sent Layla.

I needed to work on my Q&A skills. More importantly, I needed to find Layla if we were ever going to have a chance to right the balance in the world. I'd broken one of the sacred tablets Sotuk, my father and the Hisatsinom creator god, expressly forbade breaking. So far, there'd been earthquakes, fires, and lots of other chaos now unleashed on the world, and it was going to get worse.

But none of that was as pressing at the moment as avoiding the huge, pearlescent claws that lashed toward me, barely missing me. This demon was worse than the last.

"Ow," Zeke groaned. A moment later, he said, "The stuff coming off is poisonous."

I didn't answer because a big glop was headed in my direction. I managed to duck the goo and freeze the snotty substance before it hit my skin. Did I mention I was Water? The element that went along with Zeke's Earth. I wasn't actually made from H_2O any more than a normal person, but with my powers I controlled all liquids in my vicinity. Rather, I was *learning* to control liquids. That included Jabba the Great Horned Slimeball's goo.

"Zeke?"

I darted around the giant lizard's blobby middle section. A wound covered most of Zeke's left arm, fire engine–red, like a burn. I yelped, falling back when the lizard swiped his massive tail at me.

"Honani?" I called, gripping my pendant. Honani, the spectral guardian assigned by my father years ago, was my liaison with the spirits who'd helped me force Coyote back down into the first world. The clay's coolness warmed past the point of bearable and I let go.

Much as I didn't want to bother my spirits so soon after their battle with Coyote, I needed some support.

"Here." My spectral guardian appeared in front of me. "That demon fouls the air." Honani's haughty nose flared in disgust.

"The goo is toxic. To humans—or so Zeke said. Would you swirl around the demon's eyes? We need the demon dizzy or at least distracted."

"On it," he said, and gave a sharp salute. Yuck, I didn't want him treating me like Fearless Leader or—oooh!—Wonder Woman!

Nope. Still too weird.

Within a moment, twenty or so of the spirits zoomed from my pendant. They gathered around the demon's warty, dome-shaped head. Its many eyes swiveled, each trying to latch onto one of the spirits.

While the lizard staggered, trying to focus on the myriad targets, I focused my energy on everything liquid inside its huge form. Just in time for the beast to try to slam its slimy, warty body into my side. Stumbling backward, my leg—the one I'd hurt in my fight with Coyote—buckled with a whimper-inducing pop.

I moaned out all the air I had in my lungs as the hot place in my mind, where my power seemed to dwell, lashed out. The lizard lurched, gurgling. It's three eyes focused on my face, malevolence pouring off its body, and it stiffened as the ice formed a film over the demon's organs. *Yes*. I focused on the exterior and pulled moisture from inside the demon and the air around it.

Zeke threw his spear into the demon's chest. He stepped back and made a running leap, this one much higher than the fence in his yard he'd cleared with such ease. Like a basketball player about to dunk high. With an easy grab, Zeke yanked the spear free. The demon's front legs gave and it collapsed onto its bleeding chest. Zeke slammed the gore-covered tip of his spear into one of the monster's eyes.

My spirits congregated in front of me. I dipped my head as I placed my hand over my heart. "Thank you."

They babbled, excitement clear in their tone, as they returned to the plane on the other side of my pendant.

"How's the leg?" Zeke asked.

"I'm fine." Mostly.

The lizard tried to whip its tail forward, but its insides and oozy exterior froze, the ice stiffening before forming a thick, impenetrable crust. Zeke spun, leapt over the pus-covered appendage, and drove his spear into another eye. That blade, whatever it was, slid with ease through the icy exterior.

The demon tried to stand on its legs, but teetered and crashed onto its scaly chin. Toward me, of course. I yelped as I backpedaled again, grimacing at the soreness in both my legs. Already, the beast's legs crumbled into piles of white dust—the same as the other demons we'd faced and beaten.

The only positive in this mess I called my life was Zeke. He remained steadfast, battling demons for me. Thanks to him, I fought demons in the Fourth World instead of in Tokpella—or wherever gods sent dead, naughty Halflings.

I'd spent the last hour of our ride—before the demon leapt from a dusty patch of juniper-covered mesa into our path—pondering Zeke's parentage. He hadn't told me who his parents were and didn't want to. Each time we came close to the subject, shame wafted off him. Of course, his reaction only made me more curious, but he had to want to tell me. So far, his secret remained tucked inside his recalcitrant self.

Odd though our relationship was, I trusted Zeke more than I trusted anyone. Even my mother, who'd lied to me my whole life. Or Layla, who'd kept her own counsel not just from me but from Zeke and my mother. Thanks to Zeke, the gods who wanted to use my power to take over the world hadn't been successful. Yet.

There'd be others who would try. Coyote was simply the first in a long line of greedy *idiotas* who refused to be satisfied with the gifts and power they already had.

Shakola, the cloud goddess, sat at the top of the list of power-hungry haters. If no one else stepped forward to try to rip my magic from my resistant body, she would always be there, trying to kill me or at least trying to steal my powers. And Zeke.

Yeah, I was part of a love triangle. Well, sort of. Any way I viewed it, there was too much going on emotionally for a girl who'd never been on a date.

Honani knelt his amorphous form at my side. He placed his freezing hands under my elbows and yanked. He lacked a skeleton, so the lift was like a huge gust of controlled wind. I sucked in a breath but managed to keep weight on my leg. Not broken, then. Good.

Zeke finished cleaning his spear tip. The New Mexican wind carried away more of the demon's dust as Zeke's boots crunched over what was left of the lizard's ashy skeleton.

I grabbed his arm, my concern greater than the tingle shooting through my hands when I touched his skin. He jerked once before his muscles bunched in an effort to remain still.

"Gross." I wrinkled my nose. "All the skin is gone."

"Not all. I'll put some salve on it," he said.

"You need to wear your armor."

"No time to put it on."

"Make time."

He smiled, probably because he found my concern silly. "Not being dead took precedence."

"Thanks for finishing the slimeball," I said.

He grimaced at his arm. "You're the one who destroyed it, but believe me, I enjoyed stabbing it a few times."

Much as I wanted to help him, I wasn't versed in healing magic. That had to change. Not only for Zeke, but for myself. In the last few days, I'd broken multiple bones and my throat was nearly crushed twice.

I released his wrist. He stowed his weapons before fishing the stainless-steel salve container from his pocket. He dipped into the yellow cream, then dabbed his ointment-covered fingers over his flailed skin, his arm steady as sweat streamed from his forehead.

He stored the salve and patted my helmeted head with his right hand. "You were smart to keep this on."

I settled on the motorcycle, unwilling to tell him that, during the moments of terror when the demon rose up out of the landscape, I'd forgotten I was still wearing it. I wrapped my good arm around Zeke's waist as he turned on the engine.

When he pulled back onto the highway, dust swirled around us and I tensed, readying myself for another attack. When one didn't come, Zeke opened the throttle, revving the bike to dizzying speed.

Shifting my aching leg, I leaned my helmeted head against Zeke's back. My thigh didn't throb with the same teeth-grinding pain I'd awakened to after my fight with Coyote, but speed-healing created its own kind of discomfort. My sling caught on Zeke's back as I hugged him tighter and he sped into the midmorning sun.

I wiggled my fingers, smiling when pain didn't lance up my arm. Score a point for magic. Quick-healing was a fabulous benefit, but one I'd trade for a way to contact Layla. Much as Zeke didn't want me to, I couldn't resist the impulse to reach out to her mentally.

So far, Layla remained silent. Scarily so. Like my mom, she was a constant in my life, someone I talked to every day, if not more often. With both of them gone, I was lost.

We topped another hill, but the city still shimmered in the distance. I couldn't talk to Zeke over the shriek of the wind, which left me with too much time to think. I missed my mom. Until this week, not a day—sometimes not an hour—went by without my seeing her, talking to her.

Grief swept over me, pulling me down. To think the week started as any other: me, a migraine-impaired college graduate wishing almost desperately for adventure. *Ten cuidado con lo que deseas*—careful what you wish for—and all that.

At least I had Zeke.

I shifted in my seat, fighting against another yawn. The bike's vibrations crept up my legs, making me sleepy. As my eyes slid shut, we hit a pothole. I gritted my teeth as my leg bounced. The bone may not be broken, but the constant jarring hurt. The bike's wheel bounced through another pothole, and I bit back a moan. I was beginning to hate traveling this way.

In case Zeke's insane fighting capabilities weren't enough—and they were—he could open portals between places on earth. Our previous mode of transport was fast and reliable. Useful, even. Well, until I broke the tablet. The cascading effect from the chaos I unleashed made magic transport unwise, and definitely unsafe, and we were left with mundane methods of travel.

Zeke changed highways, zipping up the I-40 with a casual recklessness I didn't like. We were on a motorcycle. He needed to show respect for the lack of steel caging and air bags.

The familiar Albuquerque buildings slid past, nothing more than an eye-wateringly dizzy rainbow of earth-toned stucco. Zeke slowed his motorcycle, easing onto the exit ramp. He pulled into a gas station.

I released my one-handed grip on his waist and he slid from the bike with an enviable nonchalance. Thanks to my aching legs, I staggered off the bike like a drunken floozy. Zeke reached out and caught me beneath my elbow of my good arm, but the deep cut on one of my knees split open again. Huh. My body's healing capabilities must have left the simple skinned knee for later, deciding the crushed bones were a more important issue.

Not that I disagreed with such logic.

Once assured my legs held my weight, Zeke flipped open the gas cap on his Thunderbird. He tipped his head toward the convenience store.

"Wanna grab us something to eat and drink? Easy stuff for the road." He handed me a thick wad of bills. "Keep the rest. For emergencies." He turned back to the pump, tension in both his face and those broad shoulders. He still wasn't wearing his cotton-and-leather armor. A tattoo peeked out from the sleeve of his T-shirt. A wide leather cuff, tooled with intricate symbols—ancient runes, maybe?—circled his left arm.

He glanced back at his motorcycle, where his spear and sword were strapped in a hard case. He flicked his eyes toward me, frustration and something else bubbling up within their depths.

"We can't hang around, Echo. There will be more."

"Aren't there always?" I asked. The noise he made was between a grunt and an exasperated sigh. He became grumpier after every fight.

Entering the bathroom, I gaped at the image in the scratched mirror. No one ever looked great in the bad lighting and cheap, distorted glass of a gas station restroom, but I wasn't prepared for my reflection. Small cuts covered most of my exposed skin—and there was a lot of it. The top third of my right breast hung out of my tattered tank top, which, along with my ratty hair and jeans, made it look like I'd been through a battle. Because I had. Not that I planned to tell anyone else about my escapades last night. Who'd believe me?

One of the cuts disappeared as I watched, leaving fresh, dewy skin. Zeke had applied some miracle ointment earlier this morning, alleviating the worst of my problems—like fractured bones and a semi-crushed windpipe. But the ointment didn't help the dirt clinging to my lashes and splashed across my nose. My bottom lip was cracked open and bloody, and my tangled, unruly hair was worse than my younger niece's had gotten during her two-month combing moratorium. I took the sling off my arm and twisted my shoulder, flexing my wrist. Sweet! Full range of motion.

I washed my face, neck, and as much of me as possible, and did my best to flatten my hair. Straightening my shoulders, I opened the bathroom door and headed for the convenience shelves. Time to pull up my big Halfling panties and face whatever came at us next. The hours of travel between our current location, in the middle of New Mexico, and Arizona left a lot of miles for more demons to find us.

The one truism I'd learned this week: trust little and expect to die.

I pulled a couple of the liter bottles of water from the cooler lining the back wall of the store and headed down the aisles, scanning the shelves for something to eat that wouldn't petrify my insides with preservatives. As weird as some of my mom's meals were, I loved how eating whole, nourishing foods made my body feel. I didn't want to dilute or poison my newfound powers with synthetic foodlike substances. I pulled a few packs of dusty nuts from the bottom rack. Around the next corner, I found a wrinkled apple and three unripe bananas. Eschewing the apple, I grabbed the bananas and piled my meager choices on the counter.

"How do, missy?" the attendant asked, drawing out the sibilance in the word.

My neck prickled, but I managed a weak smile and tried not to stare at the space where his front teeth should be. I failed. His tongue darted out to lick his lips as his smile widened to a leer.

Ew. Puh-lease. His tongue shot forward again, and I stared too long. Was it…no way…his tongue was forked.

I inhaled as quietly as possible as I began the ritual of gathering the magical energy deep in my mind. My pendant heated, and I resisted the urge to grab it.

"Nine forty-seven," he said.

Yep, he definitely hissed the s's. I placed the money on the counter, pleased my hands weren't shaking. I shoved the rest of the bills in my pocket before grabbing my purchases. I kept a tight rein on the white-hot center in my head.

"You forgot your change."

"Keep it," I said, almost to the door.

"No can do, daughter of Sotuk."

I stopped, my breath locked in my chest. Zeke's Thunderbird no longer sat near the closest gas pump. A large pile of dust blew across the dull, charcoal tarmac.

Good thing I'd pulled up my Halfling panties, because I was on my own.

CHAPTER TWO

Something big and hard slammed into the tiles behind me. *Trust little and expect to die.* Where the hell was Zeke?

The dust outside was white. Another demon? If so, Zeke killed it. And then moved his motorcycle.

I put my hand on the metal door handle as the air rippled. I squinted against the sun and, in the reflection on the door, made out a large, reddish blob moving in my direction. I darted to the right as the black-and-coral face slammed into the glass.

The broken shards tinkled as it hit the floor.

I sidestepped the thick, scaly body, wishing I'd left the building when I had the chance. The demon positioned himself between the exit and me.

This one was a coral snake, but much bigger than a normal one. His body was at least fifteen feet long.

The demon turned its black eyes toward me, his tongue popping out to smell for my location, no doubt.

Arizona coral snake. Great. I'd categorized what planned to eat me.

Up until this moment, I'd liked snakes; when I was little, I'd wind the bull snakes from my yard around my neck and pretend they were feather boas. Weird? Of course. Pretty much summed up everything about me. The snakes hadn't minded, and I'd enjoyed feeling pretty.

I measured the distance to the bathrooms. My gaze flicked back to the snake in time to see his body coil tight. It blurred with speed, but I managed to dive to the side—right into one of those metal shelves. More glass shattered. I stood, dazed, in time to see the snake yank his head out of the drink coolers about eight feet past me. I ran toward the front door.

The snake lashed out his tail, the tip catching me in the forehead. I spun away, my back to the bathroom as I focused on the demon. His narrow black head wove back and forth like his cobra cousin. I didn't look in his obsidian-black eyes, just in case this one could spit.

The snake's body bunched, preparing for its next attack. Its huge mouth peeled back, showing its two-foot-long fangs and forked tongue flicking out of his unhinged jaw.

I focused all my energy on the snake, willing the demon to die. My magic sizzled over its scales, leaving icy tracks between where it managed to infiltrate small holes in the snake's thick hide.

I gripped the metal shelf behind me and eased my aching body upright. My head hurt. Again.

"My dad is the god who created you," I wheezed. "You should show more respect to his daughter." At the next hiss, I narrowed my eyes. "I don't like being slapped around by reptiles."

The air shifted behind me and I whirled, dropping into a crouch. My instincts were improving. I felt an arm wrap around my waist and shifted my gaze to find Zeke twisting the five-foot-long spear into the demon and yanking back as he pulled me into his side. Relief mixed with irritation as he drove his arm forward a second time, stabbing the demon once again.

"Hey! I totally had this one!" I complained, but I let myself lean into him, unwilling to admit how happy I was he hadn't left me.

"Stabbing is faster than freezing it. Unless you want to eat some of it?" Zeke's right eyebrow rose high in question.

"I'm not eating that thing. It's all frost-bitten and demonic." I clamped my hand over my mouth. I sucked some air through my nose. Bad idea. Evil smelled horrible.

"And now it's dead. C'mon, time to go. I'm sure it called in reinforcements."

I bent down and collected my purchases before stepping away from the carcass. I needed air.

Zeke grabbed my hand and led me out the back. The front door remained useless, thanks to the giant snake carcass lying in front of the entrance.

"You weren't out front."

"No, I'd moved the bike. Good thing, too. They came from the other side of the gas pumps and would have ambushed me."

I shivered. "The demon was a man."

"No, it projected a human form," Zeke said.

"Like Jaguar did with Layla?"

"He can actually *be* a man. Thanks to Pahana."

I shook my head in both frustration and confusion. "Another god. He's on the MIA list, too. Isn't he?"

"We don't want him showing up, Echo."

"Why?"

Zeke pressed his lips together into a thin line. I tugged on my hair, needing an outlet for dealing with Zeke and his odd insistence of not sharing information.

"Fine. I won't ask any more about the god. Will you tell me how Jaguar can be a man and a demon?"

"Think of a spectrum. Some beings have so little magic, they cannot access it or utilize it. Others, like you, are so imbued with power, it kind of seeps out whether you know how to use it or not."

"Not that you've helped me learn how," I snapped.

"In what spare time, Echo?" Zeke responded.

Annoyingly, he made a good point.

"The snake came after me. Called me daughter of Sotuk."

"Hmm. Well, you did great. Not many girls can handle the sight of a fifteen-feet-long venomous snake."

"You mean not many *people* can handle it?"

"Only you, baby." He tweaked my nose. I shouldn't find this type of playfulness cute. Maybe relief he hadn't left me made me stupid. His smile fell as he met my eyes. "I don't know anyone, male, female, god, or demon, who would be able to handle the situations you've been thrown in as well as you have."

My face flamed and I bit my cheek to keep from grinning like the fool he'd turned me into. "At least the snake wasn't as gross as the lizard earlier. And I guess it goes without saying I prefer the nonvenomous variety of all things out to eat me."

Zeke helped me over some boxes and shoved open the metal door, its hinges screaming in protest.

"How did you get in without us hearing you?"

"You were pretty busy dry-icing the snake. Cool trick, by the way."

I handed him one of the waters and a bag of walnuts. He uncapped the water and chugged as he led me to the Thunderbird.

"I like it. What happens to them when they die? Are they all like Jaguar and turn to dust?"

"They don't die. Not like humans, whose souls go back to the underworld, awaiting rebirth. The demons don't need to be reborn, they regenerate, which has been easier without Masau guarding the *sipapus*."

"How is it fair we need the god of the dead to guard death's doors but only for demons?" I complained. My mom and Honani were dead. Well and truly. I didn't even know what happened to my mother's body when she gave me her essence. I never retrieved her body from the sandy plane after I managed to shove Coyote into the ground. My stomach turned over, rejecting the water I'd managed to swallow.

"People stay dead." I sighed.

Zeke turned away, shoving his spear back into its travel case. He placed his sword across the handlebars of the motorcycle and secured it with a special strap. I frowned at this easy access to weapons. My life was so messed up.

"People have souls that need to be housed in an appropriate form. Demons do not. From the dust they break up into, my guess is they aren't even made of the same chemicals and molecules we are—and it explains why they look different each time I've run into one. Makes sense they'd have a different life cycle."

"No, it doesn't."

"Fairness, or at least our cultural understanding of it, doesn't mesh well with the Hisatsinom version. If we have the chance, we'll talk to your father about your concerns."

"Yeah, right. His disappearance started this whole train of events."

Zeke's lips firmed into a grimace. "No, my birth did that."

I wanted to reach up, grip his wrist in comfort, but he wouldn't accept my sympathy. I cleared my throat and made the sarcastic comeback Layla would appreciate. "I'll put it on the to-do list right below 'don't die' and 'save the gods from oblivion.'"

He shook his head but some of the rigidity left his face. "Helmet on," he said.

After clucking over the newest injury on my forehead, Zeke placed the helmet back on my head and buckled it. His eyes darkened and his nostrils flared as his gaze flicked down to where my coat flapped open, revealing my mostly-bare breast. At least the bruises were nearly gone now—thank you, salve—so the exposed flesh had returned to its original firm and supple state.

"You need some clothes that actually do their job."

He hopped on the bike. I wrapped my arms around his waist again as I struggled to sling my aching leg over the seat. Thunderbirds were not made for short women.

He gunned the engine. We wove through the light traffic on the side streets for a couple miles before he pulled up in front of a Walmart.

"It's not fancy, I know, but we can grab some more food and a couple changes of clothes for you," he said with a shrug. His gray T-shirt inched up enough to flash another chunk of his tattoo. The intricate black ink flared and swirled in a native design. If his shirt would rise a little more I'd be able to make out enough to…I tipped my head but he slid off the bike, his face fierce as he swept the area in a quick but thorough glance. He slung his spear bag over his shoulder; his sword wasn't at his waist nor between the handlebars.

"We need to get in and out fast. I want to put some distance between us and this last attack."

"So we're going to Coyote's camp?" I asked.

"Yep."

My plan, the one I'd talked over with Layla before Coyote's storm side-tracked me, had been similar. Hopefully we'd find some clues that would improve our chances of finding Layla. My heart stuttered with a fresh wave of grief.

Zeke touched my cheek. "Let's go, Echo." His voice softened, like he understood the pain leeching from my heart, filling up my chest. "We need to keep moving. More demons will come."

I buttoned up my leather coat before heading into the building, postponing my questions about the tat, the cuff, and his mercurial moods. I'd ask later, if we were still alive.

I winced when a rock dug into the sensitive skin in front of my foot's arch. Zeke wrapped his arm around my waist, holding me off the ground with ease. Show off.

"I forgot you lost your shoes. First stop. Messed up feet cause all kinds of problems." Concern washed over his features.

The Walmart greeter stood right inside the large glass doors. At least seventy, her thinning hair was jet black and she squinted, deepening her wrinkles. She smiled at Zeke, but disdain dripped from her curling lips when she saw me.

I peeled the banana I'd purchased at the gas station, taking a big bite while looking at her. Her wrinkles quivered in anger. I waved. And since Zeke still held me off the ground, I wrapped my legs around his waist.

Her glare turned deadly. Zeke's shoulders shook. Nuh uh. He was *not* laughing at me.

I unraveled myself from his body, wincing when my knee started bleeding again. He yanked out one of the carts while I tutted over my bloody knee.

"Want me to put you in the cart? You won't have to walk."

"You're ridiculous. My little show was for the greeter. She wanted to knock me down and run off with you." I took another bite of my banana as Zeke pushed the cart forward with great purpose. Even shopping was a mission—in and out as fast and efficiently as possible.

"I'm not interested. She's not my type."

"You have a type?" I asked.

"Yep."

"Do I know her?" And because I couldn't keep my mouth shut, I asked, "Is she tall and gorgeous in a godly way with flowing dark hair and scary, all-white eyes?"

"No," Zeke scoffed. "I'm not into goddesses."

"Huh." That was the best response I could form.

He inhaled deeply, his head dropping forward. "I've only ever wanted one woman."

"Who is this amazingness of womanhood?" Sarcastic? Maybe. Covering my disappointment and hurt took precedence over kindness.

He turned, his dark eyes glared into mine. "Even when your mother made me feel like I'd never be good enough, even then I only ever wanted you. Doesn't mean we get to be together."

Not what I was expecting. At all. "I don't understand."

"Leave it alone, Echo."

Seriously? Don't ask questions about the bombshell he just dropped? He gripped the cart, pushing it forward. I wrapped my fingers around his wrist and he stopped, his eyes filled with defeat. We stood there, in the entrance to the Walmart, assessing each other. He'd given me honesty. I sucked in a deep breath.

"I was sixteen the first time I dreamt of you. The connection's been strong since that very first night."

Zeke nodded.

"I didn't know you were real, and I used to cry myself to sleep, not knowing if I wanted to see you that night or forget you so I could try a real relationship."

"I'm glad for our connection," he said.

I tilted my head. "Are you? I don't know what you expect from me, and the hot-and-cold routine you've trotted out so far confuses me."

He stepped back, putting both physical and emotional distance between us. "I might want us to be more, but I can't *offer* more than my protection."

"Why?"

"You'll understand soon enough."

"That's a terrible answer," I stuttered. "Does this have something to do with the prophecy?"

"Yes." He pushed the cart and I hurried to catch up. "You need some clothes. And a shower. The greeter probably thought you were homeless."

Guess our moment of sharing had passed. Much as I wanted to gnash my teeth in frustration, I'd wait and worm more information out of him later.

"I can't help that you came out of the dust storm looking as squeaky clean as an Abercrombie model."

"Abercrombie." Zeke shook his head. "That's just mean."

"It's not nice to point out I look like I was in a fistfight. You know, 'cause I was. With a bunch of Kachina and a god. Then a ginormous lizard and a snake. Don't these beings know you aren't supposed to hit girls?" I finished my banana. Crap. Until I found a trash can, I was stuck with the peel.

"You kicked Coyote's ass, and I wouldn't want to be in a Walmart with anyone but you. Find some socks. Now."

"You're as bossy as Layla," I said on a sigh.

"We're on a time table. Not like demons aren't trying to kill Layla as we speak."

I scowled as I hurried forward. "Besides checking out Coyote's camp, do we have a plan?"

Zeke's mouth twisted in a grimace. I'd been afraid of that. Without the god to tell us where Layla was, we'd waste precious time looking.

I pulled some white tube socks off the rack. There were three in the pack. I had to resist the urge to choose the six-pack for a dollar more. Stores like this one fed my basest deal-seeking instinct.

"Coming?" Zeke called over his shoulder. He'd pushed the cart a little farther on and into the shoe section on the other side of the clothes racks. I had to run to catch up, the banana peel flapping against my jean-clad thigh. I skidded on the linoleum, and a middle-aged man puckered his mouth in disgust as he looked me over.

"We went to a party, and he lost my shoes," I said, gesturing at Zeke.

"Only after you tried to run off with the other guy," Zeke said, pulling a pair of sneakers off the shelf as he shook his head.

The older dude walked away, glancing back at me and muttering something about me stealing food and the youth today.

"Now he thinks I'm a hoodlum and a slut," I huffed. I slammed the sneakers back on the shelf. "Those are ugly and way too big. I want boots." I pulled out a pair and grabbed the socks from the cart. Where was a trash can when you needed one? I set the peel gingerly on the narrow bench next to me. Zeke snorted, annoyance filling the space between us. He grabbed the peel and stuffed the flapping banana skin on a shelf.

"Hey! I need to dispose of that properly."

"You need to focus on the shoes so we can skedaddle," Zeke snapped. His gaze flicked between me and the other shoppers. "Don't you dare pick it up."

"You're littering." I said the words nice and slow.

"Put on the boots. We're moving on." Zeke pulled the second boot from the box and began threading the laces through with efficient, angry movements. "No distractions. We need to find Layla and figure out where the Fourth of the Four is. My guess is his parent hid him away."

"I don't think so. I think his guardian was killed when the tablet was stolen. I think the Fourth was kidnapped and doesn't know he's half god. Kinda like me."

Zeke rubbed the back of his neck, his eyes never leaving my face. "Makes sense."

"No need to sound so surprised." I pulled on the second boot he'd practically thrown at me, spending more time than necessary tying it.

"I'm not surprised you made a valid point. I'm surprised Masau didn't mention the possibility to me. Or that I didn't think of it on my own. We know the tablet disappeared over twenty years ago. So the kid may be a little younger than you."

"Or he might be older than you," I pointed out. "His age isn't as important. Between early and mid-twenties. Some god or goddess"—my thoughts veered back to my least favorite cloud deity—"took the tablet and started the chain of events. So the deity became aware of the Four before the others. Like when you went to live with Masau." I tied the lace into a thick bow. "What I can't figure out is why that deity—the one who found out about us—kept quiet for so long."

I finished lacing the boots and stood, shimmying so my jeans pooled over the thick, faux leather surrounding my ankle. I hated when my pant legs rode up and material bunched around my waist.

His eyes slid up my entire body. He cleared his throat. "There has to be a bigger payout then."

My teeth sank into my bottom lip as I stared at him. His frustration was palpable. "Than killing us off you mean?"

"Yeah, than that." His eyes narrowed as he leaned forward. His voice was much quieter when he said, "Which means we're being played by someone."

I'd leaned in to touch his arm, but he straightened, his feet braced apart. While he hadn't touched me, the suddenness of the movement caused me to stumble back into the shoe boxes behind me. Zeke shook his head. "What else do you need?"

What the hell just happened? Something important he didn't want to share. I scowled at his back as he pushed the cart out of the shoe section, but I pushed off the racks and followed.

#

We exited the store lighter on cash, but I, at least, was much better prepared for the rest of our trip. The best purchase of the day? Clean underwear. Amazing what being on the run from angry gods will do for a girl's outlook.

My quick bathroom pit stop included a change into clean clothes, and I hummed with pleasure at the added protection of a bra under my new fitted tee. I'd taken advantage of the hairbrush I'd had to sprint across the store to buy, and even braided my filthy hair. I wouldn't win any style contests, but I was comfortable and fully clothed.

When I met Zeke out front, he laughed when I pulled out my new bottle of sunscreen and slathered the lotion all over my face and neck. I squirted more sunscreen into my hand and began dabbing it on Zeke's lean cheeks.

"Sunburn is nothing to joke about," I said, trying to keep the mood light.

"Besides the sting, those kinds of burns age you. Saggy skin is not attractive."

Surprise flashed in his eyes, but he stood still as I worked my way up his forehead before smoothing my hands over his chin and down his neck. His Adam's apple bobbed slowly.

"All done," I chirped. Stepping back, I slid my plastic sunglasses from the crown of my head down to my nose. I walked toward his motorcycle, needing a moment to remind my brain of our friends-only status.

"I didn't count on how much I'd like talking with you," he said. "Spending time with you."

He touched my shoulder, effectively halting my progress. Turning me toward him, he slipped his hand into my loose braid and tilted my head. A couple of high school boys nearby whistled. Zeke stepped out of my space and ran his fingers through his hair and over his face.

"Demons trying to kill you. That's where I need to focus. You aren't going to die because I'm distracted." Steel slid into his voice and his shoulders set, ready for battle. "I made a blood-vow to Masau. I won't take advantage of you."

His eyes hardened and he glared at the boys, who spun away from us, bumping into each other in their newfound rush to get into the store. I smiled, and he frowned, probably shocked by the quick change of emotions sliding across my face. I was, too.

"What the hell are you so happy about?" he growled.

"I see the problem. You won't take advantage of me."

Zeke stared at me, before running his hands through his hair. "Exactly." He paused for a moment. "How come I'm sure we didn't just agree to the same thing?"

I laughed. "We'll talk about it again, later. Not in a Walmart parking lot."

He turned from me, a muscle clenching in his jaw. "Virginity's prized among the Hisatsinom, Echo. Especially for us."

"Kissing is a long way from—"

"Us, together, is commitment. Lifelong commitment."

I cringed. Great. Now he was going to be even weirder about sex than I was. My mom had been vigilant to the point of fanaticism about my virginity, and

I hadn't understood why. Since both Jaguar and Coyote had tried to rape my magic from me, I'd decided the act itself must create a joining of powers, no matter how unwilling one of the participants. If both parties cared for the other, then the commitment wouldn't be an issue. My mother spent twenty-one years alone rather than sleep with another man after my father left. I looked at Zeke. Maybe I understood why.

"We can discuss my virginity and why it's important to you later," I said, waving my hand. "Those snakes aren't the only creepy-crawlies hanging out nearby. I'm shocked we've gone an hour without being attacked." I swung my leg over the bike and waited for him to join me. He tilted his head back and shook it from side to side.

"You're a pain in the ass," he grumbled. "Like, a seriously big one for being all tiny."

I wasn't looking at him anymore.

"Are you listening to me? We're not pursuing this, Echo."

I scrambled off the motorcycle's seat, basically tackling him to the ground. "Get down!"

CHAPTER THREE

The large, dark being moving toward us neither crept nor crawled. It flew. The bird, much bigger than me, landed in a flutter of black wings a few feet from Zeke, the Thunderbird between the large raven and us. Fluttering its wings one more time, the feathered creature turned one gleaming black eye toward me.

"Do not seek to freeze me as you did Coral Snake," he said. His voice, while harsh and sharp, was clear and deep. "There is much to tell and little time."

I blinked and he'd morphed into a warrior. He wore armor similar to Zeke's, with buckskin pants. Wait, when had Zeke's armor come back? He'd been in a gray T-shirt a moment ago.

Zeke stood from the unceremonious heap we'd been tangled in when I shoved him down. He eased himself between the god and me. "Raven," he said with a slight bow.

"Do the humans see you?" I asked.

"Not unless I want them to, sugar." He grinned, showing off a very attractive dimple in his right cheek. His black hair brushed his shoulders and his dark eyes flitted around endlessly. I stoked the hot center in my head, just in case. He glared, his nostrils flaring.

"No need for magic, young Lakin," the god snapped.

"What's a Lakin?" I asked.

"I am. That's my last name." Zeke palmed his knife and Raven squawked.

"Must I restrain you?" Raven asked. He rolled his eyes for dramatic effect. A thick wall slammed down, surrounding Zeke and me in a small cocoon. Zeke lowered his blade, but his eyes remained wary.

Ezekiel Lakin. Weird I hadn't known his last name until now—stranger still, I hadn't thought to ask. Maybe I was too trusting or just plain stupid. Probably both.

"I'm here to help you, but I expect equal respect and restraint from all this ridiculous violence," Raven said, squirming like he was preening his feathers. "I'd forgotten how cold spring is in New Mexico. My lady friends and I tend to spend our time in southern Arizona. Tucson is most pleasant this time of year. The ladies, they wear tiny bikinis . . . when they wear anything." Raven grinned, and Zeke stiffened, his lips curled up into a snarl.

"Calm down, boy. I am not here to seduce your Echo. Not today." His dark eyes focused on me as he hummed deep in his throat. "Though you are beautiful enough to duel for." He sent Zeke a narrow glance. "The man who takes your innocence will benefit greatly. If well played, you both will."

"What Echo and I do isn't your concern."

Raven raised a thick, black brow. "What would I know, being thousands of years old and a watcher of those around me?"

"What do you want?" I asked.

"Mmm. Much." His dark eyes traversed my figure once more before settling on Zeke's face. He tilted his head like a crow contemplating something shiny. "Her virginity is a prize until it's no longer available."

I cleared my throat. "Hello, standing right here." I waved a little, feeling vaguely more ridiculous for having done so, but the entire conversation was off the rails. "You're here to give us information?"

Raven's dark eyes bored into mine. He dipped his head, his jaw opening and closing rapidly. "Forgive me, daughter of Sotuk. I must ask you both to relax and listen."

"We're listening," I said. Not like we had much choice while stuck in an invisible bubble.

"Excellent!" Raven clapped his hands together. "I must first thank you for removing Coyote from my domain." Raven bowed to me. "He has long been my greatest annoyance. For this reason, I offer my assistance."

"And what exactly would your help be?" Zeke asked. He still held his knife, blade out.

"Ah! I'd act as an intermediary between the gods and you two," Raven beamed, his black eyes twinkling.

"Meaning you have a message from them?" I asked. "Or yourself?"

"Indeed, beautiful Echo. Indeed. This is from me and others, as many of us do not desire to see this world end any more than you do." Raven fluttered his arms and dipped his head. He managed to settle himself. "We desire to tread no farther along this dark, dangerous path. You need to find the Magician. He knows much about the one you seek."

"The one I seek?" I asked. "I seek more than one person. And I want more than a name of someone who might help me, especially if you're going to string this out."

Raven smiled at us but his eyes continued to dart around. "The problem is larger than you yet know. Heed this, too. Masau weakens the longer he remains jailed, leaving the doors between the underworld and the Fourth World unguarded and easily opened again."

I gaped at him. "He's *jailed*? That's why he left the portals unattended?"

Raven frowned. "He would never leave the *sipapus* unattended by choice, leaving the gateways between the worlds unsealed. Hence, the resurgence of Jaguar and the other Kachina so ready to gnaw on your tender skin."

I shuddered. Kachina were more powerful than other demons, more cunning and adaptable.

"We haven't seen a Kachina since trouncing Coyote," I said.

"For the moment, you will not, for you—what did you say?—trounced the Kachina back to Tokpella with Coyote. But those demons will not stay there, not with the *sipapus* open and you still living."

"So seal them," Zeke said.

Raven dipped his head. "I have not the inclination."

I snorted. "You mean you can't."

"No one owns guardianship or holds the keys. Powerful though you might be, you cannot seal so many portals yourself, beautiful Echo, even with Zeke's magic to help you. Coyote was aware of this, much to your detriment. But he is not your greatest concern. The other has proven falser and far more treacherous." Raven met Zeke's eyes for a long stare that seemed to pass some important message. Then he shook his arms and dipped his head. "Hurry to the Ridge Ruin."

"The one in Arizona?" Zeke asked.

Raven dipped his head. "I know not of another. I shall endeavor to meet you there."

"Why not just tell us everything you know now?" I asked. My exasperation mixed with Zeke's, and I practically yelled at the god.

"I cannot. This is a battle I may offer to aid but cannot fight."

"Can't or won't?" Zeke asked.

Raven's arms fluttered. "Perhaps both. I have no wish to end up like Masau or Coyote. If you handle this task well, I will be able to help more. Time to part. Enemies approach."

"Wait!" I said. "Do you know anything about Layla?"

"Visit the Magician," Raven said. "He will tell you much about your friend as well as the Fourth, should you not discover more on your way." He cocked his head, as though listening to someone else.

Fear for Layla warred with the joy at discovering her continued existence. I needed Layla, the only connection to my past. Already, memories slipped from me, and I feared I'd never return to Santa Fe; be a housebound but carefree girl who'd known only protection and love. During those years, Layla had been my friend—my only friend. I needed her. She'd mourn my mother's loss with me.

"Go now. Your time unmolested is at end." With a quick twist of his body that seemed to blur the lines between physics and chemistry, Raven bolted into the sky. The invisible shield lasted another second, then it, too, dissolved.

A single black feather floated down. I caught it and fingered the smooth edge. He'd left *la pluma* on purpose, I'd bet.

Zeke grabbed my elbow and practically threw me on the bike. He slammed my helmet on my tender head, causing me to wince. Murmuring an apology, Zeke slid in front of me, still buckling his own helmet, though holding his knife made the process harder.

I glanced back up at the deep blue sky. It had to mean something. I stuffed the single black plume into my jacket pocket and wrapped my arms around Zeke as he kicked off.

A shadow slid over the low-slung adobe building. The world's biggest ro-dent slunk across the flat roof. Its teeth gleamed bright and huge, its whiskers moving at a frantic pace. Zeke cursed. Maybe the northern New Mexico sun would do its part to burn the demon's belly and feet on the hot tar.

Zeke opened up the throttle to its fullest capacity as he entered the west-bound lanes of the highway.

"Was that a deer mouse?" I yelled over the roar of the engine. Zeke shrugged.

"You want me to go back and find out?" Zeke shouted.

No, I could live my whole life without knowing for sure a giant deer mouse was trying to kill me. Zeke wove through traffic. I waited until we were outside the city before leaning forward again. He stiffened when my chest brushed his back, but I ignored his tension. One, I needed a place for my hands. Two, I liked holding him despite his discomfort at pursuing intimacy.

The engine rumbled and the wind screamed. I kept my cheek pressed into Zeke's back, watching the juniper-strewn landscape zoom past. Nothing else came darting toward us.

After an eternity, my eyes shut.

#

How I fell asleep on the back of a motorcycle moving at seventy-five miles per hour boggled my mind. Talk about stupidity.

The electric blue of the New Mexico sky disappeared; the air dipped into a frostiness I associated with a winter dawn—even if it was an early afternoon in spring. Ice crystals formed in front of me, an impressive trick in the desert.

The drop in temperature was worse than going from a hot tub to snow. My teeth slammed together, my jaw locking at the unpleasantness of the sensa-tion. I forced my muscles to unclench, a much harder feat than I expected.

Horrible pterodactyl-like screeches filled my ears. Well, maybe not ptero-dactyl. I didn't know what noises dinosaurs actually made, so I was assuming. But the things flying toward us looked like the pictures I'd seen of the long-dead creatures.

Large hairy bodies, long, vicious beaks and beady eyes. Murder with wings.

Couldn't one of my would-be assassins be cute? Scratch that. With my luck, I'd fall for an adorable kitten or maybe the cute bunny in the Monty Python movie Layla liked so much. I'd bend down to scratch the cutie between the ears as the demon leaped up to rip out my throat. What an embarrassing way to go.

Zeke opened the Thunderbird's throttle all the way, and the frigid wind shrieked over us. My hands clamped tighter onto his armor. When his muscles bunched, I mirrored his actions, moving in tandem with him with surprising ease.

We were traveling faster than seemed smart and way too fast to get my bearings.

He skidded, the Thunderbird sliding to the edge of the black rock after which the area was named. El Malpais National Monument, an otherworldly jumble of volcanic rock and ice caves. The place looked alien and inhospitable.

Zeke jumped off the bike, sword and spear held out in front of him as the first enormous pterodactyl/bat thing dove toward him. Closer up, the demons were shaped like enormous bats.

I struggled off the motorcycle, cursing at my short stature. I fell over, my hands slamming into the rocks next to the cave where Zeke had parked. I cursed again, this time in a high-pitched squeak as I scrambled upright. My hands were bleeding.

"Go inside the cave," he yelled.

Zeke pierced the bat-thing with his spear while he twirled his sword. He was such a showman. He quit spinning his sword and ripped the blade across the belly of another furry-bodied creature. Its squawk cut off as the demon disintegrated. The rest of the bats swarmed overhead, calling and clawing each other.

I cowered behind the chrome body of the motorcycle as the demons zoomed toward us, their beaks and claws razor sharp and way too close. Zeke cut down three more of the creatures. I needed a weapon.

The rocks next to the Thunderbird didn't look like they'd be enough of a deterrent, but then they'd cut deep gouges into my hands.

"I'm not leaving you alone. There are so many of them."

"Then help. Do the ice thing you did to the snake."

Right…I had magic. I stoked the spot in my head, making it as hot as possible as I gathered a handful of rocks. I went for smaller rocks, reasoning my poor hand-eye coordination skills improved with a larger target. I'd totally sucked at tennis during my six-week Serena Williams–wannabe phase.

I stood up as one of the bat demons dove for my head. I screamed, ducking again. From my peripheral vision, I saw Zeke hurtle his sword into its furry body as he yanked his spear from the throat of a disintegrating corpse at his feet. Great. I'd distracted him. He'd lost a weapon, and I sighed, remembering I hadn't been as much of a tennis competitor as the girl who'd worn leg braces for her scoliosis. How I'd ended up with magic was beyond me, considering I lacked both athleticism and coordination.

The bat-demon disintegrated as it fell into one of the open lava tubes behind me, contaminating the ground for all eternity, no doubt. Zeke's sword clattered to the ground as I stood, more determined than ever to help. After pouring some water over my pile, I froze the rocks in my hand until they glowed blue. Thanks to my online physics research—during one of my rebellious phases—I knew that the energy emitted from a flame was called quanta. Bluish light had high-energy quanta whereas reddish light emitted lower energy quanta. I wanted the coldest temperature possible. Not the same as a searing-hot flame, but dry ice stored a lot of energy.

I counted six more sets of wings. The human-sized bats clearly included larger brains than their tiny brethren; they circled above Zeke's reach with his spear and settled between us so he couldn't retrieve his sword.

I nibbled my top lip, considering my options. I decided on a buckshot approach—enough to annoy and fluster the beasts. I flung the handful of super-cooled rocks at the beast's middles in an effort to make contact with the biggest target, and I concentrated on decreasing the temperature as the rocks sailed through the air. Dull thuds were followed by faint hisses and a stronger stench of decay. I didn't watch; I dove for Zeke's sword, catching the weight with my left hand. Lighter than I expected, it was well-balanced, easy on my wrists. Still, I had to add my right hand as I swung the blade in a wide arc. Not for the weight but for accuracy.

While the arc lacked grace, the blade slammed into one of the bat's shoulders, catching the demon at the wing joint. The creature wrenched sideways, hitting another demon as they both careened into nothingness.

I brought the blade up, more as a protective measure, as another bat passed right over my head. The sword impaled the creature through its neck. Its beak peeled back in a surprisingly human grimace as it, too, began to turn into dust.

Zeke reached around me and plucked the blade from my hands. I relinquished the weapon with pleasure, my arms shaking from the effort. While the sword hadn't been heavy, I wasn't used to that type of workout. I would've dropped the dark, smooth blade on my foot at some not-so-distant point in the future.

"Wow. You really moved through those things."

He grinned, a gorgeous upward sweep of lips that flooded his eyes with warmth. I thanked every god I remembered when he drew me toward him. I sighed into his chest, enjoying the friendliness of the embrace.

"You're no slouch in the warrior arena, either," he said. "We gotta go."

"Okay," I mumbled. Much as I wanted a few minutes to stretch my legs, I refused to slow us down. The attacks came with too much regularity.

After cleaning his sword, he studied the terrain, then the sky. His eyebrows drew together.

"More will come. Since the snake and lizard didn't work, air power makes sense."

"How can that make sense?" I asked.

"I bet this group was the vanguard."

I slid my fingers between his, needing the contact, hoping to comfort us both. At least I needed *comodidad*. Those things were freaking scary.

He led me to the motorcycle then waited until I was comfortable in the saddle before he settled between my spread thighs.

"Vanguard. Great. So there'll be more."

"Always. Echo. We're not going to be able to outrun them. Someone's put a bounty on your head. They want you dead."

CHAPTER FOUR

I fumed, annoyed by his cavalier attitude. Like I'd wanted a bounty placed on my head. This whole situation was ludicrous. I was simply me. Echo Ruiz. No one special. My pendant's temperature rose as my agitation grew. I patted it, mumbling to Honani that I was fine. Still alive and kicking, anyway.

We drove to Gallup without having to face another attack. Zeke pulled over again. The terrain remained desolate, the black asphalt radiating thick plumes of heat that kept both Zeke and me tense as we tried to look beyond the heat-warped horizon. At least we were out of the badlands and heading back into the mountains.

When the motorcycle slid to a stop, I managed to dismount without falling down. I patted my braid and took a tentative step away from the Thunderbird. My feet ached from my hours last night without shoes, but they were much better. My body had healed the lacerations. Life was good—my arm worked and I walked without assistance.

"You think you can manage to keep out of trouble long enough for me to fill up the tank?" Zeke asked, a hint of a smile flitting over his lips. "I don't want to get caught somewhere and run out of gas."

I faced him, my hands on my hips. My bladder was near to bursting. Worse, I feared insect guts were splattered across my face. I'd had a nasty run-in with something winged—thankfully, much smaller than last time, but no less unpleasant—about fifty miles earlier, nearly causing me to fall off the stupid motorcycle as I flailed and spat.

"I can pee without you rescuing me."

"Prove it," Zeke said with a grin.

"I can't keep up with your moods," I sighed. "You switch from grunty badass to flirtatious sweet talker faster than I can blink. In case you missed the memo, I'm the *loca* here for God's sake!"

I clapped my hands over my mouth and glanced upward. Had I offended my dad? I waited, breathless, for the lightning to strike down on me.

"You are so messed up right now. It's not like the tribes didn't believe in one supreme being. Which would be your father, by the way."

I glared at him. "Along with a bunch of other deities. It's confusing, and I spent years learning the hierarchy."

"That's not what this little tantrum is about."

Much as I wanted to pout and flounce away, Zeke waited with a patience I didn't deserve. I answered him with as much truth as I deemed smart. "You try being the only child born out of wedlock in a conservative community. I'm not sure I could be any more guilt-ridden than I've been my whole life."

The planes in his face firmed in frustration, his dark eyes hardening. "You aren't a bastard. In case you missed that detail: your folks married under the old laws."

He tilted his head toward the leather circling my neck. The necklace was identical to the one my mother used to wear, ugly clay pendant and all. I shoved my hand into my pocket, grasping her broken necklace—my only memento for either of my parents.

"And you've got the goods to prove it, unlike some of us." He paused, his brows drawing down. I thought he wanted to say something more, maybe tell me about his past, but instead he shut down. "Go to the bathroom."

I stomped to the entrance of the grungy convenience store, aggravated that everyone else knew more about my life than I did. I slammed through the glass doors, considering Coral Snake's attack in the last gas station a moment too late. I drew myself up, poised on the balls of my feet. The two people I encountered in this place were human and totally disinterested in me, the pseudo biker chic wearing cheap Walmart jeans. Not that I blamed them.

If I was supposed to save the world, I wanted a better wardrobe. Come to think of it, I was still annoyed Layla had nixed my theme-song idea. How cool would I be walking if The White Stripes sang to the world not even a Seven Nation Army could keep me down?

Oooh, I'd given myself chills thinking about it. I loved that song. For a week straight, I'd played it on a continual loop, annoying Layla to the point she threatened not to come back. Grief tried to balloon in my chest so I focused on sending a back-off message with my eyes. That would be useful, a skill to work on during the long, boring hours of road travel.

I added the idea to my insanely long mental to-do list. Each time my thoughts veered toward either my mom or Layla—a constancy, really—I forced my thoughts to the list of things I planned to accomplish in the years—or maybe minutes?—I had left on Earth.

No, it didn't really help, but I lacked any other tools to deal with my grief. Once in the bathroom, I relieved my overfilled bladder. Hitting potholes with a full liter of water swishing around my insides wasn't an experience I wanted to repeat. Talk about a form of torture. I washed the bug guts from my sunglasses and splashed some tepid water on my face, wishing my eyes weren't so gritty. Sleep, the uninterrupted kind, already proved a distant memory.

Zeke walked out of the men's bathroom as I came out of the women's. We turned in unison and headed out to his motorcycle. I slid my glasses back on my nose and wondered how much longer I'd manage sitting on the bike. Flagstaff was about seven hours from Albuquerque, which meant we still had a few hours of travel left.

"You hungry?" Zeke asked.

I nodded. I shook from low blood sugar and exhaustion, but I hadn't wanted to slow us down any more.

"A meal, then."

"Any place with vegetables is great."

Zeke glared at me. "Don't tell me you're vegan," he said, his voice dripping with scorn. "I saw that hummus and carrots you were eating the other day. Food like that isn't going to cut it, not with all the magic you've been using."

I'd eaten that more than a week ago. Before I officially met Zeke. Stalkery, sure, that he'd been watching me, but also kind of sweet. "Hummus and carrots is a balanced meal, full of nutrients."

"No, hummus is a shitty snack."

I threw my leg over the bike and winced as the wound on my knee split open yet again. When I'd fallen off the bike in Malpais, I'd cut my leg in exactly the same spot. The previous injury had almost completely healed, but now, without more salve, I was back to my normal healing rate, and the cut hurt.

I hoped blood didn't seep through my pants leg. My jeans were ugly enough without bloodstains. A few strategic rips might help them, though. They were so…denimy.

"My knee is bleeding again. I'll need to put some salve on it."

Zeke pulled the container out of his pocket, his hands pushing the denim up my leg as I finished speaking. Uncapping the lid, he dipped his fingers in and dabbed the ointment over my knee. His breath hit my exposed skin, causing it to ripple with pleasure.

"I'm not eating soy and raw zucchini," Zeke said. He stared at the cut, seeming to will the gash closed. "I want real food that tastes good."

"I'm not a vegan or a rawist or anything extreme like that. I tried for a while, but I didn't have the discipline for it," I said on a sigh, once again saddened by my pathetic self-control in regard to both Zeke and food. "Can we go? I'm really hungry. For something with protein." I kept a straight face when I added, "You know, like walnuts. Or spirulina."

He smoothed my pant leg down and stood, sliding the container of ointment into his pocket once again. He slung his leg over the Thunderbird. "What you named there, that's a horrific salad. You need to eat more if you want to able to keep up the magic."

"Wait. A question." Because I wanted to see his face when I asked, I clambered back off the bike and went to stand next to him. "Before, with Layla, we'd talked about looking for the other tablets and their keepers. I want to find Layla more than you do, but shouldn't we be focused on the tablets?"

"No. When you broke the one, we lost the ability to find the others."

I winced. "So we don't think whoever took the first one—along with the Fourth—broke that one. Not if breaking the tablet caused all the fires and earthquakes and disruption in portal travel?"

Zeke nodded.

"But there's supposed to be a secret locked within them. To release the god, Pahana, who'll open the door to the Fifth World."

Zeke's face tightened so that his nostrils flared white. "There isn't a Fifth World."

"How do you know that? I've read about it."

"Think, Echo. Four is the magic number. Four elements, four seasons, four Halflings, four worlds."

I tugged at my bottom lip with my thumb and forefinger. "Fine. Then why the story about Pahana and the Fifth World?"

"I don't know. But it's a recent phenomenon, the idea of a Fifth World. We do not want to free Pahana. He ushers in Armageddon."

"But I thought—"

"You don't want the *god* Pahana," Zeke snapped.

I wished he'd remove his sunglasses; I wanted to see his eyes. He fiddled with the key, putting it in and pulling it from the ignition. I waited.

"The literal translation of the word is a cloaked white brother. We'd do better with *a* pahana."

He'd handed me a bone I needed to pick. "You mentioned him before. Why not the god?"

"He's not what he used to be. Back when they created that pact."

"How do you know that?"

"Because I do." When I opened my mouth, unable to drop the topic, Zeke turned away. "Not now, Echo. Please."

I crossed my arms, wanting to push. But I heard my mother's voice in my head: *No reason to push an argument that you can't win.* If I forced Zeke to admit whatever bothered him—and his emotions were wafting off him faster than a nuclear explosion—we'd both end up more hurt by his revelations.

"You'll tell me later though?" I couldn't drop it.

He shrugged. "Get on the bike."

Something cold slid across my skin, deeper than a chill. And with it came darkness. The shadow of an enormous red-tailed hawk lay over us. This one's wings spanned five times more than the ones that normally circled the park near my house, searching for rodents, snakes, and smaller birds.

"You know what that thing is?" I whispered.

A beady, black eye turned in my direction, and the bird shrieked in pleasure. Damn its hawk hearing.

Zeke tugged me onto the motorcycle. He slid into place as he turned on the ignition.

"Trouble," Zeke called back as we shot out of the lot toward the road.

"Man Eagle?" I asked. The story about that demon freaked me out more than most of the others I'd read. If the stories were true...or even partially true...

"Do you want me to stop and find out for you?"

"No way."

Shuddering, I gripped him tighter, not caring where Zeke took me. Right now, all I wanted was food and a solid lead, maybe a good nudge in the right direction. And if I wasn't so paranoid about dying, I'd really want a good night's sleep. I glanced up at the shadow easily keeping pace overhead. I'd be lucky to still be alive at dusk.

"Can you freeze the demon's insides?" Zeke asked.

I tried, but I couldn't focus on the hawk. The bird darted away or Zeke turned and I'd lose the connection. My eyes streamed with tears from the speed, but I managed to catch sight of a billboard. One block to the east. "Go there!" I yelled, pointing first to the sign then to the right.

Zeke nodded.

The shadow kept pace overhead as Zeke slid between the traffic, earning lots of honking and a few really dirty names. He continued to weave in and out of the cars to the strip mall's parking lot. This had better work.

I jumped off before he'd slowed down completely, forcing my feet to keep moving. I tripped and pitched forward, but somehow managed to right myself and hurtle through the door of the Catholic Superstore.

"Excuse me," the indignant clerk said.

"Holy water. Now!" I reached into my pocket and pulled out a twenty-dollar bill. "There's a demon outside waiting to find a body to possess!"

"Oh, please," she muttered. But she hopped off her stool so fast her large bottom continued to jiggle for a few steps. Her blue broomstick skirt stuck to her thighs. My breath puffed out in tiny gasps.

The woman handed me a couple of small flasks, her multiple chins waving indignantly. She wanted me out of her shop, pronto. Slamming the money onto the counter, I snatched them out of her hand. "Thanks."

I launched myself through the door in time to see the raptor in a dive, its two-foot-long talons open and ready to rip into Zeke.

"Padre, ayudame," I whispered. A plea for godly-father help sounded mighty fine right now. Without breaking stride, I threw the first bottle. The glass hit the bird just below its neck, shattering on impact. I uncorked the other as I ran. Drawing the water from the bottle, I created a ball of the substance. Another three steps and I threw the water, aiming behind the giant bird's beak.

My breathing increased, too rapid to sustain, and my vision started to gray. Those familiar migraine dots popped into my periphery. No, I couldn't stop now. I pulled air into my lungs, deep and hard, before exhaling in a hard puff. I concentrated, using that hot, flickering center in my mind, my hand fumbling to close around my pendant, my anchor, as I focused all my energy on the water coating the bird.

Honani's presence there, in my pendant, centered me.

"Do you need me?" he asked.

"No," I gasped. "Got this."

Honani's grunt might not have been one of approval, but I chose to ignore any negative connotation. I did have this moment—and I was growing stronger with each test, each fight.

My vision cleared enough for me to see the feathers shrivel; the bird turned its black eye toward me and squawked, ruffling its wings that, thankfully, were half-gone. I tried not to pant as I put my hands on my knees. Blood dripped from my knee down my leg. The bird's head disintegrated.

Zeke's arm slid around my shoulders. He helped me to the bike, where I plopped on the seat, still wheezing.

"What was that?" he asked.

Shock radiated both from his tone and his slack jaw.

"Tired," I mumbled.

"You're cold. Too much magic," he said. He touched his palm to my forehead. "What did you do?"

My chin rose, defiant. I'd taken care of the problem. He gestured to the decomposing corpse. "What did you throw on it?"

"Holy water," I said with a shrug.

He handed me a bottle of water. My ability to talk normally returned, but my shaking hands made bringing the bottle to my mouth difficult.

"That doesn't explain what happened," he said, exasperation lacing his tone.

Instead of answering him with the truth, I dug in my heels. Maybe because I was so exhausted, both mentally and physically, or maybe Zeke brought out the worst of my stubbornness. Probably all of the above.

"Demons can't survive the Lord's blessing."

"And you know this how?"

"I've been to a church." At Zeke's raised brow, I lifted my chin. "A few times. Enough to know holy water is imbued with divine properties."

"But that's not Hisatsinom," Zeke muttered. His eyes darted to the Catholic Superstore.

"Who's to say what is and isn't. And why are you carving up religions into tiny bits anyway? Why not go along with the fact our people"—I pointed back and forth between us—"believe in a supreme creator like Judaism or Christianity or other native cultures?"

"If you take that view, then how do you explain Masau or Coyote or…" Zeke spread out his hand. "You know what. Never mind."

"So you don't want to know that I froze the water to sub-zero temperatures as soon as it hit him?" I asked, trying hard not to giggle. I failed, especially when the shock registered on Zeke's face. "Like you suggested earlier with the bat-things. I hadn't thought of going straight to the source."

He opened his mouth, shut it. Glanced back at the store then at the hawk disintegrating on the ground. "You froze the water. All over the bird."

My chest puffed up with pride. "Sure did."

"Nothing to do with being holy?" he asked, suspicion lacing his tone.

I shrugged. "Who knows if the water is actually consecrated by a priest. I didn't want to have another fight at a gas station. One was enough for today."

"Huh."

"What does that mean?" I asked.

"I'm not exactly sure how I feel about all this," Zeke said, his words drawn out.

"Doesn't matter. It's dead, and that fight's over. Just a hawk, not Man Eagle." Disappointment nipped at me. Not that I wanted to meet Man Eagle or any of the other big baddies, but knowing he was back in the netherworlds where he belonged would've made this interaction worth it.

Zeke still spluttered, at a loss. He snagged the water bottle from me.

"Why not just use this?"

"It's not holy," I said, smirking.

"Got that. Simple water." He took a prolonged sip.

"I wasn't sure how much I needed. I'm still getting a handle on my Water aspect."

"Thanks for taking care of the hawk," he said, glancing back at the shriveling carcass.

"You're welcome. To be honest, I wasn't sure freezing the water would work, but it's the best defense I've discovered so far. If nothing else, I figured it'd piss off the thing long enough for you to stab it." Over his shoulder, my eyes met the gaping sales clerk.

"Did you see that thing?" I asked.

She shook her head, but her eyes turned to the place on the ground where the carcass sifted into a pile of ash.

"It wanted your soul," I called. "Because you were the most devout among us."

The woman backed away, letting the door to the Catholic Superstore slide shut. The lock slid into place, and I chuckled. "Why could she see the carcass?"

Zeke shook his head at me, trying to frown through his amusement. "Its magic wore off."

I glanced at the pile of dusty white powder. A breeze blew some of the residue into the air. "Makes as much sense as them existing."

"You feeling okay? You're really pale."

"I'm starving." I placed a hand over my loudly gurgling stomach.

"That's from using so much magic. Let's find some real food."

#

Zeke drove deeper into town while I fought waves of dizziness. I'd never been this hungry.

About a mile or so down Main Street, he pulled into another strip-mall parking lot filled with cars. Zeke managed to maneuver his Thunderbird between a couple of beat-up pickups. He hefted his spear bag over his shoulder as I sorted out my trembling legs enough to stand and walk unaided.

As we moved through the rows of cars, I realized he was no longer wearing his armor. Maybe he'd stored it in his bag while in the restroom. That tattoo peaked out from the cuff of his T-shirt. Hmmm, ink added to his bad-boy image. Considering how little I'd dated, which would be not at all, my deep-seated attraction to this man made sense.

Who was I kidding? Zeke's rebelliousness, his willingness to skate the fringe of our legal system, to maim and kill demons, gods, humans, and anything else to keep me safe. That was barbaric, sure, but also sexy.

"This needs to be quick," Zeke fretted as he held open the door for me. "I'm starving. Those six walnuts weren't much of a breakfast." His tone veered toward accusatory.

I shrugged as I stepped onto the wooden-plank floor. The scent of cooking meat hit my nose, and my salivary glands went into overdrive as my stomach contracted. Zeke made a whimpering noise in the back of his throat.

A young woman, not much older than me, stood behind the hostess podium, applying sparkly pink lip gloss. She put the container down onto the podium slowly, never taking her gaze off Zeke. I stepped closer, needing to mark my territory. Annoyance drilled into my chest when amusement rolled off Zeke in thick waves. *Pendejo.* I mouthed the word at him.

He narrowed his eyes but his lips twitched. "I know what that means."

I crossed my arms over my chest. "Good for you."

"You don't really think I'm stupid, do you, Echo?"

I glared harder when he laughed louder.

"How many?" the girl asked, confusion dripping from her. Her voice was smoother and richer than melting brown sugar.

Sometimes being able to feel other people's emotions was a waste. Tuning the girl out as best I could, I waited for Zeke to quit laughing. He had to ruin my moment by smiling at her.

"Two," Zeke answered, wrapping his arm around my waist and smiling politely. I decided I could be more understanding of the other woman's infatuation. Though I was still considering whether my powers would allow me to mute and blind her temporarily. The thought had merit, perking me up.

"Right this way, darlin'," the hostess said. She swung around the welcome booth.

"Thanks, ma'am, for calling me darling, but so you know, I'm *with* him," I said. "Not that you aren't pretty."

The woman turned back with wide, horror-filled eyes. "I'm not into girls," she said. "I was talking to him."

My eyes narrowed while the center in my mind leapt a little. I was as weak as my magic. Dammit, I needed fuel. Bad. Zeke squeezed my waist, probably because he'd noticed the blip in power. I pretended great interest in the menu when we sat down.

"I understand," Zeke said.

I glanced up. His hands were folded on top of the menu, his eyes sincere. He reached over and took one of my hands in his. His long, thin fingers brushed across the tendons in my hand before settling down to rub the sensitive skin between my thumb and forefinger. I stared at the thin, silver scars crisscrossing the backs of his hands. There were a few deeper gashes, now healed, that had left thick scar tissue.

"You understand nothing."

"That act right there? I totally know where you're coming from. I had a fantasy of ripping apart that guy in the convenience store when he watched you walk into the bathroom."

I gaped at him. Amusement tilted his lips and his dark eyes sparkled. Great, now he felt superior. I snapped my mouth shut and gave a faint nod. When a waitress set down bucket-sized red plastic cups overflowing with ice and about a tablespoon of water, I shoved my straw down to the bottom and drank in greedy gulps. Ever since I'd created that huge rainstorm to stop Coyote's attack, I couldn't seem to drink enough water.

I shoved my drink away. "Well, that woman looked at you like you were an ice-cream cone she wanted to lick."

"I can't help her desires, Echo. And I already told you, I'm not interested."

I crossed my arms over my chest, realized I must appear defensive, and placed them in my lap, leaning forward. "Why don't you want to want me?"

He leaned back in his chair, his head thrown back in a laugh. I pouted, my eyes trained on my thick red cup. Sobering, Zeke clasped one of my hands in both of his.

"To clarify: I can't have a relationship with you."

Disappointment clawed through my belly, churning up the emotions building there. "Because you don't like me now that you've gotten to know me?" I sighed, hating to admit the next truth. "Not many people do."

He studied my face, causing mine to heat in embarrassment. I didn't know how to converse with him, let alone play the game most people seemed to delight in to show a guy they liked him. I needed Layla. If not my bestie, then at least some reality TV to show me how to handle this situation.

"Maybe I'm the problem. And you don't really know me," Zeke said, his voice matter-of-fact.

"Because you're afraid to tell me more about you." He stilled so completely, I'd bet he wasn't breathing. "Hmm. Thought so." We were quiet, gauging each other's reactions. Of course, I cracked first. "Fine. I know you've saved my life too many times, usually at risk to your own safety, which tells me that your heart is bigger than you want to admit. And I'm beginning to think *you think* I've been forced to like you. By my mother, the gods. Let me point out that doesn't fit in with your previous statement that my mom didn't want us to even know each other."

"The gods will do—and have done—worse, much worse, than try to manipulate emotions." His voice was soft, regretful, but strong with conviction. "Look, it all comes back to this: I promised my foster father I'd protect you. I promised your mother, too, in Sotuk's name."

I frowned, attempting to make sense not only of his chivalry but the complexity of the system. "Then what about what Raven said today?"

His response was supposed to help clarify my own. Zeke shifted, his gaze laser-sharp as he searched my eyes. "His theory seems like a justification for taking what I want."

Warmth built in my chest and spread over my neck and cheeks. His gaze held mine steady even when I wanted to look away.

"I don't want you to feel pressured into anything with me because I've saved your life," he said.

Frustration coiled around us. Zeke shifted back in his chair and sighed. Emotion drifted off him, laced with disappointment. Sometimes I hated this newfound ability to feel others' emotions, especially Zeke's. I forced my face upward, meeting his eyes again.

"Let's talk about the Magician," Zeke said. "He seems to be our best lead, especially if he can point us to the Fourth."

"Raven said he may be able to help with Layla."

I glanced around at the people who were eating, drinking, laughing, paying a bill. Such normal little things; I wasn't sure I'd ever achieve enough serenity to find my way back to a place where I could do those, not with the intensity of my emotions. Each moment seemed to ping me between some rush of happiness to be here with Zeke and anguish over my mom and worry for Layla.

Before I could consider how in…something…I was with Zeke, I locked up the niggling worry. I returned my gaze to his face. All relaxed, he appeared like an indolent twenty-something-year-old.

"Do you know anything about the Magician?" I asked.

"You decided on your meals?" A thickset, middle-aged woman with unnatural orange hair stopped by our table.

"Two cheeseburgers. Lots of fries. And whatever veggies you can pile onto the burger. Echo loves veggies, so adding more tomatoes and an extra side of green chile would be great," Zeke said. Shock coursed through me at the realization that I liked Zeke taking charge, ordering for me. I'd forced a god down into one of the lower worlds; I shouldn't want a man to protect me.

When he smiled at the waitress, she blinked and grinned back. I groaned. Zeke winked at me as the woman trundled away.

"Feeling shaky, Echo? That's from using so much magic. You need protein. And grease. You need to power your energy and hummus won't cut it."

"Why would I want to put grease into my body?" I asked, crossing my arms over my chest.

"Because you need lots of calories to do what you did again. Fat burns slower than even those complex carbs you're so fond of." He leaned forward, eyes serious. "And here's a bit of information: Magic will tap you out. You can—and will—die if you push too hard. Yours is some of the most impressive power I've seen. Ever. But your magic, like mine, has to be fed. With fat as well as the leaves and scraps you'd normally call a meal."

"You're saving me from demons only to kill me from heart disease." I huffed and flopped back into the seat. He rolled his eyes at me but I caught the faint smirk he tried to suppress.

"You need to refuel if you're going to be able to take down more gods. Even with the extra magic your mom gave you," Zeke said, his eyes roving across the crowd. "Because that energy needs fuel, too."

My breath caught, aching, in my chest as my throat closed over a knot of emotion. "Why wouldn't my mom tell me that?"

His eyes fastened onto mine. I didn't want him to see the grief I'd been trying to suppress all day. "For the same reason she tried to suppress your magic and make you nearly invisible to normal people."

"In an attempt to control my life?" I snapped.

Zeke shook his head. "Seems to me she was trying to save you."

That lump of emotion rolled through my chest and up into my throat. But

I wouldn't cry. I would not give that bastard Coyote the satisfaction of how much I missed her, even if she had lied to me.

"I didn't mean to upset you," Zeke said, his voice soft.

I was not weak, nor would I allow Zeke to treat me like a fragile flower. "Hunger makes me emotional," I said in a casual voice. I flipped my hair over my shoulder. "I'll eat the burger. Let's talk about rescuing Layla." I frowned at an older man whose eyes were clearly on my chest. Maybe Zeke was right and, like him, I drew more attention than I deserved, now that my mom's spells had dissipated. Zeke turned, trying to figure out why I was scowling.

"The Magician?" I prompted.

Zeke swiveled back to face me. "He was a leader who lived and died about eight hundred years ago. Best guess is that he died in his forties. Big man. Maybe his size killed him? Who knows. Based on the hundreds of items in his grave, he was powerful. A stick swallower."

"A shaman who handled fire," I said, leaning my elbows onto the table and cupping my chin in my palms. "Could he be one of Masau's children?"

Zeke shrugged, stabbing his straw into the cup. "Maybe. He lived in the large pueblo at the Ridge Ruin. Over twenty rooms, multiple kivas and ball courts."

"I never really understood the ball courts."

"Kinda like an early version of soccer, but the ball wasn't allowed to touch the ground."

"So two soccer pitches?" I asked, surprised.

"They oriented them in different directions, maybe for different purposes and probably not just for games. For its time, the pueblo—called the Ridge Ruin—was an important location. The most important location in the vicinity."

"My professor said the Magician's burial mound was one of the biggest and most important archaeological excavations in the Southwest."

Zeke smirked. "Some claim it's better than King Tut's tomb."

"If he's a child of Masau, I think going there could be a problem," I said, speaking slowly as I tried to grasp the workings of the nether worlds.

"Why?"

"I read a scholarly paper on the site excavation. The Magician's grave was dug up in the late 1930s by an archaeologist with the Museum of Northern Arizona. Disturbing a powerful shaman's grave, especially by whites unfamiliar with his historical importance, that wouldn't make his soul happy."

"What happened to the excavators?"

I pulled out my phone and pulled up my web browser. "Nothing. Do you think the Magician would've tried to avenge himself?"

Zeke lifted one eyebrow. I fiddled with my napkin.

"Raven's idea sounds worse by the second," Zeke sighed.

"Do you have a better one?" I asked. Fear for Layla burst outward, coating my skin. "We're out of options right now. We're headed in that general direction and the distance between Coyote's camp and the Ridge Ruin isn't great."

"I'm not arguing against going, just pointing out we're not well-equipped. I don't know what we're walking into up there."

"I can't lose Layla, too. I can't."

He covered my hand with his much larger one and linked our fingers. His calluses scratched at the sensitive skin between each finger. "You're not going to. We'll find her. I'm working on a plan. Just so you know."

"Why do I think I'm not going to like it?"

"Because you won't. I'm not saying anything more right now." He crossed his arms over his chest. His tattoo slid out from under his sleeve. Just enough to peak my curiosity.

"What's up with the tat?" I asked.

"Something I did one night when I was lonely."

I gaped. From what little I knew about tattoos, they hurt. "You did that to yourself?"

Zeke shook his head. "Masau helped."

"I want to see it."

"I can't show you the whole thing right now. Goes over my shoulder."

"Tonight. You'll show me tonight."

Zeke smirked. "I do believe you're trying to get me naked," he said.

"Fair's fair." My cheeks flamed. "You've seen me in the buff."

A slow smiled slid across those wide lips, his teeth flashing white against the golden skin of his face. "Sure did."

I waved my hand as if I was dispersing smoke, but I was really trying to cool off my overheated skin. "So do you have an actual plan? To talk to the Magician?"

Our food arrived. "Looks great. Thanks," he said. The older lady grinned, showing her crooked teeth. Zeke shoved a fry into his mouth and munched. I waved the waitress away with a smile.

"I want to contact someone who can help us meet the Magician tonight. The Ridge Ruin is a protected site," Zeke said. "That means there'll be park service people around. Until the park closes, anyway."

I paused, the cheeseburger halfway to my mouth. I set the sandwich down and glared. "I don't want to fight with a park ranger."

"We'll wait until they close up for the day."

"Who's the friend?"

Zeke shook his head. Once he'd swallowed his bite, he said, "I'm not sure about the friend status, but I'm pretty sure we'll learn something from the meeting."

"I don't understand."

"I know." He met my gaze, his face implacable.

Should I push him? My mother's decisions to not let me interact with men really stunted my ability to gauge this situation. I didn't want to be emotionally stunted. I settled for a different approach. "So we're going to break in to an ancient burial site?" I asked, barely able to push the question past my stiff lips. Dread bubbled up, chasing away my hunger.

Zeke lifted his burger in the air. "Eat," he commanded.

He waited until I took a small bite and chewed. I hummed in the back of my throat. He grinned.

"Yep. A little B and E should keep the excitement in our relationship, don't you think? A bit of adrenaline to add to our boring days of fighting off demons and dodging angry gods."

"I'm beginning to think you're crazy," I mumbled. I tore through another bite of my burger. My stomach gurgled in appreciation as the food hit its empty confines.

Zeke laughed. "As a fox."

#

I still fretted about our upcoming felony as we drove into Flagstaff. We were going to backtrack about twenty miles to the small mountain town of Winona. From there, we'd follow the roads into the state park at Homolovi, where the Ridge Ruin sat in all its former glory.

Zeke put on his blinker and took the first exit for Flagstaff. He prowled the streets until he found a small, clean motel. "I don't know about you, but I'm exhausted," he said. "Let's get a room. We can catch a few hours' sleep before we need to be at the park."

"Shouldn't we go straight there?" I asked around a giant yawn.

"We haven't slept in over thirty hours, Echo. My reflexes are shot. You fell asleep on the back of a motorcycle. Sleep isn't a luxury right now. It's what's going to keep us alive."

I nodded, too lulled by a full belly and the constant vibrations of the motorcycle to do anything more. Zeke unclipped my helmet and pulled me behind him into the small office. I stood in the shadows, blinking with bleary attention at the overweight man with bristling white hair sitting behind the desk.

"Eighty-seven ninety," he said without looking up from the small TV. Sounded like a basketball game, but I didn't really care.

Zeke put down the correct bills and waited for the guy to hand over a key. He glanced up and his puffy eyes flitted between the two of us.

"You old enough to be here with this fella?" he asked, worry evident in his voice.

I smiled, pleased this stranger cared about my well-being. "Of course. I'm really ten years older than he is," I whispered with a wink. "Great skin. But don't tell him. Might scare him away."

"Thanks," Zeke muttered, shooting me a glance from the corner of his eye even as his lips curled up at the corner. He grabbed the key from the counter and ushered me out the door, the night clerk frowning.

"I always wanted to do that."

"Lie?" Zeke asked.

"Oh, hush. I didn't hurt anybody."

Zeke grunted, his eyes scanning the parking lot. I helped him pull our backpacks from the small storage bins on the sides of the bike. He set the alarm from his key fob and shepherded me into the room.

A large bed took up nearly the entire space. An old analog TV sat on a small, chipped table. I headed toward the only other door, which led to the bathroom. After taking care of my most urgent needs, I crawled into the bed.

Zeke stared down at me for a minute, his body tense. "That dude wanted in your pants, same as all the others. It's beyond old, watching them mentally undress you."

"Don't care," I groaned.

"I thought you wanted a shower," Zeke said.

"Do. But I'm too tired now."

"Call Honani," he said.

I forced my eyes open and glared at him. "Why do I need Honani?"

I tried to swallow a huge yawn, but it nearly split my face in two. Zeke grinned. He stepped forward and brushed a thick lock of hair from my cheek, rubbing the long, dark strands between his fingers before bringing it to his lips and kissing it. He stepped back, letting the thick wave fall from his fingers.

"Because I need to sleep nearly as bad as you do, and I can't do that if I don't know if there are demons coming for us."

I yawned and my jaw cracked under the pressure.

"Honani?" I asked, using that special place deep in my skull. Power pulsed there, an oddly comforting ripple as I sent my request. I wished I had the energy to take off my shoes.

The spirit warrior showed up immediately. "You survived the day!"

His hug reminded me of falling into a three-foot snowdrift without a coat. After letting him pat me a couple times, I huddled under the covers, shivering.

"Zeke wants to know if you'll keep watch for us while we sleep," I said. Honani drifted back to the edge of the bed. Zeke came out of the bathroom in his T-shirt and boxers. I perked up, my eyes flickering over all of Zeke's exposed skin.

Only part of the tattoo I'd already seen was visible under the edge of his shirtsleeve. I needed to see the whole image.

"Ooh, shirt off. I want to see the tattoo."

"Later," Zeke said, waving me off.

"I don't want to be here if you're going to bang her," Honani said. His body flickered, like he was fading in and out of this plane.

"Honani! That was so rude. I'm better than a bang."

"I bet you are," Honani said with a smile.

I rolled my eyes. "You've been dying to say that."

He snorted a dry, ghostly laugh. "Good one."

"I can dish, too." I snuggled into my pillow.

"So you can," the spirit said, still chuckling.

"I want you to wake us up around midnight," Zeke commanded. "Can you do that or am I making a huge mistake trusting you?"

"My job is to keep Echo safe," Honani said, his voice as pissy as Zeke's had been. Irritation at their silly attempt to out-man each other caused me to shove a pillow over my ear.

"Ten o'clock. We need to travel to the Ridge Ruin then. Don't let the demons get close."

Zeke slid into the bed, careful to stay on top of the sheet. He flopped backward and yanked the blanket and comforter up over his head.

Honani's disbelieving expression reflected my own. Honani pulled his chin back against his neck as if to say *What's his problem?*

I shrugged. Then yawned again.

"Of course, Echo. I'll keep watch now. You need to rest. You look terrible. That is why Zeke ignores you."

"She doesn't look horrible," Zeke snapped.

Honani grinned. He drifted over to the locked door and settled between it and the console holding the television. I flopped down and tried to ignore that, for the first time in my life, I shared a bed with a man. That didn't work. I wiggled around. Zeke grunted. I scowled at him even though he'd buried his head under the blanket.

I turned onto my side, trying to find a comfortable position. Zeke's arm slid over me, cocooning me in his warmth. I smiled. Just what I'd needed. Oblivion slammed into me.

I slept hard, dreaming of a big mountain cat with saber teeth. The cat sat still, regal, daring me closer. Honani called me, but I ignored him. The cat knew something about Layla. I needed to get to the cat.

Zeke called my name. I couldn't answer him. I wanted to. I tried. My mouth didn't work right. Uh oh. Something told me following the cat wasn't a good idea.

"Can you do anything?" Zeke asked. "Echo!"

Who needed to do what? I tried to open my eyes, to struggle against the floating sensation, to tell Zeke I was fine. I just needed a minute. But I wasn't fine—I was untethered, a kite lost to a strong gust and about to be batted down by a cat. Where was the cat? I moved farther from Zeke and Honani.

"Her soul has wandered," Honani responded.

Really?

The farther I moved from the motel room bed, the more amorphous my being became. This was my *coyopa*. That was a word I'd read used for a drifting mind or maybe the soul, as Honani said. In less than a blink, I moved outside the motel, pulled quickly beyond the mortal world. I needed to find my way back into my body. Fast.

I did not want to go for a joyride.

"Zeke?" I whispered. "Honani?"

Nothing. Just chill and mist.

There was the cat. He turned to look at me over his shoulder, whiskers twitching.

CHAPTER FIVE

The mist rippled around me like a fog machine gone haywire. One minute I was in a gray, blank space. The next, a thick haze wrapped around my legs and arms like thousands of pieces of spider silk, tangling and weighing my limbs down.

The cat was gone, but I remained very much *here*. Wherever here was.

On the other side of the haze, something tried to pull me through the damp barrier. It felt like…scared though I was to admit it, the thing pulling me felt like Layla.

I hesitated, thinking back to my coursework on dreams and *coyopa*. The part of consciousness that transcended the physical realm. In the book my mother had, I'd read the mere act of entering a memory as a *coyopa* could change the course of history. I didn't want to do that.

I was drawn like a fish on a line out of this soft, safe place toward Layla. Thoughts of her pulled the line taut. I wanted to fight, because I worried the cat was a demon and this was another ambush, but I didn't. With each thought of Layla, the closer she seemed to be.

Her fear coiled around me. Where was the cat? Should I stop? I couldn't stop. I needed to find Layla.

Her presence became more insistent and louder. I could actually hear her voice now, calling. The hair on my arms and head lifted as both fear and hope crashed through me. Only to be crushed as logic screamed at me that this couldn't end well. *Coyopas* weren't meant to leave bodies during dreamland. And what if Layla wasn't the one calling me?

Whoa. I tried to drag my nonexistent feet. Everything about this situation smelled of danger.

Mist wrapped around me, tighter, trying to force me into a cocoon. I'd never been interested in gambling, and this form of roulette was even more dangerous than holding a gun with one loaded chamber to my head.

"Echo…be my Echo. And I'll be your shadow."

Layla had made up that silly song in response to some mean girls' teasing. While I'd appreciated her support then, I couldn't believe that's how she chose to call me.

Actually, I could. It was our song, something just for the two of us.

Fighting off the mist, I waded forward, surprised to see a round, stacked-rock tower jutting out of a low mud-and-daub building. The tower stood at least four stories tall, the narrow rocks set like interlocking bricks interspersed with small open windows. Thick wood beams shot out at ten-foot intervals all the way up the tower.

The edifice seemed both ancient and new. Mist slid out of a gaping door-way set in the front of the building. Forward progress became impossible. Layla's voice drifted across the space. I couldn't see her. I plowed through the thick fog. And fell. Just like Alice. I was sucked into the *sipapu*. At least I had no stomach to rebel against the suction-like moment before I fell from the gateway onto the rocky plane.

Images began to take shape in the mist, like shadow boxes. "Layla?" I whispered.

She wasn't here because she wanted to be. No, this place seemed to be waiting, almost holding its breath. Malevolence and fear brushed over my skin, causing nasty tingles. I'd be lucky if the mist was the worst of what lay between my friend and me. I stumbled into a circle of fog-free, dead ground.

There she was. Layla's back pressed against a steep rise of rock. Her hair, a tangled mass falling over her face and back, blocked her eyes. Bits of dirt clung to the thick, blond hanks. Her clothes were ripped and as dirty as her hair. The wooden staff in her hands was taller than she and not much thinner. Even disheveled, she glowed like a golden beacon in a sea of nightmares.

An entire army of demons surrounded her on the other three sides, slavering and pressing forward against some invisible leash.

The need to rip apart bone and muscle exuded from the stiff set of their necks and the thick drool pooling at their feet.

The assortment of wings, feathers, talons, scales, and furry animal bodies didn't seem to connect to each other. The masses were like those jumble books parents give to preschoolers so they can make their own croco-ele-pus. But these beasts were the result of godly imagination, masses of sinuous muscle and the crucial features of sharp teeth and claws designed to rip apart and destroy.

The beasts pressed in harder with each new gash and howl of agony, hazed in bloodlust. Problem was they were inching nearer to Layla even as they fought each other.

Layla roared. She was like a Viking goddess—how I imagined Freya as she fought her foes. She held the long piece of wood with an easy certainty that intimated long use.

A few of the beasts lunged. A cry of denial tried to burst forth but I clamped it down. Or maybe my lack of body held in the sound. What could a *coyopa* do?

Layla slammed the staff toward the most aggressive bunch of the nasty creatures, blowing them into insubstantial bits.

Immediately, the group behind took their place. She stumbled against the rocks but forced herself upright in a quick jerk.

Even across the distance separating us, Layla's eyes were dim, the silver almost gone. Just like my mom's eyes had faded as her magic drained from her body. My mind seemed to convulse with the negation of the tableau unfolding below me.

No wonder Layla had called for me across time, space, even physical planes. Screw those books. No way I'd allow Layla to die. Not without me doing *everything* I could to help.

A beast, a cross between a wolf and a saber-toothed tiger, padded on large silent feet behind Layla, tilting its head as though measuring distance. Layla was too distracted by the frontal attack to notice.

I remained too far away to help. I wasn't sure what would happen if I waded into the demons. Could they see my ethereal figure, or was I invisible to them? A mere speck of dust in their horror-filled world?

Cataloguing the situation was the easy part. The threats were obvious and they outnumbered Layla nearly a thousand to one.

Without a sword, spear, or staff, I had only my head: a jumbled mass of disorganization and scattered ideas. I struggled to capture enough of a thought to form a plan.

The saber wolf above Layla crept closer, its thin, talon-sharp claws catching on the rock with each step. Another joined the first, angling in from the other side, too far away for me to ice-attack them together.

A group of those giant bats Zeke and I had battled earlier today launched themselves over the other beasts, straight toward Layla, who was pinned against the outcropping.

Her staff wavered for a minute. Then Layla huffed and stood straight. She raised the staff and screamed, the sound rife with rebellious hate. Her last stand. I felt her emotion. She planned to die, taking as many of these murderers with her as she could. I'd never been prouder of my friend, nor more terrified for her safety.

Another shadow slunk out from behind the rock, as huge as the wolves, poised to pounce—on the saber wolf. The cat who'd called me here. With predatory feline grace, the cat leaped, locking itself in a fierce fight with the wolf.

My magic flamed to life, and I barely controlled and directed the large bolt of ice-cold energy toward the second saber-toothed wolf just as the demon jumped toward Layla.

The beast yelped in agony only to be swallowed by the ravening white mist. That's why it was so hard to move here—all that negative energy tried to adhere to the sentient beings like Layla and me, needing something to propel forward, away from this barren place.

The cat shook the wolf one last time before he leapt back over the rock, out of sight. I didn't watch its descent because another wave of demons edged closer to Layla, clawing at each other in an effort to eat her.

"Screw you for thinking otherwise," I snapped at the demons, the mist—all of it. If I'd had a jaw, I would have locked it hard enough for my teeth to crunch. The mist curled up and over my *coyopa*, colder even than Honani's embrace. Prickles of anguish blossomed wherever it came into contact with my presence. Not my physical body but the sense of it, much like my awareness of Honani's stature and physique. He wasn't solid on my plane just as I wasn't solid here—I was still tethered, in part, to the Fourth World.

The mist licked over my consciousness, but it couldn't force me to its bidding, because I was master of my spirit—of all spirits, according to Zeke and Layla.

"I say this is purple haze. Not white mist," I said. Not because I cared about the song or even the color of the fog wrapping around me tighter with each heartbeat. No, I needed to use words—I'd always hated to be alone, fearing demons and scary creatures. My mom had soothed me, allaying my concerns. But she'd never, not once, said demons didn't exist.

"No one in my world has even heard of you," I called out louder. The mist pressed closer, trying to stifle my voice. I called louder to both the haze and the demons beyond it. "And that's where you belong: extinct and unremembered."

The mist slid from me, unable to stick. I blasted that fog with my version of a winter storm. The wave of frigid energy surged into the ranks of the monsters, flash-freezing them in quick succession.

With loud creaks and a few crashes, the beasts toppled, breaking into demon flotsam. My smile grew. My power was stronger and more pliable here, and I liked it.

A huge tidal wave swept across the plain as soon as I thought it, decimating more of the demons that had started to thaw. The beasts clawed and howled, ripping at each other and the rock, trying to regain purchase of higher, dry ground. They flipped and scuttled through the torrent of water, unable to withstand my power.

"Echo!" Layla screamed. She'd zapped more of the beasts, which were still advancing toward her with her staff. She gestured toward me. The fog was back, thicker than before.

"Echo!" she screamed again, still gesturing and blasting, wading through the inch-thick fog that clung to her. A huge, furry beast slammed into me, pinning me to the ground. The demon was strong—much stronger than I was.

Gravity, like magic, didn't work the same here, and the beast holding me down grew heavier the longer he held me. I'm not sure why that surprised me. Everything about this new world I lived in surprised me, usually in a bad way. Like now.

The beast's teeth sank deep into my *coyopa*, where my shoulder would be, and dragged down toward my chest. It yelped and released its hold. My essence, a rich purple, leaked from the wounds, drifting past my face to taunt me.

Why did it stop?

My hold on reality slipped as the demon batted me around like a kitten with a ball of yarn. Its mouth and long, yellow teeth were mere inches from my consciousness.

I focused my waning energy and slammed the magic into the beast. The purple essence swirled around us, enveloping the demon. A saber-toothed wolf, like the one who'd planned to take down Layla. This one had sought me out, decided I posed a bigger threat to its brethren than Layla.

The demon lunged, long canines biting into my middle sending another bout of agony through my soul. I twisted, trying to heave the wolf from my body as purple tendrils coiled around the beast, freezing its coat and nose and finally its eyes and mouth, just as I had the giant snake at the gas station. Not enough.

The cat slammed into the saber-wolf, and the canine jerked, its claws catching the injured spot in my *coyopa* once again. I screamed and my mind splintered. When I collapsed against the thick, blanketing mist, the wolf was gone. The cat nuzzled in closer. He didn't act like a demon. In fact, concern wafted from him, lingering over me.

"No, no. Echo. You can't fade. Stay with me, E." Layla's voice was warped somehow. She sounded close to tears but so far away. "Echo María Ruiz, focus on me now!"

I tried. "My shoulder," I said through gritted teeth. The cat leaned forward, swiping the wound with its tongue. For a moment, the burn built into an inferno.

"Make it stop," I gasped.

"No, the cat seems to be helping. Lick her again," Layla said to the cat. The rough tongue scraped over my cuts, working its way down toward where my stomach would be.

"You're a mess," Layla admitted, her eyes full of fear. "You shouldn't have cuts when you're not even really here." She touched one, her eyes wide with fear. "So many of them. And they're so hot."

Now that she mentioned it, my temperature skyrocketed. Layla swirled her hand, pulling my purple essence back toward the deepest gash. The cat licked it. Layla shoved its head away.

"I'm so sorry I thought of you," she whispered. "I didn't mean to pull you here, I just wanted you to know I felt him."

"Who?"

The cat growled and licked the wound again.

"The Fourth." Her eyes met mine, her chin trembling. The cat quit licking, his large head turned toward Layla as if he wanted to ease her distress. "He's here. I feel him, but it's muted. He's close but I can't see him, find him."

"You sure?" I gasped. I didn't feel anyone else—and I was the only one of us who could tap into others' emotions. Maybe my senses were dampened by the demon's attack. Holy *frijoles*, I hurt. The cat slunk backward, it's long black tail curling around Layla for a moment before he disappeared.

She picked up the staff she'd settled next to me when she dropped to her knees to address my seeping *coyopa*. "I can't believe you took out all the demons," she muttered, patting my shoulder, seeming to force my essence back into me. "You've become even stronger."

"Glad to help. I was getting the hang of the mist before that thing attacked me. What did you mean about the Fourth? Where'd you get the pet?"

Layla nodded, but her eyes were on my shoulder. Layla's face fell in shock and anguish. "He found me. The cat I mean. He brought me the staff, prowls around me. It's like…like he's stalking me."

"Has he hurt you? Where are we?"

She shook her head. "No, he's helping. My magic's stronger here." Her surprise and delight mingled together, drifting over me.

So was mine. But that wasn't what I wanted to know. Plus, my energy slid out of me. No, not my energy. My essence. Me. Layla's face contorted into a mask of sheer concentration.

"We'll fix you," she muttered. "I'll find the Fourth, then I'll find you. Oh, Echo, stay with me."

"I don't think you can fix me." I sighed.

"I have to. I need you to talk the Fourth into coming out of hiding." She turned her head searching. "He's close."

"So tired," I muttered.

Tocha. The name drifted over me, a caress. Zeke. He called me again. *Echo, don't die.*

"Help me. Focus on the wound. Stop the flow." Her voice held a note of panic. Weird. Layla didn't panic—she preferred to snark.

I drifted off, not really aware of my surroundings. Everything hurt so much. Worse even than after Coyote tried to kill me.

"Echo, you bring your spirit back together now!" Layla bellowed. Her eyes swirled to life, flaring a bright, fierce gray. My retinas seared with the full extent of Layla's power; she put everything she had into that command.

I smiled weakly. This was the part of Layla I was just beginning to know. My magic center flickered. I'd used so much energy already, but I'd try for her. I told my magic to do what Layla said, to go to the deep gouges in my shoulder and halt my soul's escape.

Fight for me, Zeke called, his voice cracking. *Come back. I need you back.*

"You can't die for me, not now." Layla's bright gray gaze darkened and her face crumpled. "I need you to help me, E. I didn't know…Look, you must heal. Then come find us. I can't save him alone. You saw what I'm facing." She shivered, her normally bright silver eyes too dull. "They'll be back. They keep coming back."

"Quit ordering me around," I croaked. "I'm sleeping somewhere, so this is the best I can do in my semifunctional state. Granted, I didn't know I'd fight an army in my sleep."

Her mouth slid into an O while her eyes widened.

"You're *sleeping* with him?" Layla asked, her voice sliding toward sly. "We definitely have to catch up."

I wished. Much as I wanted to tell her she was wrong, my throat convulsed. Holy *frijoles*, my shoulder hurt. Layla's gray eyes burned brighter than melted pewter.

"That's it—Zeke! Go back to Zeke. Think about him, just him. Really concentrate. Can you do that for me, E? Concentrate on Zeke. That's the only way we can get you back to your body."

I needed to tell her because I couldn't tell him. "I don't understand him. But I like him. He doesn't want me. Or want to want me."

"Find him." She used that ordering voice that pounded against my *coyopa*. I had to obey. My eyes rolled back in my head. Agony and sadness rippled through me in some slow wave, like the first tremble of ocean tides before a big storm.

I pictured his face: Those dark eyes smiling down at me while his lips flipped up in that little smirk. His straight nose and firm jaw.

I'm pretty sure I died.

CHAPTER SIX

"Echo. *Tocha*. Come back." Zeke. Fear and something more…Concern? Pain? Those emotions slammed into my consciousness like a head-on collision with a train. The need to ease his concern drew me up out of the fog of pain along with the nausea I always experienced when moving through planes. I hated that form of travel.

"Wake up," Honani screamed into my ear, which caused the one part of my body that hadn't been incapacitated to throb.

"You must want to come back here to this plane," Honani continued. "Echo. Please."

I tried to roll away from Honani's icy hands clamped on my cheeks. The vicious pain that had once been my shoulder forced me fully awake, and I screamed. Well, it would have been a scream if I could breathe properly, but I couldn't.

Hanoi released my face, causing me to flop back onto the bed. As my shoulders hit the bed, pain radiated into my chest, neck, head. For a girl who'd lived most of her life with relentless migraines, these sensations were beyond indescribable.

I'd lost all ability to control my lungs; I tried to drag air in through my mouth and nose but couldn't. Black dots formed in front of my eyes, then blocked out my entire field of vision.

"Echo," Zeke murmured, his quiet voice reaching me through my panic and agony. "Breathe. You got this, *tocha*. Breathe."

His warm, callused hand slid across my cheek. I focused on his touch. The heat there finally permeated my fear, and I took a breath.

"Good. Again."

I turned my head into his neck and shuddered hard. Before I realized it, tears streaked my cheeks. Zeke held me, whispering to me—silly nothings about my bravery and beauty.

The blackness receded in centimeters. The next breath wasn't as labored, the next less so. I settled into my body, which lay across Zeke's lap, his arms wrapped around me, his torso blanketing mine. Honani fluttered just behind my head, making my hair follicles hurt from the cold radiating from him. He was subzero for sure. I guess stress did weird things to ghosts, too.

"Why...*tocha*?" I managed to ask.

Zeke ran his hand over my hair, cupping my cheek. "You scared me." His gaze flicked up to the ghost warrior behind me. "Us."

Honani moved so he hovered at the foot of the bed. Gray permeated his normally bright turquoise aura. I reached out my good arm and touched his fingers. The warrior glanced up at me, his eyes filled with shadows.

"I didn't think you would come back from that place." Honani's lips tightened. But his chin still wobbled. The answering emotion welled up in my eyes. This strong, mighty spirit worried about me. The closest being I had to a brother—any family, really—death notwithstanding, his concern touched me more deeply than I wanted to admit. Tears pooled in my eyes, but I didn't *want* to cry. Somehow crying meant I had to accept my mother's death. What Coyote had taken from me. I slammed my eyes shut, forcing the tears to stay in me.

Zeke tugged me closer to his warm chest. This time, the pain seared through my physical body, settling deep in my shoulder and down my arm. His arms circled my torso, holding me close, his jaw resting on the top of my head. This moment was caring, and I soaked in his willingness to share a part of himself with me.

"I didn't either," I said. My voice sounded strained, even to my ears.

Zeke lowered me back against the pillow. He ran his fingers over my cheekbones, my throat, back to my lips, my hair, my eyebrows. His eyes followed his fingers as though he was memorizing my features.

His face was so close, his warm breath on my skin. I needed him to kiss me, hold me. To help me feel alive, valued.

"You're okay," he whispered, tracking the curve of my lower lip with his thumb.

"What's *tocha*?"

"Means hummingbird in an ancient dialect Masau taught me. You remind me of one. You know, small but tough. I just…You'll be fine," Zeke said, his deep voice cracking with the strain. "I need to see. Can I see?"

I nodded. Zeke carefully slipped his arms from underneath me. His heat leached from my skin, and I shivered from the extreme cold. Zeke's hands shook as he peeled my shirt from my shoulder in a gentle motion. How such a large man used his hands with such precision was beyond me.

The cotton of my T-shirt stuck to my new wound. Zeke pulled with more urgency, and the movement caused me to cry out and stiffen. Zeke reached under his pillow and pulled out his knife. The wicked-sharp blade was prismatic but also dark, trying to hold the light inside.

He slipped the blade under my shirt and flicked the handle upward, baring my entire torso. He peeled the edges of ruined cotton from my body, exposing the four deep gashes that started at the top of my shoulder and ended at my bra. The skin on my shoulder looked like it had been attacked by a poisoned chainsaw, all torn and swollen. My stomach wasn't as bad, but the cuts there were inflamed and working toward infected, though they were already closed over with thick scabs.

Zeke hissed out a breath before his eyes met mine. I couldn't make out his pupils. That scared me more than anything else had, and my breathing escalated again. He ran his big hand over my hair, cradling me with exquisite care.

"How did you manage to close the wounds?" he asked.

I shuddered, still able to feel the cat's tongue abrading my soul. Layla hadn't stopped it, but she did use her powers to shove as much of me back inside as possible. "Layla!" I gripped his wrist. I paused for a long moment, waiting out the nausea and pain. "She's in some place with a tall tower and an army of demons attacking her."

"The Ridge Ruin?" Zeke asked.

"I don't know. I kept falling, to a field strewn with rocks. There were demons everywhere."

I dipped my head toward the wounds. A single tear leaked involuntarily from my eyes at the movement. Tears were pathetic. They wouldn't change my mother's death, my pitiful response to the hurt. I mashed my lips together and willed them to stop.

"Cry," Honani said. "Many warriors do after battle. It's a physical release of the adrenaline from your system."

Zeke brushed his thumb under my eye, trailed his fingers down my damp cheek before he sat back on his heels.

"Do you know where I went?" I asked, my eyes flicking back and forth between them. "The place felt ancient. Layla said she felt him—the Fourth—there."

"No. I don't know all the places the dead gather," Honani said. He sounded perturbed. "Not a good place if demons have overrun it."

"We have to find them. We need to help them," I said, my voice reedy and weak.

"Soon," Zeke said. His eyes were brighter and a small smile tugged on the corner of those wide, mobile lips. "I'm glad you're back."

"Will Layla be able to move from there? She needs to." After experiencing that mist's near-human ability to manipulate feelings, and the sheer volume of monsters in that place, I couldn't imagine Layla's exhaustion and terror.

My need to rescue her ratcheted up. She'd found the Fourth. Something about Layla's hesitancy in mentioning more about him worried me.

As soon as I could move, I was going to the Magician. I'd beg him for information, whatever I needed to do. I had to save Layla, as she'd saved me. No way I'd leave her there. No way I'd give up the lead on the Fourth. Not with Layla's concern for his safety.

Honani inched forward. "Not yet. She doesn't have the power. Especially now. She helped you heal. From what I understand, that's her strongest capability."

Zeke nodded, his brows furrowed as he poked at my shoulder. He traced the deep, vicious cuts with the tip of his finger. "I don't understand how you survived that demon's attack. I have scars from them, but they've never gotten my soul. That's what they want, you know. What they feed on."

No, I hadn't known that. I didn't want to know. Soul-eating was disturbing.

The cat licked me—to get my soul? "What happens if a soul's rent apart?" I asked.

Honani shrugged but his aura paled even more. The idea made him really nervous. "Pain, I'm sure. At some point, a profound loss of consciousness." Honani paused. Not new information. "I know only what the dead tell me—to fear the possibility."

"You would no longer be human," Zeke said. "I mean, if the demons ripped you apart. Maybe bits of you would float around, trying to attach to something stronger than you."

I was quiet, digesting what I'd learned. Had my mother chosen the better path? She'd merged her essence with mine. New layers to the puzzle of living, dead, sentient and not slid over each other, but answers weren't yet clear.

Zeke continued to poke at my shoulder, his face falling into disbelief. He shook his head. "The wound is completely sealed."

My eyes met his, bewilderment and something like admiration in their depths. "Is that bad?" I asked, my confusion and fear ramping back up.

Zeke picked up my hand, gripping the fingers tight enough that each pulse of blood to the tips became painful. "It's good. I think. There's no way for your soul to continue to leak out of your body. That has to be positive. Right?" He turned toward Honani, who shrugged again.

"I know little about demons," Honani said. "They are difficult to kill and they don't like to stay dead."

"You think the wound should be festering?" I asked.

Zeke touched the wound once more, and while his touch hurt, I didn't need to suppress the desire to scream this time. "If the demon ripped your flesh, well, you could heal from that, but the process is long and painful." He looked down at the silvery scars on his hands. Zeke spoke from experience. "I think the wound would spread, pulling at your soul if you were in danger, not healing over and knitting together so well."

"This is painful!" I said, indignant.

"Having just seen you come back into your body, I don't doubt that," Zeke said.

I glared at him while he continued to tap his chin. "Souls only function in their entirety. When one is ripped, there's no way to mend it. That means you lose you. But you managed to patch your soul back together. I—I don't even know how that's possible. Maybe that has something to do with your father."

"Wouldn't that be Masau's area?" I asked.

"Then perhaps she has some control over the finality of death itself," Honani murmured.

"That doesn't make sense!" I exclaimed.

"Why ever not?" Honani asked. His aura pulsed a feisty green.

"Do you think I would have let my mother die if I could have prevented her death?" I was indignant. Angry. And too naked. I tried to pull my shirt closed and hissed out a curse when I jarred my shoulder. Shards of glass seemed to fall through my skin, lacerating the inside. Zeke pulled my shirt closed and stood, reaching for his jeans. He slid into them.

"The key word there, Echo, is *prevent*. She was dying. Well on her way to dead. You couldn't stop that, but maybe you can slow the process down. You talked to her, there, at the end, right?"

I nodded.

"Who's to say that's not because of your powers? And you definitely staved off death tonight. At least for yourself." Zeke motioned toward my shoulder, his eyes roving the area.

"You keep saying that. I don't know what I did or how. Layla yelled at me to fix it, so I did my best. She seemed to use her mind mojo to make me, even though I didn't understand the what or how. Maybe my mom's essence helped somehow. It all happened so fast."

I sighed, picking at my shirt. "If the wounds heal, I'll scar, huh?" With my shoulder a mass of bite marks and deep, angry gouges, my wardrobe choices would no longer include strapless and sleeveless tops. "I really hate that saber wolf demon. He's severely limited my wardrobe options."

Honani and Zeke both stared at me, openmouthed. "You're incredibly lucky to be alive. To be human still," Honani said.

"I got that already, *ese*. I'm just saying that stupid demon managed to maul my most important bits, and I'll have to wear the ugly reminder forever. How unfair is that?" I huffed. "Gah! My stomach." My guts—which were still inside—pitched at the red, angry gash.

Zeke laughed. "I guess this means you're feeling better. And the wounds won't leave much of a scar once I smear them with the salve. Can you sit up? Or will the movement hurt your stomach too much?"

"No, no. I can manage." I gritted my teeth but did fumble into a sitting position. The movements caused sharp pains to stab through all my cuts.

"It's almost dawn," Zeke murmured. "We should take off soon."

"I thought we were supposed to wake up in the middle of the night," I said.

Zeke raised his brows and glanced back at Honani. "We were. We tried, but your *coyopa* was too deep into its joy ride."

"Not joyous at all. That place was scary." I shuddered, followed by the need to bite the inside of my cheek to keep from moaning again.

I wanted to find out how Layla ended up there. And how could the Fourth be there? Too many questions that I couldn't answer.

Standing hurt more than I anticipated. Zeke didn't see my shudders of pain, because he was digging through his pack for the jar of yellow ointment. Honani rushed forward to help, then stopped just short of touching me. Did he think he'd get demon cooties? His lips folded inward and he frowned, his brow pulled low with ferocious annoyance as he hovered.

"I'm okay," I told him. A big fat lie. My body seemed slower, as though I were still moving through that thick white mist. I sat on the edge of the bed, hands on my knees. My gaze landed on the pale flesh of my belly, highlighted by more of the gouges visible through my tattered tee.

I tried to work up the energy to stand and grab another shirt from my backpack that sat across the room in the small chair, next to the door. Maybe four steps.

Nope, not happening right now.

Zeke darted a quick peek back at me. "Maybe it'd be better if we got cleaned up first and then I put this on you. I don't know if water can wash out any of those wounds but cleaning can't hurt."

"Why don't you go first? I just need another minute. To catch my breath."

I waved him toward the bathroom with my good hand.

"You sure you're well enough to be up?" Zeke asked, coming back to stand next to me. He tucked a thick strand of hair behind my ear before his thumb traced the curve of my cheek.

"I'll be fine. Just taking it slow." I smiled at him, though my eyes wanted to cross and my body already shook. Zeke jerked his head in a sharp nod, his eyes filled with concern.

"I'll be quick," Zeke said as he entered the bathroom. He gave me another worried glance before shutting the door.

"You should tell him," Honani whispered as he hovered at my side.

"I'll be fine," I repeated.

Honani's aura faded once again. "Perhaps. But we both know something happened with that demon. Its stench surrounds you."

I took a few deep breaths, trying to find equilibrium. I touched the pendant hanging around my neck, a token from the father I'd never met. The saber-toothed wolf's attack ended when he came into contact with the pendant. Had the magic flowing through the pendant caused him to stop? I cupped the piece, willing the souls inside to heal whatever was wrong with me.

The clay stayed cool. Of course. The pendant worked when I wanted it to before, when the spirits sensed danger.

I raised my head as Zeke opened the bathroom door. His damp hair stuck up all over his head as though he'd toweled his head roughly. His gray T-shirt clung to his shoulders. I sighed.

"What's wrong?" he asked, his eyes flicking over my face and nearly naked torso. I recoiled back into the bedding as his eyes sought my wound.

"I-I don't know."

"You feel bad?" Zeke asked, sitting next to me. "Or can't you walk?"

I nodded. Honani tipped his chin in encouragement. "I feel…off."

Zeke ran his hands over my shoulders. The calluses on his palms slid across my skin, but the sensation of touch remained distant. My heart rate escalated.

"I don't feel like I'm me," I said. The explanation was poor but the best I could manage.

Zeke helped me to my feet, an arm around my waist, just below the angry scratch marks on my belly.

"Here, let's get you into the shower. You'll feel better when you're clean. Afterward, I'll put ointment on those cuts. It'll speed up the healing."

Concern lashed across my skin, but that, too, seemed removed. I gripped Zeke's wrist, nauseated.

"Does the demon own the part of me he ripped?" I asked.

"What happened to it?" Zeke asked.

"I'm not really sure. I think my soul wrapped around its body." The purple was hard to miss, especially when the color had flowed back into me when Layla and I managed to close the wounds. "Then the cat chased it off." Confusion painted Zeke's features. "What?"

Maybe I'd imbibed the demon into my body. My stomach heaved, no longer nauseated but in all-out rebellion. I didn't want a demon polluting me, maybe even the way I thought.

"We'll see, Echo." Zeke maneuvered me around the bed and into the bathroom.

My legs felt like they were clamped in fifty-pound weights. My breath puffed and my heart rate escalated like I'd run a marathon in the eight steps I forced my legs to take. I stood in the small tiled space. He closed the door and I sat on the toilet for a few minutes. Standing with slow, careful movements, I turned on the water and finished undressing.

My shoulder muscles continued to seize and relax in a thick shudder. I adjusted the temperature to the hottest point on the dial and bit my lip against the sting of water on my skin.

The heat helped enough for me to shampoo and condition my hair with my good arm, finally ridding my scalp of the last of the grit from Coyote's dust storm. Had that really been two days ago?

Turning off the tap, I grabbed one of the thin, white towels from the rack.

I hadn't brought clean undergarments into the bathroom with me and Zeke hadn't thought to either. I squeezed as much water from my hair as possible, shivering slightly where the wet mass dripped down over my hips. I secured my towel around my chest, just below the red weal that marred the lightly tanned skin of my shoulder.

I stumbled out of the steam-filled room on weak legs to find Honani and Zeke glaring at each other. Honani started at my head and worked his way down. Zeke started at my feet and slowly worked his way up. Heat crept up my chest and across my face.

"I need some clothes," I said, motioning toward my bag with my right arm. I leaned against the wall, glad for its support. "But I also need that medicine."

"Sure." Zeke snagged my backpack and the small pot of ointment. How soon would he need a new jar?

"Can you get more of that stuff?" I asked, tipping my head toward the container.

"Sussitanako makes it. Layla keeps a supply. Your scarring would be nonexistent with her recipe."

"Who's?"

"Sussitanako's."

Zeke stepped close enough so that my towel brushed his chest. "Be still while I run the ointment over your shoulder." His dark eyes glazed as he reached up to touch my raised, red skin. He spread the cream with slow, deliberate strokes.

His touch was more tangible now and too intimate, especially given my state of undress. I eased back from under his hands, causing his fingers to brush across the top of my towel. I gripped the edges, trying to hold them tight together as Zeke's eyes followed his hands. I grabbed the ointment from his hand. "I'll see to the rest of them on my stomach. Thanks."

I stepped back and turned toward the bathroom. My towel slipped and I managed to catch it over my breasts, though my back exposed to my waist. I shut the door. Not that the lock did much good—the barrier was barely thicker than a tissue. Sound traveled through easily.

"Leave her alone," I heard Honani scold. "I do not wish to tell her family you've hurt her."

"We've already finished that conversation," Zeke responded, as I heard the front door slam shut.

Something didn't feel right, but I had too much to worry about right now. Whatever was going on between Zeke and Honani would have to wait. I forced my focus back to my wounds.

The heat from the shower and Sussitanako's ointment soothed much of the inflammation, and I dressed. Once I zipped my boots, I picked up my brush and backpack.

I opened the bathroom door to find Zeke stepping back into the room balancing two cups of coffee in one hand and some kind of breakfast sandwiches and what looked like a smoothie in the other. I finished brushing my long hair and slid the brush into my bag before snatching my cup of coffee from his hand. I enjoyed the heat and dark roast flavor on my tongue and down my throat. I smacked my lips.

"It's not going to win any awards, but it's better than nothing," Zeke said. He handed me one of the wrapped sandwiches and the smoothie.

"I think there's real fruit in that," he said, tipping his head toward the smoothie. "The sandwich isn't natural or real food, but it's calories. You keep using magic at this rate, and you'll fade away in less than a week." He took a bite from his own sandwich, chased by a healthy swallow of coffee. "We gotta get on the road."

I tore into the first bite. "What's the rush?"

"While you were off saving Layla, I went on my own nocturnal trip and saw a line of demons heading toward us. We need to get away before they catch up."

"Why don't they travel via *sipapu?*"

"Because you messed that up when you broke the tablet. Same reason we aren't moving around that way."

"I didn't mean to."

"I know that. But it's slowing us down."

"At least it's also slowing down the demons."

"So far," Zeke said. "But they were gathering more with each mile."

I nibbled at the edge of the bread. "How do they do that? Find us, I mean."

"By smell," Honani said. "It's like Echo-location." He sniggered but turned the sound into a cough, his face contorting into a grimace.

I frowned at him, but didn't blast him for acting like a child. If he needed his pathetic jokes, he could enjoy them. "How'd you know that?" I asked.

Honani shrugged, his eyes distant. "Your bigger problem is they're here."

CHAPTER SEVEN

Zeke snagged his spear. He grabbed the sword and scabbard from the bed, buckling the sword sheath on in a quick, efficient flick of his wrist.

"Grab my bag." He darted to the window. "Aw, hell. That's an entire battalion out there. Someone's getting serious about killing you, Echo."

"I'm hoping to disappoint the god or goddess for another fifty or sixty years." A weird sensitivity drifted over my skin, like an awareness of the energy moving toward us. Like ants crawling on my skin—I was itchy, tickly, not terribly comfortable.

Just another way my life had changed over the past week. I had a feeling a morning out on the back porch sipping coffee wasn't going to be in my future any time soon.

"Can't you give us more warning?" Zeke demanded, turning to glare at the ghost warrior.

Honani shrugged. "Been busy."

"We should've left hours ago," Zeke growled.

Honani's aura glowed a brighter green. "Then wake when I call you."

"Fight later, you two. We need to get rid of a lot of demons right now." I picked up Zeke's bag and slung it over my good shoulder. Mine was already there; the two bags banged together, making me work to keep them in place. I slung Zeke's bag back up and glanced from the front door to the bathroom. No window in there.

"A spirit has to like you to come to this plane," Honani sniffed. "I stay for Echo. Not for you. Few of us are comfortable with all these glaring lights living people insist on using. Then there are people moving through you, which is an uncomfortable sensation for us both."

"They're getting closer," I said. The fiends shuffled in to surround the building. I sucked at the dregs of my smoothie and tried to send out go-away vibes. The demons snarled in my mind, filling the space with threats and images of how they planned to kill me.

Yeah, it was scary, but I also learned demons are capable of very little imagination. Rip, bite, slurp. Repeat.

I shot out some of my thoughts, which were way nastier than theirs, including lots of fire and ice javelins. My images projected spectacular and gory deaths. They paused, agitated and unsure.

Wait.

I'd *communicated* with these things. I'd never been able to feel them before. I concentrated harder.

My pendant stayed cool against my chest. This was wrong. So wrong. Maybe that demon destroyed the pendant's link to me. Or, worse, the pendant no longer recognized me as its owner.

I gripped the two bags tightly and stumbled back from the energy pulsing from the hundreds of demons, just outside. More even than what surrounded Layla last night. More than I could take out with my ice trick. They snarled into my mind, shooting more images of me bloodied, dying, dead. I fought back with another shot of me icing them, this time adding some actual frigidity. The front line of demons whimpered and collapsed as their organs froze.

The agitation grew as did the in-fighting and aggression. "In case you didn't know, there are more behind us. It's a good sized army."

Zeke cursed. Honani's eyes grew even wider. He dipped his head once in acknowledgment, still staring at me.

"How'd you know that?"

"They're really riled up," I whispered.

"We're going to fight our way out," Zeke said. He gripped his spear and sword tighter then rolled his shoulders. After twisting his leather cuff at his wrist, his cotton and leather armor slid over his body. Huh. So that was how he went from fully armored warrior to normally dressed citizen in the blink of an eye. Coolest trick ever. Better than Superman, who was stuck in his Lycra all the time. I wanted something like that.

"It fits in there?" I asked, fascinated.

"Later," Zeke said.

One of the demons lunged forward, shoving its two-foot-long claws through the metal door. "I forgot to send death images," I moaned. The demons pressed forward en masse and I sighed, realizing our pissing contest was over.

Since I'd already imagined it, I created a swath of sharp ice just outside the motel room door. Not quite right. I honed the chunk to a narrow, deadly edge. Better. Balancing the weight wasn't easy, but I managed to drop the ice onto the front line to slice through dozens of bodies, leaving demon ash and jagged chunks of ice in its wake.

"Yes," I exclaimed, careful not to move my shoulder.

"That was a good one," Honani said. "But you'll tire out soon. And then what's the plan?"

I frowned. "What do you mean?"

"Determination isn't the same thing as intelligence, is it?" He sounded bored. I glared at him, but he just smiled at me.

"Are you saying I'm no smarter than those things out there?" I demanded.

"Of course not." The beasts howled as bodies slammed into the building. I stumbled backward. "But you can't keep them out there forever."

"So?"

"You could call for backup," Honani said.

"My pendant isn't responding," I mumbled.

"And you fear...what?"

"That the demon..." Which one? The wolf or the cat? "Whatever it did to me—destroyed my connection to it," I said. So what if the necklace was my last link to my parents, the last gift I'd ever received from my mother? Getting out of this situation was more pressing than yet another layer of grief to add to my stupendous heap.

"I could go into it. Perhaps unlock it," Honani said. His aura faded to a pale turquoise.

My hand trembled. "Will that work?"

Honani gripped my hand still fisted over the backpack strap, his cold caress a comfort against my overheated skin. "I don't know. But I'm bound in service to you. So I'll find my way back to you for as long as you need me."

"I can't lose you, too," I cried.

"Whatever you and Honani are blubbering about, save it for later," Zeke gritted out.

I slammed against Honani's vaporous form, my arms hugging him briefly. "Be careful."

"Always," he replied.

And then he flew into my pendant. My too-cold pendant.

"Echo! Do some more of that dry-icing. Or something. Please." Zeke stabbed his spear into one of the demon's scaly middles and lopped off the long-clawed paw of another.

I was terrible at multitasking. I couldn't hold on to my magic—even something as simple as projections—and carry on a conversation.

I tried to turn on the ice again, but I worried about Honani.

Claws shredded the door. Zeke pressed forward to meet the newest onslaught. He slammed his spear into the next paw that swiped past. The beast on the other side howled. For a breath, nothing happened.

The rest of the demons pressed forward, hatred rolling off them.

"There are too many of them for us to handle," Zeke said. He gripped his spear in a white-knuckled grip. "We're simply reacting. And we're pinned down here. Terrible battle strategy."

I closed my eyes and focused my thoughts. "Come on, Honani. Come on."

Zeke sucked in a deep breath, held it for a long moment. Finally, the air hissed from between his teeth. "We're going out. I'll clear a path by opening up the ground under them. Stick close to me."

"Give me a minute."

"We don't have a spare minute!"

Calling up spirits wasn't as easy as Zeke assumed, especially when the demons outside were trying to get my attention. But then, maybe fighting or portal travel wasn't as easy as he made it appear.

"Honani, come back. Please."

I heard the faint whine as Zeke slashed with his sword. "Faster, Echo. There are a lot of them and they're all pressing against the door. We're going to get overrun, and then we're beyond screwed."

Zeke shoved his spear into an open, slavering mouth. The demon's tongue had spikes. I winced.

"I'm doing the best I can," I yelled back. "Honani, I command you to return to my side. Now. With an army of spirits."

The pendant around my neck warmed to the point of discomfort. Holy tamales, the heat intensified further. I refused to lessen my grip, breathless with the hope I'd made some type of contact.

No Honani, then quite possibly no spirit army.

One of the demons lunged forward. I threw my smoothie cup at it. The beast stopped, apparently shocked by the bits of pink goo dripping from its matted fur. I couldn't help it, I giggled. Talk about being reduced to the ridiculous.

"Your mother is part of you. She gave you her essence. Use that," Zeke suggested.

"I don't know how," I moaned, even as I turned the pink smoothie into ice. The beast froze without making a sound. One down, many thousands to go.

"Here they come," Zeke whispered.

"Mom? We need help!" I yelped the last word as the wall in front of me collapsed into chunks of drywall and two-by-fours.

This beast reminded me of an anteater, but bigger. Way bigger. I slapped the demon hard with my right hand, but the movement jarred my left shoulder and both backpacks tumbled down my arm. The beast and I both squealed in pain, but at least the massive anteater disintegrated. I stayed in one piece, though I had to grip my shoulder as waves of nausea rolled through my stomach.

The pain slowly receded as cold air tugged at my pendant and whirled through my hair. Goose bumps formed on my flesh as the spirits circled protectively around me.

"Thanks for coming back, Honani. Spirits," I murmured. "Could you, maybe, destroy the bad guys before they kill us?"

The spirits swirled around me in a show of spirit love before hooting and brawling with the monsters. I'd been worried about asking the spirits to come—I didn't want any of them to suffer as I had by losing their immortal souls. This group consisted mostly of warriors who carried spears, bows and arrows, and even a few tomahawks. They formed a neat wedge formation and plowed through the hundreds of demons, leaving a wake of gritty dust.

One of the spirits rubbed a hand down my back. The caress and her aura reminded me of my mother. I turned toward the spirit, trying not to get my hopes up. Not my mom, much as I wanted her to be. Still, I smiled at the woman who stood next to me, her blue-gray eyes shining. She seemed familiar, but I'd never met her.

Losing Mom ripped at my heart, shredding my concentration. Much as I wanted to, I resisted the urge to grasp the woman's hand and press her palm tight to my overheated skin. My limited experience with spirits pointed to the fact they could touch me if they chose. However, when I touched them, their connection to this plane slipped. Honani, who spent more time here now, was the only exception—and only when he wanted to be. My best hypothesis was I acted as both the anchor and the door between this world and theirs.

"We're related." My voice cracked with the emotion I tried to keep under control. A yellow aura brighter than the sun surrounded her. Except for the chilling cold, she was perfect.

"*Mi amorcita*. You've been so brave. Yesterday was terrible to watch. Today hasn't been much better." She turned and roundhouse-kicked a beetle between its pincers. Perhaps there were benefits to death; this lady was totally spry. And effective—the beetle fell backward into an approaching group, its nasty insect feet flailing. I took a moment to freeze-crisp the lot of them before returning to my conversation.

"So who are you?"

"Your *abuelita*. Your mother's mother."

That explained her comment and why she seemed so familiar. Her oval face, the stubborn little chin, those were my mother's features. But *Abuelita's* eyes were gray, not the warm bourbon tone my mother's had been without Sotuk's magic floating through her system.

"Are you…I mean, do you have magic, too?"

"*Aiee.* Of course! I'm the reason your mother learned of the Ancient Ones."

"Okay."

A few demons scuttled from the rowdy group of spirits, two of whom were flying a few inches above a snake, a Red Racer I guessed, pelting the snake with trash from the nearby Dumpster. The snake hissed, picked up speed and slammed into the edge of the building. The spirits high-fived and hooted as the eight-foot-long snake disintegrated into dust. I added direct frontal hits into my mental file of how to obliterate monsters.

Talk about efficient use of time. If only calling the spirits forth wasn't so difficult. Turning back, I focused on my grandmother.

"I didn't want Mom to die."

"I know this."

"I'm sorry I let you down."

"You did no such thing, *amorcita.* You're at the beginning of a journey. One I wish you didn't have to undertake. Already, you have been through so much." *Abuelita's* clear eyes darkened with sadness, but she smiled. "You must leave now, but call for me again. I look forward to catching up. And I'll do what I can to help."

"What happened to my pendant?"

"You were right. The demon-wolf tried to sever your connection." She lifted the chain, showed me the tear in the leather. I gripped the spot in my hand.

"Why didn't it work?"

"Ask the cat. When next you see it."

"He's a demon."

"Doubtful. But you have seen enough to know not all creatures are hate-filled, just as all aren't good."

"Can you get messages to Mom?"

Abuelita's aura faded. "No, *amorcita.* She is gone. None of that!" she said when my chin quivered. "She chose to give up her powers. Your mother foresaw bits of what you'd go through. She made her decision, hoping her powers would amplify yours. She made peace long ago with her choice."

The pain in my chest didn't want to stay contained. I nodded, clamping my jaw tight. *Abuelita* pressed her cold hand to my cheek, her eyes soft and sad. For me. I sniffled.

"Her sacrifice was made in love. The very best kind, Echo." She rubbed my eyebrow like Mom used to. I pressed my cheek harder into her palm, finding warmth in her frigid touch. "The Magician can explain better and in more detail than I."

"But he's sketchy." At her elevated brows, I raised my hands in a defeated gesture. "I don't trust him."

"Smart. But he is your best option in a sea of poor ones. Lord Raven risked much to send you down the right path. Meet with the Magician. He can help you find the Fourth."

"Great," I muttered. "The Magician's the one sending these armies to slow us down, isn't he?"

"No. He's as much a prisoner of his fate as you are. You are the daughter of Sotuk and Almira. You can free the Magician. My guess is he awaits you with bated breath."

"At least someone will be glad to see me."

"Please. Watch for those who wish you harm. And the traps laid between you and your goal."

"Is it possible to keep secrets from the gods?" I asked.

Abuelita shook her head, her lips a grim slash. "Not without much, much effort. Be safe, Echo María. I'm not yet ready for you to join me on a permanent basis. You're too young and lovely to slouch around the underworld. I'll help as I can. Honani, come, the warriors wish to speak with you."

"Later, perhaps," Honani replied. His aura flashed once again to bright turquoise, his smile huge. "I enjoy beating up the demons."

"This will not wait. *Venga, hombre,*" *Abuelita* said. Her Spanish still sounded so Midwestern, even after nearly fifty years of marriage and nearly exclusive Spanish-speaking to my *abuelo* and mother. How I knew this, I couldn't say. Just that bits of her past transferred to me at her touch.

Adeline Jones Ruiz would always be what she was—a mix of heritages born from love for an unlikely match.

Which made me wonder if my godly father played a role in their meeting. I was pretty sure Sotuk had. He'd worked from his end to ensure the right mix of bloodlines.

My mouth dried out. No wonder Zeke remained leery about my feelings. He and I, just like my mother before me, were some type of social engineering project.

My father used me—as a knight, perhaps—on his chessboard as he attempted to out-strategize the god or gods who wished to destroy the Fourth World.

I startled out of my depressing thoughts when Honani wrapped me in one of his signature hugs. "See you soon, Echo," he said.

"You'll come back?" I'd missed him in those moments he was gone.

"As I already promised," he said with a bow.

I blew him a kiss. He nodded, his face grave, and turned toward Zeke. I had a feeling my spirit warrior gave him a "take that" face, but I decided I didn't want to know. Honani and Zeke needed to work out their issues themselves, in their own time and in their own way.

Abuelita seemed relaxed, her arms hanging long and easy from her shoulders, her chin tipped at a jaunty angle. I wanted to lay my head on her shoulder, but doing so would ruin the illusion I'd built in my mind. Her eyes brightened, answered by a pulse of light around her body.

"Do you know why my pendant—"

"I know naught of the magic your father provided you. But I do not believe the demon could break the connection. *You* must do that."

I pressed my lips into a firm line, dipping my head. "Stay well," I said. A small smile was all I could manage.

"Do I not get a hug from my amazing granddaughter?"

My arms folded around her as my breath hitched. She smelled of cinnamon and laughter, but she'd faded to an amorphous specter. I held on until not even the misty tendrils were left.

My arms fell to my sides. Zeke's expression turned solemn as he clasped one of my fisted hands.

"Another adventurous morning with you," he said. His mouth tilted up on the left side—not so much a smile as an acknowledgment of our situation. I nodded and rolled my shoulders. Ah, that's why my *abuelita* had asked for my touch.

"She did something to my shoulder. The wound doesn't hurt nearly as much."

"Excellent."

"Do you think healing me cost her too much of herself?"

"No more than she wanted to give. I'm glad you were able to meet your grandmother."

I let go of his hand and slid my arms around my torso. He followed me, closing the space and wrapping his arms over mine, around my waist. He rested his cheek on the crown of my head. My breath shattered.

"She said my mom found peace with her choice," I said.

"Your mother died for you, Echo, first and foremost. I'm sure she also wanted a chance to rebalance the Earth."

"But she sacrificed so much." I rubbed my hands up and down my arms. "You didn't see her face, Zeke. She was in so much pain."

"If I'd been so lucky as to have a mother like yours, I'd be proud of her sacrifices and her love. She was selfless when the need was greatest."

"I-I miss her. So much." I rested my forehead against his chest and inhaled the scent of his armor and the underlying scent that was Zeke's. My heart's raging tempo slowed to a less painful one. "I can't ever even tell her. She gave me every bit of herself she could."

Zeke kissed my hair. "She's in you. Not many people get to carry such a gift."

We stood there for another minute, and I drew strength from his warmth and the constancy of his heartbeat. Once my emotions steadied, I tilted my head up and smiled at him. "I needed to hear that. Thank you for fighting for me. Now, let's go see this Magician."

He grabbed our backpacks from my shoulder and headed toward his Thunderbird.

"What do we tell the motel manager?"

Zeke frowned. "I don't know. This is the first time I've destroyed someone else's property."

"Do you think they have insurance?" I asked.

"Let's hope so. I can put some of this back together because it's of the earth." He was quiet, eyes squinted. The wooden framing reattached and the drywall repaired itself. The wooden window frame knit back together. While chunks of paint were missing and cracks remained in the brick façade, the building no longer looked the complete demolition site of moments ago.

"The best I can do," Zeke puffed out.

"Nice job. You really know how to show a girl a good time," I said, trying to lighten the mood. "Being near-dead is our thing now." I spun my finger by my ear. Zeke grabbed my hand before sliding his palm against mine.

"No, that's not going to be our thing. We're going to survive this, Echo. You know how I know?"

I shook my head, my eyes never leaving his.

"Because I cannot imagine a world without you in it. Your smile. Your gorgeous copper eyes. Your sarcasm. Your long hair. Even your crazy eating habits." He slid his hands up into the thick mass of my waves, combing his fingers through its damp weight.

Wow. That was…wow. I hadn't expected him to say that or for his cheeks to redden as he met my gaze. He handed me the tube of sunscreen. His wide lips curled up into a wicked grin.

"Slather me up, *tocha*. We got some ground to cover, and I don't want to worry about those age spots you're so concerned with."

I chuckled as I rubbed the cream into his skin. "Ah, but now I know about that magic ointment. Maybe age spots and skin cancer aren't as big a deal as I thought." I quirked my lips. "That stuff's keeping me patched together."

"That's what it's for."

"I'm really worried about Layla," I said. "She was so tired. And that was before she healed me."

Zeke's frown deepened. "Your grandmother said to go to the Magician.

Raven said the Magician could lead us to Layla. So that's the plan."

I heaved out the breath I'd been holding. "Good." I stopped next to his motorcycle. "Why didn't the demons destroy your bike? I would have."

Zeke smoothed a stray line of lotion off my cheek before stowing our gear. "The bike's been reworked and is covered in repellent," he said.

"Whoever made the stuff should go into the bug repellant business. Even the DEET spray we use now doesn't work well. Your guy would make a killing."

I settled my helmet on my head and tilted my chin up. Zeke stepped closer and clicked the buckle shut. "I'll keep that in mind if I ever need a career change. I'm pretty proud of my invention."

"You made it? Did you get a patent?"

Zeke rolled his eyes. "No, Echo. I don't have a patent because most people can't see demons and fewer want to admit they exist."

"Did you go to college? Are you a chemist?"

He grinned at me. "So curious. I can tell you're feeling much better now that you're back to rapid-fire questions. Yes, I went to college. My degree's in civil engineering."

"That's...not fair to the rest of the men in the world," I decided. "Being brainy and deadly."

"Are you complaining?"

"Nope. I'm keeping your secrets all to myself. No sharing. That way the rest of the male population doesn't get jealous."

Zeke shook his head and chuckled. He stowed his spear in its case and his sword across the front of the handlebars.

"But you should really consider safeguarding your demon repellant stuff. Can we wear it?"

Zeke narrowed his eyes, considering me. "Not in its current form, but that's an idea. If I get a chance, I'll try to make it safe for people."

"At least clothing. Our helmets, stuff like that. May slow the demons down, make them take longer to find us." I shrugged. "That'd be a nice change."

"That we can do." He pulled out a can and sprayed my helmet and my feet.

"I don't want to get the liquid on you."

"I'm fine," I said.

After Zeke sprayed his accessories, he met my gaze, his filled with concern. "You up for this ride? Coyote's den isn't too far. I'd like to do some reconnaissance."

I wasn't sure. My shoulder felt better. Still, sitting on a vibrating bike didn't appeal. But I didn't have a choice.

"Sure." I blew out a breath. "We need to get to Layla."

"Not sure this is going to net any Halflings, but I want to see the terrain. Maybe it's where you were last night."

I clambered onto the bike, completely forgetting about my shoulder. "Who's to say?"

Zeke settled in front of me. He waited until my arms slid around his middle before turning the key. "Hopefully you. Soon," he yelled over the engine's rumble.

#

My shoulder throbbed its displeasure. How tainted with demon was I? My body flashed between hot and cold, seeming to both accept and reject the lacerations.

My head and muscles screamed in protest to the harsh conditions. By harsh, I meant traipsing across a plateau near the San Francisco Peaks under cerulean skies and near-perfect seventy-five-degree weather. I shoved another pine branch out of my way as I catalogued my needs. When Zeke said he wanted to do some reconnaissance, I assumed we'd go and see if there were any clues at Coyote's place. Nope, we'd walked in and out of his home; I'd seen the pit where he'd held me captive. I smiled a little. That's where I first officially met Honani. I loved that ghost.

We found exactly nothing. The building didn't resemble the structure I'd visited last night. Not a scrap of humanity, let alone magic, remained within Coyote's house or the surrounding area.

"How's that possible?" I asked as we completed the largest circle around the perimeter yet.

"He's a god. I'm sure he had safeguards in place for all eventualities."

"I still don't get how Raven knew to send us to the Ridge Ruin but Coyote didn't know I'd kick his butt."

Zeke frowned, considering. "Aren't there multiple decisions made every second? And isn't there some idea of endless possibilities interconnecting throughout time? If all that's true, that would be a lot of potential outcomes."

I sucked on my lower lip. "You mean string theory and the physics of time and space."

Zeke pushed a branch of scrub pine out of our path. "I guess. I haven't studied it much. But if I can open doors on Earth to get to other parts of Earth I want to go to, then I'd bet there's something to that string theory."

"All sounds related," I sighed. "So does that mean we have more or less autonomy in our own destiny?"

Zeke shrugged. "Right now, I wish I could open a portal. That would save us time."

My cue to stop talking. When I broke Sotuk's tablet, I shook up all the magic, displacing demons. We'd felt multiple small earthquakes during our ride today—especially the closer we traveled toward Zeke's house, the epicenter of the original magic detonation. Thanks to my mistake, Zeke had to abandon his favorite mode of transport.

Echo, be my Echo...

I stopped, tilting my head.

Echo...

"Layla!"

Zeke let go of a branch and it snapped back into his neck. He didn't flinch, his eyes too busy searching for threats. "What?"

"I heard Layla."

"How?"

"Shh!"

Echo. Be my Echo.

Definitely her silly song. I darted left, following Layla's voice. I sprinted around a bush and leapt over a boulder, my heart pounding even harder than the exertion warranted. Layla. My friend, the reason I was still alive today. I had to get to her. She'd been so tired, so scared last night. Had the cat hurt her? I ran faster, ignoring my quivering muscles. Layla.

My chance, my best chance to help her, as I'd promised.

Zeke's arm wrapped around my middle, banding me to him just as my feet hit nothing. I dangled there, slow to comprehend Zeke had saved me again.

"What's that?" I gasped.

His chest rose and fell against my back. "Trap."

*Echo…*I pointed my toe and touched the brush covering a deep hole. Stale air drifted upward, coating us both in its dankness. Zeke shuffled back.

"Layla's down there," I said.

Zeke peered over my shoulder. "Do you know where *there* is?" He set me on the ground but kept his arm around me. Almost as if he didn't trust me not to throw myself into the pit.

"Somewhere dangerous," I guessed.

Grasping my arm, he stepped up beside me. He picked up a rock and tossed it into the pit. We leaned forward, trying to see into the thick darkness. Nothing. No sound of the rock hitting anything.

Echo…

"I hear her now, too. Definitely Layla's voice," Zeke said softly. "Bad news. Real bad."

"What?" Alarm slicked my skin with a layer of sweat.

"Someone set this here for you to find."

"Got that." I locked my knees to keep them from quaking. "So now I'm going in there and getting Layla out. The Fourth, too, if I can find him."

"You can't."

I turned to face Zeke. When our eyes locked, the emotion in his rocked me back. "I have to," I whispered. "She's my friend."

"It's a *trap*," Zeke said, his voice rising in alarm. "Just look at it."

"Layla used her magic to help me, Zeke. I left her down there, if not powerless, then close to it. And scared."

He clenched and unclenched his free hand. "You said she has a kitty friend."

"It's a mountain cat. I'm going in, Zeke." I wanted to sound decisive but my voice held a note of pleading.

He sighed, a harsh sound. "We do this my way."

I raised my eyebrow. "Which means?"

He stooped and grabbed a handful of rocks. Standing, he threw them as hard as he could into the hole. I held my breath, though I wasn't sure why. Nothing.

With a triumphant smirk, I stepped forward. A small, fuzzy blue head rose from the hole. Long antennae flicked forward as obsidian eyes turned toward us.

The fuzzy ant crawled forward. Not big—at least not for a demon—but it's stinger was as long as my pinkie finger.

"What is that?" I asked, already backing away.

"Velvet ant," Zeke said. He gripped his spear, the tip of which was twice the size of the ant. But within seconds, hundreds more poured out of the hole. The dust-colored ground undulated, a mass of red, blue, and black. Their exoskeletons clicked over the rocks.

That song I'd learned as a child: *The ants go marching*…played through my head. But, holy *frijoles*, those things were scary, the stingers dangerous.

"Let's go," Zeke said.

"I'm not leaving Layla," I said. I jutted my jaw out with a stubbornness I needed to get through these next few minutes.

"Those things aren't ants. They're a type of wasp, and they can kill you with their venom, Echo. So move it."

"No!"

I narrowed my gaze and focused on the tiny insects. There were a million of them, maybe more. Layla was more important than a sting or fifty. Not that I planned to let that happen.

Ice. Lots of ice. The pressure built in my mind and I released the blast of cold at the insects. The first ones were on the tips of my boots. They quit marching, covered in a thick layer of frost.

My lungs spasmed. That had been close. I did not want ants, especially the XXL stinger kind, crawling on me.

"That really is the best trick," Zeke said. He wiped his forehead with the back of his arm.

"Don't like bugs?"

"Not those." His hand tightened again. "I was stung, many times, as a child."

That would do it. Much as I wanted to take his hand and offer comfort, I knew he wouldn't like it. I stepped forward—onto the frozen ants. The resounding crack was loud, like the sound of a glacier calving like I'd heard on a YouTube video during one of my vacation-dream moments when I was fifteen. I'd never gotten on the cruise ship to Alaska, and this experience today was not a close second to my dream of glacier-watching.

I stepped forward again, all my muscles tensed against the need to scream over the sound. Another step, then another, brought me within looking distance of the edge. I peered over and saw…nothing.

"Can you feel her?" Zeke asked.

"No. She hasn't called me either." Tears of frustration built in my eyes. "Honani?" I asked. The warrior popped into the space between Zeke and me. "Do you think she was ever there?"

Honani's eyes were filled with sympathy. "She is not in the pit. Nor is her essence nearby."

"Using Layla was a way to get you here," Zeke said, his voice gentle with understanding.

"To kill me," I mumbled. "Since the demon attacks haven't worked."

Another loud crack rumbled through the air. Dread pummeled my guts. "Did you, maybe, shift your feet?" I asked.

"No."

We pivoted at the same time, instinct kicking in before the earth shifted under us.

"Run!" Honani yelled.

Chaos whipped around us, under us. My feet pounded across the splintering ground. Zeke stayed close, shortening his stride to match mine, but his focus was on the ground beneath us. The dirt stabilized under our feet. A large boulder tumbled toward us, but Zeke slowed down, his gaze locked on the boulder. It stopped, as did the rest of the smaller rocks.

He stopped in the relative safety of a thick copse of pines.

"What was that?" I gasped.

Zeke's frown turned ferocious. "Another attempt on your life." At my continued silence, he explained, "An earthquake. An intentional one placed right there."

"And you used your Earth magic to stop it?" I asked.

Zeke nodded.

"I'll go back and examine the pit," Honani offered.

Honani returned moments later. He shook his head. I offered up the pendant and he sank into the clay.

"I'm sorry," I said to Zeke. "You told me not to."

He touched my hair. "Don't apologize for being a good friend. I envy Layla your closeness." He cleared his throat. "Let's head into Winona to find something to eat."

Walking back to the motorcycle parked in a nearby copse, I begged every deity I could think of to keep Layla safe. Not that my prayers would do much good, but her mother might still consider her a useful pawn. Maybe she'd watch over her daughter until I could get there.

I swung my leg back over the motorcycle. While I would never love this mode of transport, its power and continued existence were definite pluses. So what if I had to grit my teeth and press my shoulder into Zeke's back to ease the ache from each bounce?

My shoulder was definitely the loudest of my unhappy body parts by the time we reached the small mountain town.

Zeke motored down the one main drag. My eye caught a trendy little café with signage promoting its plant-based cuisine.

"There!" I practically screamed. Who cared how an eatery that understood how to cook something besides meat got in this tiny town? I wasn't looking a gift rutabaga in the leaves. I frowned. That didn't even make sense in my head. I must be woozy from lack of decent nourishment.

"Really? I want real food," Zeke yelled back.

I poked him between his shoulder blades. "That is real food. The realest. Pull in."

I ran inside and ordered the biggest salad on the menu, breathless both from my painful jog and the idea of tasting fresh produce. Zeke followed more slowly, eyeing the clientele and their plates.

"Maybe I'll grab something on the way out of town," he said, fear flickering through his eyes when a server began juicing wheat grass. "I saw a fast food place."

"Relax, I ordered you a veggie burger. You'll like it."

"Sorry to break this to you, but a burger—by its very definition—cannot be made out of vegetables."

"That so-called meat served at your fast food place isn't actual food at all. At least this way you're eating something that closely resembles its heritage and isn't sludge."

"You've been brainwashed by some hippy contingent," Zeke grumbled. "You should've grown up in Arizona where people are normal."

Happy with my fresh carrot-apple-ginger juice, I failed to rise to the bait. I slurped up the last of the dark orange liquid, humming as the flavors slid across my palate.

Zeke poked at his bun. "Got any ketchup?" he asked, frowning at his plate.

The waiter, a few years older than we were, handed over a bottle. "We see boyfriends dragged in here all the time. Trust me, man, the burger's pretty good."

Zeke sighed and took a tentative first bite. I smirked when he took a much larger second bite. I snagged an onion ring from his plate.

"So what's the plan now that you've seen the place?"

"Figure out what's protecting the perimeter of the Ridge Ruin," Zeke replied around another bite. "We need to see if there are other traps like the one we ran into. We'll get closer. It'll be some steep hiking. If your shoulder can take more, that is."

"I'm managing. Though, could I put more of that salve stuff on my newest set of gashes? They feel…hot."

"Let me see them," Zeke said. He sat down his burger and moved closer, like he planned to pull off my top right there.

"Hands on the burger, *guerrero*. I'm not into that kind of PDA. My boobs have been out in public too much lately. These girls are shy. You need to respect their desire for discretion."

He smiled again. "I prefer private viewings myself." His eyes flicked over my face, then he grabbed my hand, turning my palm over and running his fingers over the sensitive skin on my forearm. "Any other symptoms? How's your head? No blood poisoning I can see."

"My head is still on and hasn't ached since Coyote kidnapped my mother. It's working well enough to tell me you're crazy. Stop worrying about me. I'm fine. Mostly."

"I'll give you the salve after we eat."

"I need to know the plan when we get to you-know-where."

Zeke shook his head and grinned. "You'd make a terrible spy. We get inside and talk the Magician into telling us what we need to know."

"I don't trust Raven. Or the Magician," I said. My sigh was hard enough to ruffle my spinach leaves.

"I don't like the situation much either. Have a better suggestion?"

I shook my head. "I'm worried about Layla." I set down my fork, my appetite fleeing as I considered my dream from the night before. At least I'd already eaten all the chicken and most of the greens. "That place wasn't right. It felt, I don't know, soulless. And there was this cat. A big one."

Zeke rubbed his forefinger over his upper lip. I heard a slight rasp as his skin caught on the fine scruff there. "We have to work on one problem at a time."

"But it's so slow."

"Eat up. Quickly. We need to get back out to the Ridge Ruin. That's our best chance to get Layla back." Zeke wiped his mouth. He slapped my hand when I reached for another onion ring. "Those're mine. They're payment for eating fake meat. Tell me about the cat."

I ignored the sting on my knuckles and dipped the thick fried circle in his pile of ketchup. I bit into it, contemplating him over the treat.

"Not much to tell. He killed another demon-wolf. Like the one that shredded me."

"Demons kill indiscriminately. Nothing new there."

"Seemed intentional. Like he protected Layla. Then he protected me."

Zeke munched, contemplative. I pushed my plate away, my gaze going to the stark Northern Arizona landscape visible out the large picture window.

"There's been lots of excitement in our relationship," I said. "It's only been four days since we officially met, but in that time, we've fought gods and Kachina, nearly died and destroyed an irreplaceable relic."

"Been busy," Zeke agreed. "Bet we could pick up the pace now that you've learned how to use your magic."

"I'm still learning what I can do. Sorry, but a weeklong crash course isn't the same as years of honing the craft as you've done. Anyway, I think I'd like something a little slower-paced. That doesn't require committing a felony on native lands."

Zeke rolled his eyes. "I'll take you on the slowest, most boring date you can imagine once we get through this."

I blew out a breath and tossed my tangled hair over my shoulder. I really should've braided the mess earlier. Now I could give some kind of zombie bride pointers on how to appear more dead. "I'm holding you to that. You know, you're a bad influence. Sneaking around and B and E is the kind of night I never wanted to have."

Zeke leaned far enough for me to count the individual brown flecks that spiraled out from his pupils, getting lighter just at the outer-most edge—an unearthly blue that haloed Saturn in the deep dark of the huge, Southwest night sky.

His eyelashes had a hint of blond at the tip. They were so long and full, they had to bump against his sunglasses. Who'd ever created this guy had gotten all the parts just right.

"I know how important Layla is to you. I understand you're scared. I'm not exactly pleased with the turn of events, either. I thought shipping Coyote off would allow Masau to break free from his prison, wherever that even is. But none of that's happened yet, so we're going to keep moving forward with our current information and hope we're fast enough and smart enough to stay alive so we can find Layla." Zeke's eyebrows pulled low with concern. He shook his head. "Finish up. We need to move out."

I ran to the bathroom to wash my hands and rub on more ointment. I took the time to braid my ragged hair. Zeke waited for me at the door.

Three women stared at him, eyes wide and cheeks flushed. His godliness was not helping him keep a low profile. I pushed my way through their lust to stand next to him. His smile widened when he saw my frown.

Well, fine then.

"I hope you took your meds," I said. "You know how violent you get when they wear off."

He chuckled and pulled me closer, squeezing my waist before pressing a brief kiss on my lips. "I'm all out. You'll have to take your chances."

Still in shock from the touch of his mouth to mine—why would he stop? I didn't want him to stop!—I let him snag my hand while I turned to raise my brows at the women behind me. Their faces were a mixture of confusion, disappointment, and desire. I shrugged.

"I guess another busted rib is worth it." I sighed. Two of the girls focused on their plates while the third, an older woman in her thirties, shook her head, clucking.

I trailed behind Zeke on the way to his bike. "You are going to get me in trouble," he said, but he was still smiling.

I clambered onto the Thunderbird, but Zeke didn't slide onto the seat in front of me immediately. Instead he reached into the side of his bag and handed me a dagger. "That's a gift from your father." Zeke waited for me to take the handle.

The blade was well-balanced for my hand. Carved with flames on the bottom, hummingbirds soared across the top of the handle.

"This is yours," I said.

Zeke shook his head. "No. It was always meant for you."

"Is that where you got the name? *Tocha.*"

Zeke's confusion cleared as I showed him the handle. He shook his head. "No, but I can see why you'd think that."

I traced the intricate pattern on the handle. "Why are you giving the knife to me now?"

"Because you're going to need it."

"I already needed it," I said, trying to sound patient.

"But you weren't ready." He ran his finger along the blade and the colors exploded from the darkness as it shifted in the light. Score one for Zeke. Especially since I wasn't sure I could use the weapon now. But something about the velvet-ant attack bothered him. Not that he'd actually said anything about it. No, I could feel his concern.

"You have more control now, more understanding of what you're fighting for." He met my gaze. "Why you're fighting."

"To save Layla. To ensure my mother's death means something."

"But also to balance the world." Zeke ran his hand from the blade up over my fist, holding me even as I held the knife. "Good, evil, right, wrong. The potential is in all of us."

"I could use the knife to hurt someone who doesn't deserve it."

Zeke cocked his head. "Will you?"

Not intentionally. I didn't like death. Something he'd picked up on immediately. And why he'd given me the blade, I'd bet. "I've been meaning to ask. What's the rock used in the blade? It's very sharp."

Zeke smirked, shaking his head. "Diamond."

I nearly dropped the knife. "What? This thing is…And your spear…How? It's black. Where'd it come from?"

"Near the Kelsey Lake Mine."

I shook my head, confused.

"That's what the government calls it, but it's older than the United States. Millions of years old," Zeke said. "It's on the Colorado-Wyoming border. The mining company found nine of the Kimberlite pipes. None offered much in the way of sellable diamonds. That's because they didn't find the most valuable pipe."

He grinned and motioned to my dagger, then to his sword and spear, hooked to the side of the Thunderbird.

"These weapons were made thousands of years ago, and they've been passed down to each generation of godly children. I own two weapons: the sword and the spear. Masau gave me that one for you. He didn't want me to hand the knife over until I deemed you ready for combat. He worried you'd get yourself killed."

"So far I'm doing okay in the living department. Still kicking."

"Don't I know it. I plan to keep you there—kicking. Just not at me, please. As far as I know, these three are all the weapons the gods made."

"That doesn't make sense," I said.

"Why?"

I glanced up at him with difficulty. I'd liked his dagger from the first moment I'd held it, back in his house when he told me not to touch the blade. I'd liked the way the hilt fit my palm so much, returning it had been difficult. Even now, after holding the knife for just a few minutes, there was a connection.

"Why, Echo?"

"Four," I blurted out. "Like you said. There are always four. Worlds, directions, weapons, godly children. Just makes sense."

"Hmm. I haven't seen or heard of another," Zeke said. "We'll try to search for it, too."

"What do you think the weapon would be?" I slid the dagger through my belt loop until the wider hilt caught against the denim. I worried I'd cut myself but I didn't have a better place to store the weapon. "There isn't a sheath for this one, is there?"

Zeke shook his head as he slid his helmet over his short hair.

"Why give them to us?"

"Because the gods don't really need them. They can destroy demons, humans, animals, even trees and rocks, with their metaphysical powers. It's one of the perks of being godly. The weapons were supposed to be kept and used by their most trusted human lieutenants."

"Their children?" This blade was a priceless gift. From my father. A deity I'd never met, who, until a week ago, hadn't cared I even existed.

With all the other distractions—Zeke, losing Layla, my mother's death—I hadn't had any time to process my relationship with my dad. Rather, the complete lack of relationship. I was the daughter of the Creator God. He was the reason I could call up spirits, make water bend to my will.

I sucked in air, trying to find some equilibrium. My emotions seethed just under the surface of my skin, careening from anger to fear.

"So these weapons destroy the demons? They can't reanimate?"

"That's the idea. Though Coyote figured out how to regenerate Jaguar, so I guess nothing's one hundred percent effective."

The white-hot center in my mind flared before he finished the sentence. Zeke stepped back from the burst of energy. "Of course not. That would give us a chance to balance out their evil. A chance to *win*." I took a deep breath, unable to meet his gaze. I didn't want to see pity, or worse, fear.

"We better leave," Zeke said, eyes darting, body tensed, waiting for demons to appear after the nuclear reaction my emotions set off across this plane.

CHAPTER EIGHT

The next group of demons attacked less than twenty minutes later; I was surprised they took so long to pinpoint our location. Zeke sped out of the café parking lot and turned away from the San Francisco Peaks, away from our true destination. The misdirection wouldn't matter. Demons were smart; they'd know where we were going—or at least that we were going onto the rez.

I held on, both physically and emotionally ill. Zeke continued to risk his life to save mine, and I'd put him in danger yet again because I couldn't control my feelings.

That wasn't fair to either of us.

This time the monsters exploded up through the ground, snarling and lunging. I appreciated the different approach. The beasts, or at least whoever controlled them, showed mental growth. This batch of fiends was uglier than the rest. Their saber teeth were thicker than my wrist and longer than my forearm and drool pooled from their foaming mouths. I decided they were more gross than scary, but my decision was definitely a judgment call. I couldn't stop staring at their feet, which were half again as big as a bear's, with three-inch-long claws. Claws much like the ones that had ripped my soul apart.

My heart rate ratcheted up as I thought back to the agonizing minutes when I was sure I had died.

Zeke hopped off his motorcycle and slashed and hacked at the cats before we rolled to a stop. He'd killed three before I fumbled my way off.

Ignoring my shaking legs and sweaty hands, I gripped my new weapon. Six inches of blade put me in close proximity of claws, but I'd take the weapon over the distance.

I'd kill these vermin without magic. I would rip them apart like they wanted to rip me. I was Sotuk's daughter, which gave me strength and whatever else my parentage meant.

With my first slash of the blade, the handle conformed to fit my hand, filling my palm and balancing perfectly so that I thrust and parried with amazing speed and accuracy. I killed five of the demons within a minute. That cooling sensation I'd come to associate with my spirits crept steadily down my arm. The blade began to glow with that same white-hot energy that pulsed so brightly in my head.

I actively tamped down my brain's natural response to this threat. This was just me, amped up with my more acute magical senses. While I didn't understand how I'd done this or what was happening, exactly, I liked the vicious cold I'd produced.

The best high got even better when I ripped through another animal trying to creep up behind me. I'd sensed the beast's presence and met the attack before the demon managed to spring. I was ice-cold and so ready for the next attack I could anticipate it.

The saber wolf had definitely left some sort of an imprint in me. Maybe that should freak me out, but right now I enjoyed the ability to sense the demons before they reached me.

The chill tingling across my skin flared as I gave myself over fully to the sensation, starting with my pendant. Ice licked across my chest before wrapping around my dagger and arm. With a flick of my blade, a mini blizzard enveloped three of the cats. They collapsed into a heap of ash and snow.

I executed a pirouette and stabbed another one of the beasts. I pulled my blade free. Zeke fought to my left, employing both sword and spear. The muscles in his arms and shoulders bulged with the effort. He hadn't taken the time to call up his armor; I didn't like to see him exposed, especially knowing what these beasts were capable of.

One of the demons flanked Zeke. This one was bigger, blacker than the others. Dark as the big cat who'd killed the saber-wolf attacking Layla. The one who'd licked my wound, healing me. But…that beast was in Tokpella with Layla.

Why would he be here?

The animal crouched, its muscles quivering with the need to pounce and rip into Zeke, much as the beast did to me last night. Yet he didn't. My feet propelled me forward before I'd registered the movement. This creature drew me unlike any of the others. Like we'd connected. Because of my new demon-senses? No, I didn't think so.

Its golden eyes met mine for a brief second. Something moved in their depths—something much like a plea. But not for himself.

"Wait!" I cried.

The animal dropped to the ground. He sheathed his claws, bits of the cat's dark pelt he'd ripped apart still stuck on his paw that was mere inches from Zeke's back. The other demons prowled outside the cocoon of ice I managed to slam between us and them.

"Are you? The cat...Last night."

He cocked his head. No saber teeth on this one, but his canines were just as deadly. He was bigger than the others, probably close to two hundred pounds of sleek muscle. He tilted his head, and flashes from his mind popped into mine. For years, he'd fought the desire to kill, the need to tear flesh and destroy everything around him.

"You're not a demon."

He dipped his head. Whether in acknowledgment or defeat, I wasn't sure.

"Not all demon," I said. "You licked me. But you...you put demon in me, too." Awe and disgust slithered over me as I met those eyes again. I saw flecks and a familiar ring of brown. Like my eyes. Or Zeke's. "To save me?"

His gaze flicked to Zeke, who danced through the demons, slashing and stabbing his way to victory.

"What are you?" I asked. "Why are you helping Layla?"

The cat settled onto the ground in s sphinx position, back legs primed to pounce. Still watching me, he rolled over, exposing his soft belly. An image of him on the rock above Layla flashed through my mind.

I crouched down next to the cat, placed my hand over its heart. "Is she alive?" Those golden eyes held mine as he sighed. Not a promising response.

"Can I save you?"

"Echo!" Zeke's anguished yell barely penetrated my concentration. Another hell-spawn prowled inside the icy sphere that crumbled around us. I'd focused too much of my attention on the cat at my feet. Before I managed to stand or even raise my knife, the new threat launched itself at me. My cat moved in a blur of fur and muscle, meeting the attacker midair. He ripped it's throat out with one deft flick of his canines. As he landed, his hackles rose and a deep growl rumbled from his chest.

Zeke charged toward my mountain cat, unaware of the other demons accumulating between us.

"Go!" I yelled.

The cat glanced over his shoulder, his whiskers twitching as if he wanted to say something. The image of Layla, too pale and dirty, formed in my mind again. My throat tightened but I managed to choke out, "I'm coming. As soon as I can. Stay with her. Please."

The cat dipped his head before jumping forward just as Zeke's spear crashed into the place he had been. In less than a blink, he disappeared, and Zeke and I were now surrounded by the rest of the beasts. I turned in a slow circle, ensuring that none of the other's eyes affected me. They were all empty—just as the rest of the demons had always been.

I shivered hard, trying to rid my body of its reaction to the now-departed beast.

"What was that?" Zeke rasped. His chest rose and fell rapidly under his armor.

"A friend, I think," I said as I rushed another cat trying to hamstring Zeke. "He helped me. He's helping Layla. Gotta concentrate."

A jagged layer of ice coated its chest seconds before my dagger ripped through sinew and bone, piercing its heart. The large, rough-furred body shuddered and melted under me, and I stumbled. As I gained my footing, four of the demons snarled just outside the blizzard I'd managed to rebuild around Zeke and me.

Their dark eyes flickered orange and intense. Teeth bared, they showed off not only their long sabers but also the rest of their dirty, needle-sharp teeth. None of them had the near-human gaze. Good. These were going down.

One of the cats padded forward. I brought my left hand upward, clutching my blade in my right. Icy blades surged from my palm, white-blue and deadly. I threw them, never worrying I'd run out, as I turned to the next demon. I wouldn't give them the opportunity to run. Hitting the last of the four, I crouched, preparing for another attack.

Zeke leaned against his spear. Sweat matted his hair and dripped from his temples and nose. "Thanks."

"The chill, like the water, that's from my father. Isn't it?"

Zeke returned his sword and spear to their traveling case and wiped the back of his hand across his forehead. He scrubbed his hand through his wet hair.

"I don't know."

"Come on, Zeke. You pushed me earlier but now you don't want to talk about him?"

"I don't know Sotuk. I've never met him." He met my eyes. His were clear and calm. "What you did here, this was different from the magic in your head. I couldn't feel you turn the energy on. So I'm going to assume this comes from some other part of you."

I slipped my dagger back through the belt loop of my jeans. "I think the cold is a defense mechanism that comes from my body. Like it's *in* me and I can let the power loose." I paused, cleared my throat. "Let's get out of here. I can't even imagine what the cars driving past saw."

"Not many cars in this area, but the magic is strong enough to cloak our activities from the masses. That's part of why I was surprised when you told me you could see me while I fought that demon on the Plaza."

"That was a dream, not me actually there, so maybe I can't detect you if you don't want me to. I don't understand this—this magic shroud."

"First, I can't do it. The cover surrounds the demons and monsters."

"But not you and me?"

Zeke shook his head. "We're human even if we're also part god. We're tied to this plane because it's our home. That means no hiding, no distorting. This is our reality."

"I think I'm officially on overload."

He pressed his lips to mine. My hands tangled in Zeke's hair, but he pulled back much too soon. That didn't qualify as a kiss. Barely a peck. I huffed in frustration as he tilted his head so his forehead pressed against my helmet. His eyes slid shut and I sensed his struggle to get his emotions under control.

"Echo—"

"Don't you dare say anything," I snapped, pulling away. "If you tell me you didn't want to kiss me, that touching me was a mistake…" My chin trembled. "I'll…I'll hit you."

His sigh was harsh, so was the laugh that followed. "I have no self-control where you're concerned."

My teeth sank into my lip as his statement flooded through me. He didn't like how I made him feel.

I didn't have anything to compare my feelings for Zeke with—my mom had been overprotective to the point of sabotaging my one and only potential relationship with Zeke.

Her reasons were solid. She worried about me having sex with the wrong person. I'd read about a theory where souls attached during intercourse. I didn't know if strong emotions were necessary. I didn't know if one party could force the other's soul to attach.

But I did know that I wanted Zeke to want me as much as I wanted him. If we ever pursued the passion that flashed bright between us, I assumed we'd mingle our souls and our magic. I didn't know if that would weaken one of us and strengthen the other. No matter the outcome, I'd never forget Zeke and our time together. I met his chocolate eyes, saw the longing in them, felt the shame roll from his body as he ran his thumb down my cheek.

He pressed a soft kiss to my cheekbone. I breathed him in, relaxing into his hold even as his shoulders eased under my fingers.

Raven wanted Zeke to claim my virginity, something I'd gladly cede to Zeke—almost had yesterday just feet from where my mom died in the battle with Coyote.

Which made me wonder if my soul hadn't already connected to Zeke's. Perhaps, for me at least, sex wasn't necessary to transfer power and even ownership.

Perhaps I'd already lost the piece of me my mother had tried so hard to protect.

CHAPTER NINE

Zeke remained quiet and tense, his emotions jumbled. He stopped the bike near one of the long plateaus and asked me to wait there.

"Why?"

"So I can set my plan into motion."

I tipped my head back so I could meet his gaze, but he'd already walked into the trees, keeping his back to me. He dropped to his knees, head bowed, hands on his thighs. He'd moved too far away from me to gather and process all his emotions except for soft tendrils of concern. Much as I wanted to relieve his worry, I didn't know how.

This, whatever we were building between us, was too fast, too intense. Because I was such an emotional child, I'd had to work hard to learn some semblance of control. The trauma of the constant sideways looks from my *tías*, the inability to connect with children my own age, my lack of a father—all of those shaped me and my need for emotional security. Zeke had become that for me, but we walked a razor-thin line; my missteps could get him killed or have him reject not only my body but my continued friendship.

I slid from the Thunderbird, massaging my shoulder. The wounds from the demon attack were now thin pink lines, thanks to that second round of healing emollient I'd put on during our lunch break in Winona. I rolled the damaged joint once again, just to test the edges of the wound, but I didn't even get a twinge.

I slid into downward dog position, hoping the familiar yoga moves would alleviate some of the stiffness. My butt and shoulder hurt, and my stomach growled.

Dammit, Zeke was right about eating protein and fat. The constancy of the need to fill my belly frustrated me; I'd never been interested in meals before, let alone establishing set eating times. Now I acted no better than my little cousins. Their days cycled around their empty stomachs. Layla used to laugh and say kids understood what was really important.

I missed her. And I was terrified that she wouldn't last another night in that place.

"Now that's an image," Zeke said.

His emotions were calmer than I'd ever felt, and I glanced at him over my shoulder, my rump still high in the air. His eyes traveled up my legs before coming back to my face. I stood.

"Trying to keep the blood flowing. You're in a good mood."

"We're getting some help. Let's get moving."

"Does the place we're heading serve food?"

Zeke smirked at me. "Do you really think I'd take you somewhere without food?"

"Yes."

"Do you like nachos?"

My stomach gurgled and I moaned. "Can we order two big plates?"

"Guess that salad earlier didn't really fill you up."

We were back on the motorcycle and my butt ached in protest. How did people ride horses for days on end before cars?

"I feel healthier."

"Healthy isn't going to keep you alive."

"Maybe not, but healthy food keeps me fit." I tucked my hands inside his T-shirt. "Hmmm, I think that veggie burger did your abs some good, too. They're so defined."

Zeke chuckled as he pulled back onto the road. "You are such a pain in the ass."

The intense Arizona sun had finally set by the time we pulled up in front of a bar I could only categorize as a dive. I stared at the low-slung cinder block exterior with dubious fascination until Zeke took my hand and pulled me off the bike. I'd never been in a bar, let alone a place with a motorcycle-to-car ratio of five to one.

Unsure what to expect, the bar met my television-defined preconceptions. The large room was covered in a gritty film from spilled drinks and nicotine.

I didn't catch a whiff of cigarettes, though; the scent was a toxic cocktail of old beer and pheromones. I tried hard not to let my face show my deep-seated distaste for this place.

Anytime a man, most of whom had a large gut and a smarmy gleam in their eye, so much as glanced at our table, Zeke inched closer. I couldn't understand why he'd bring me here. This place was, in a word, awful. But the nachos were pretty good. I'd inhaled half a plateful before I managed to slow down.

I smiled a little as Zeke scooted closer again, scowling at a new patron who'd leaned an elbow on the edge of the bar. At this rate, Zeke would be in my lap before we finished our meals. I snorted at the image; Zeke was easily twice as broad as me and outweighed me by close to one hundred pounds.

"What's so funny?" Zeke muttered. A fierce scowl transformed his face to anything but friendly.

I wiped my fingers on a napkin. "Just thinking how much better you'd be able to hide me if you were sitting on me."

Zeke choked on a bite of nacho, his response a mixture of a cough and a nervous laugh. After taking a sip of water and composing himself, he changed the subject. "Help me. If you see a tall, thin woman, wave her over."

"That's your best description?" I asked.

He hesitated long enough for my stomach to tighten. "She has long black hair with a streak of white in the front."

I stilled, the napkin falling from my numb fingers. "That sounds an awful lot like the cloud goddess."

He nodded. "Shakola's the only deity I can call upon with any ease. She set up the connection years ago."

I stood so quickly, my chair toppled back into the person behind me. A big burly man who also stood, growling out a "hey."

"You called her here to meet us?" My voice came out in a squeak.

A frown tugged his eyebrows low over his nose. He leaned in. "Part of my plan. Trust me."

"You brought me to meet my mother's *murderer*?"

"Trust me, *tocha*." He looked beyond me. At her. The cloud goddess.

"Ezekiel, I've been worried about you. These last few days have been an agony."

The woman embraced Zeke as he stood, pressing tight against him. He hugged her back, probably with a tender expression on his face. I couldn't see much of Zeke thanks to her mass of dark hair.

My hands were in fists and I used all my self-control not to launch myself at her. Shakola turned her pale, slanted eyes toward me. The light color—almost as if she had no pupils at all—was startling in her tanned face framed by hair the same length and color as mine. Thankfully, she and I didn't resemble each other in any other way.

Shakola's eyes narrowed. Once she'd catalogued every imperfection of my face, she turned back to Zeke, her hand still on his arm, caressing. "Introduce us."

Zeke helped the woman into her seat across from me. She turned to smile at me, a bird of prey. Unfortunately, she considered me the mouse. My magic flared.

"Echo Ruiz," I said before Zeke could do so. "The daughter of the woman you killed."

"This is Shakola," Zeke said, his voice firm and his eyes sending me a warning.

Oh, hell no. He didn't ask me to be nice.

"You were right; she possesses lots of raw power. Barely controlled." Shakola turned back to me and smiled again, like a rhesus monkey. Those primates only smiled to show their power, moments before they attacked their prey.

I drew a deep, slow breath, refusing to rise to her bait. As I wrestled to keep my magical center quiet, Shakola angled her body toward Zeke's. She leaned in, showing me how little she thought of me, period.

My magic flared hotter this time and she glanced at me from the corner of her eye, a dimple appearing in her cheek. Zeke turned to glare at me as well, but his message was different—*why the hell are you giving demons our location?*

I stumbled backward, mumbling an apology at a biker I bumped into. He shrugged, turning back to his group, though he cast a furtive, longing glance at Shakola.

"I cannot help you much. Not if she's so incapable of controlling her magic."

"Leave Echo to me," Zeke said.

My eyes had to be huge and my mouth dropped open. I wasn't five. I didn't need to be managed. His face paled, his mouth mashed in a thin line. His eyes touched mine, pleaded for patience I did not have.

"You had to know Masau sent him here to protect you years ago. He was the perfect choice. Clearly, he's done his job well. You still breathe." Shakola sighed. "Though it would be best if you didn't. Not just for Zeke but the rest of the gods."

I wasn't quick enough to school the flash of betrayal that flowed across my features. Zeke dropped his gaze, his hands fisted on the tabletop.

"Stop antagonizing her," Zeke said.

"I'm testing her control," Shakola practically purred. "As someone should have years ago."

"I need information," Zeke said. His jaw locked down hard, frustration rolling off him. He was angry with *me*? My magic slammed against the confines of its box.

"I want to know more about the Ridge Ruin and the Magician," Zeke continued. "Who's holding him, why, and what's surrounding the perimeter, guarding it."

Shakola shrugged. "There are tests, many tests, some more painful and deadly than others. Consider what we know about the instigator." Her pale eyes slid to me, reinforcing her connection to Zeke—that they were confidants. "I've arranged for another protector for the child. She should be able to fend for herself until he arrives. She does, after all, possess all that untapped power."

"That's not going to happen." Zeke's voice was hard. "Echo's my responsibility."

Shakola leaned forward. "She need not be. I'll free you of that terrible bargain. Send the girl to Sussitanako's spawn if you're so worried. I'll help you with your quest."

Shakola's words flamed my jealousy and my worst fears. Zeke settled in, intent to converse with my mother's killer. I slammed my hand against the table, unable to sit still and quiet any longer. Not even Zeke's presence would keep me from letting loose my magic on the conniving liar.

But I kept it under control. "Bathroom," I mumbled, keeping my face averted.

Zeke called my name, but I'd already shoved through the crowd, putting as many bodies between us as possible. I didn't want him to see the anger and confusion on my face, I didn't want to think about how readily I would have slept with him at any time over the last few days—if he hadn't rejected me.

I practically ran the last few steps to the bathroom, refusing to let the tears fall or the magic out. I breathed in a steady rhythm, concentrating on keeping my mind calm and still. I was failing, but the spark hadn't leapt to torch me or the bar. Yet.

I struggled to get a breath into my lungs, fighting with the rage and humiliation threatening to consume me. Shakola tried to kill me with demon dogs at our first meeting. She'd told Coyote where I was located, which led to my mother's kidnapping and subsequent death. She'd brought Jaguar to Zeke's house, the Kachina intent on raping and murdering both Layla and me.

"You didn't know he was still working with Shakola. Zeke led you back to the bitch. Now you know. Now you get out. Because she won't win and he doesn't matter," I told myself.

But he did. My heart crumbled in my chest as one realization crystallized: Zeke, my most important confidant, my partner in crime, would never be the lover I'd learn intimately. Until this moment, I'd cared for him not because he kept saving my life—though I was indebted to him for that—but because he genuinely mattered to me.

I cared about his thoughts, his feelings, whether he got his favorite cheese on his hamburger. I wanted him happy. After seeing him with Shakola, seeing that my happiness didn't register with him, my naïveté slammed into me like a fist to the nose. Layla had tried to warn me—said Zeke made Jaguar look like a kitten—but I hadn't listened. He'd used me.

He'd continue to use me. I couldn't let that happen.

I stayed in the stall longer than necessary, planning my escape. No way I'd stay with Zeke now. He'd had—still had?—a relationship with Shakola. His betrayal cut deeper than I expected, maybe because he'd assumed I wouldn't care.

When I came out of the stall, I splashed water on my dry, gritty eyes. I straightened my shoulders and forced my cheeks to relax so my mouth didn't pucker in such a telltale sign of displeasure. Finally, I didn't appear so upset. I pushed through the door, determined to keep my newfound resolve.

"'Bout time," Zeke growled. He materialized out of the shadows. Danger wafted from him, mixing with anger and frustration. The emotions licked at my mind. How had I missed these strong vibes before?

Maybe because these were directed at me, not at Shakola. Because I kept Zeke from what he wanted—spending more time with the very goddess responsible for so much of my heartache.

I pressed my body back against the wall, needing space from Zeke's seething emotions.

"I nearly came in there and dragged you out. I can't believe you ran off like that."

"My mother's killer intentionally antagonized me. Because you didn't warn me, I wasn't prepared for your girlfriend to be such a bi—" I cleared my throat when Zeke's chin dropped to his chest, his eyes darkening with dangerous promise. I didn't like that expression turned on me. "And there was a line," I said, raising my chin and daring him to contradict me. No one else had come into the bathroom while I was there and no one else walked out.

"Are you ready?" he asked. "We need to get out to the Ridge Ruin. There's more than just demons protecting the property at night, and I want to get a feel for what's there, especially after the ants earlier."

"Did you ask Shakola about those?" My voice sharpened with displeasure. She'd already been suspect, but now, after seeing her and Zeke together, she skyrocketed to first place on my list.

"No." He ran his hand up and down the back of his neck. "We're going to need as much time as we can get to free the Magician. Shakola said he disappears each morning and those trying to get in must restart the tests."

"I'm not going anywhere with her," I said.

Zeke's nostrils flared and his mouth firmed to a dangerous slash. "Don't be obstinate. We must to talk to the Magician. Layla's weakening. You've given away our exact location. We're trapped, Echo. And Shakola said there might be humans in the coming group. That means a blood trail."

I was disconcerted long enough to step closer to him. "You could go to jail if you hurt one of the humans?"

"If the police figured out I committed the crime, yeah."

Zeke tucked a strand of hair behind my ear. My stomach tumbled first with pleasure, then with something much less pleasant. He'd played me. This whole time. He used my feelings to get me to do what he wanted; another, subtler weapon.

"Why doesn't *she* do something to distract the humans?"

"She won't help me anymore as long as I'm with you. She says you're dangerous, and after your projection a little while ago, I can see her point."

"Oh? I'm unreasonable because I don't want to be near the goddess who caused my mother's death? Who would've happily let Coyote rape me?"

"*Tocha*, don't," he said, his voice low.

"Don't what? Point out the truth?"

"C'mon," he said. He grabbed my hand, and the same ripple of awareness flashed through my system along with a driving need to get closer. Pain shot up my arm and straight to my heart. I didn't want to go with him and Shakola. I didn't want to go anywhere with him ever again.

"No, Zeke." I tugged my hand from his. "You go ahead and take care of whatever you need to, wherever you need to. With her. I'll figure something out."

"I told you, I'm not going anywhere without you," he said. His teeth were clenched so tight, a muscle ticked in his jaw.

That place in my head flared to life. I tried to tamp the flicker down, but I remained perilously close to losing it. "I can't be with you!" I hissed. The surprise in his eyes slowly shifted to hurt.

"You don't want to be with me?" he asked.

"I can't be around you. You've been using my emotions. I don't know why I trusted you. You're no different from Coyote. From Jaguar. Leave me alone."

I backpedaled, slamming into the wall behind me, trying to distance myself from my desires and Zeke's emotional turmoil. My magic didn't want to remain contained much longer. I tried to breathe through the rising emotions, but I was losing. He'd kept so much from me. He brought in that goddess, knowing what she'd done to me, to my family. Gah, I'd been so stupid.

"You alright, missy?" The same burly man I'd run into at the table stood off to my right. Several others stood behind them, all wearing red bandanas and lots of tats on their arms, necks, bald heads, and even some on their faces. "This guy bothering you?"

The guy cracked his knuckles—that seemed so ridiculous and cliché. People didn't really flex their biceps and ready their fists. Did they?

Zeke narrowed his eyes as if daring me to affirm the question. Shakola walked toward me, her beautiful face shadowed but her pale eyes glowing. Triumphant smile on her face, she focused on Zeke. Hate rose up fast, hard. I gripped the hilt of my knife, wanting nothing more than to wield it.

Zeke stepped in, his hand closing over mine, squeezing until I winced. My heart beat twice in rapid succession.

"Don't."

"You brought her here," I panted. His scowl deepened. Why didn't he understand?

"You can't leave. We need to talk!" Zeke yelled, his voice filled with frustration and maybe even fear. I'd figured that out myself, and I put my hands to my ears and sprinted, not registering that the crowd parted around me.

CHAPTER TEN

I shoved through the door and stumbled out into the cold night. I moved in the direction away from Zeke's bike, walking as quickly as I could, staying in the shadows next to the highway. I needed a place to stay, to plan. I was worried about Zeke and the men who planned to kick his ass. More, my entire body hurt from the depth of Zeke's betrayal.

"Honani?" I choked out of my pained throat.

"Why are those men fighting with Zeke back there?" Honani asked, appearing next to me.

I shut my eyes. I didn't want Zeke hurt. "Isn't Shakola there?"

"She is, yes. She's watching the men hit him."

I frowned. That didn't make any sense. Honani moved so that he floated in front of me. "That's why you left? Because of her?"

"Yes."

"She's the reason your mother was captured."

"Yeah, I know. That's not the only horrible thing she's done this week."

"I doubt you not. Her eyes are so...flat. Lifeless." Unease pulsed off him.

I nodded, wrapping my arms around my waist. "She's awful, but she and Zeke have known each other a long time." I spat the last word because the anger would fuel me better than the horrible ache building in my chest could. I threaded my fingers through my hair.

"Ah. You figured that out?"

"She made their shared days very obvious."

Honani was quiet. The gravel crunched under my feet. My stomach hurt, both from the greasy nachos and from Zeke's callousness.

"Would you believe that their relationship wasn't sexual?"

"No."

Honani sighed, his aura fading to an avocado hue. "I figured you'd say that."

"Will you help me? I need to get to the Ridge Ruin."

Echo?

Zeke's concern laced the word. He called me again. I took a deep breath and shut down that part of my brain.

Honani patted my shoulder, his discomfort shimmering over us both. "Not your smartest decision."

"If you're going to criticize me, you can go away, too."

"I am your protector; I cannot leave."

"Then help me. I don't want to see him again," I said, my voice fierce. I sniffled once.

I stumbled and let go of my middle in order to stop my fall. A rock gouged the flesh on my palm. I lay there for a moment until the pain of my ripped flesh galvanized me.

Screw it. I sat on the side of the road and put my head to my knees. Mom, Layla, Zeke, the only life I'd ever known and didn't know how much I'd miss—I ached for all of them. For me, too. For being naïve enough to believe in love.

Honani stood nearby, discomfort etched on his face and in the dark color of his aura. I heaved a breath and stood up. The mission hadn't changed. Find the Magician and make him some deal to free Layla. No one would ever accuse me of not keeping my promises. If that meant sneaking into the Ridge Ruin to talk to the Magician tonight, then that's what I'd do. Right now. By myself.

Because I was never, ever falling for Zeke Lakin's lies again.

#

"Find out where Zeke is," I said.

Honani glared, clearly not liking my tone, but he obeyed. I wiped my cheeks and stretched. I checked my knife, thankful for its presence.

"Shakola is tending to him in the back of that place."

"Good." I walked back toward the parking lot. "Now, I just need an easy mark," I muttered. "There."

Middle-aged, the man had a healthy appetite for beer based on his girth. His thinning hair blew in the soft breeze. He wore a brand-new leather jacket with the name Bob emblazoned on the chest. He stood next to a Honda motorcycle, the low, sexy curves built for speed and overcompensation. I pegged the owner as an executive with bad-boy grandeur. Perfect.

I smiled enough for my little dimple to flirt its way out of my cheek. His eyes roamed my face, down over my chest and hips.

"What type of bike is that?" I asked.

"Honda Blackbird." He patted the thick, black leather seat, an air of pride drifting from him.

I twirled a long stand of my hair as I edged closer. "Go fast?"

His smile grew wider, more lascivious. "Tops out at one-ninety."

Fast enough. "I need a ride," I said.

"Oh, baby, I can give you a ride," Bob said. Really? He had to go straight to suggestive?

"What is it with older men and beautiful women?" Honani said. "I know the man has a brain, but he's not using it."

The bar door crashed open and Zeke staggered out, arm wrapped around his midsection.

"I'm mad at you, too," I snarled at my so-called ghost friend.

"Me?" Bob balked.

"Why?" Honani said.

"You lied to me. You said he was in the back."

"I did not lie!" Honani said, scandalized.

"Who are you talking to?" Bob asked. Confusion made his jowls jiggle.

"My ghost protector," I said.

"Um. What?" Bob asked.

Zeke's eyes zeroed in on me and even with the distance between us, the heat of his gaze licked over my skin. I stiffened when Shakola stepped out behind Zeke, her pale hands sliding to his waist. "That's my boyfriend." I tipped my head toward Zeke. He dripped blood from a gash over his eyebrow and his nose, and his expression was killer. "He's mad at me. So are you going to help me or what?"

His anger radiated across the lot, slamming into me. What did he have to be angry about?

"Get your ass over here now," Zeke bellowed.

"I'm not getting in the middle of your problems," Bob sputtered.

Wrong answer for the horny coward. My eyes tripped back to Zeke and Shakola. I was out of time. I yanked my knife from my belt loop and pressed the point under Bob's chin. "Either give me a ride or give me the keys. Either way, I'm not staying here."

Bob paled, his lips opened slightly as he breathed hard through his mouth. "Take it, then."

I hopped on the motorcycle and shoved the key in the engine. "You can pick the bike up near Winona."

Zeke shuffled nearer. Shakola's eyes glinted with unholy pleasure. Time to get out of here.

"Can you make this guy not think I'm stealing?" I asked Honani.

"I'm dead, not a miracle worker."

I growled low. Pulling out part of the wad of cash Zeke gave me, I shoved the bills into Bob's hands. "Thanks for the rental."

"The kickstand," Honani said.

I shoved the thin metal rod up with my heel and thundered forward, taking immense pleasure when small pebbles shot back from the spinning tires. As I headed out of the lot, I raised my middle finger, making sure Zeke saw the gesture as I zoomed onto the road.

Driving a motorcycle at excess speeds proved way more fun than sitting behind someone else. The wind whipped through my hair and I pushed the engine to a high whine, forcing the vehicle faster and faster, needing more space and time between Zeke and me. This bike flew over the terrain, the tires gripping tight to the road.

As I neared my destination, I slowed, saddened my ride needed to end. I turned off the bike, put down the kickstand and tucked the keys under the black wheel cover.

"Can you get me some new clothes?" No way I'd continue wearing anything Zeke bought for me. Just as I wasn't going to talk to him ever again.

Honani licked his lips. "Why?"

"If you think for one moment I'm going to forgive Zeke for what he did . . ." I bit down on my trembling lip. "I'm done with him. So are you going to get me clothes and some gear so I can rescue Layla, or are you going to stand here and fight with me until Zeke shows up with that…that goddess," I snarled the word, "and I try to kill her?"

Honani scowled. "You are angry."

"You have no idea. Clothes, Honani. Something dark so I blend into the night. And some gizmos to help me get into the ruins."

"What are you going to do when Zeke shows up?"

I flipped my braid over my shoulder and jogged toward the cover of the nearby trees. "Not my problem."

CHAPTER ELEVEN

I slithered through a sparse piñon corridor, feeling audacious, thanks to my new night goggles and black cargo pants filled with all kinds of crazy out-doorsy accessories, all courtesy of my nimble, thieving ghost buddy, Honani. I loved that man.

But having a virile man, even a spirit one, pick out my clothes wasn't the best plan. Ah, well. Beggars and choosers and all that.

Honani had brought back a sweet charcoal Burberry coat that I'd partial-ly buttoned over a glittery black bustier. Honani's wardrobe choice differed from mine with him veering toward Fredericks of Hollywood. But the top was freaking Armani, and I wasn't turning down the opportunity to feel sexy while I committed a felony.

My second felony of the night.

I was practically a ninja. Oooh, no. A hit woman. I was totally going to James Bond someone tonight, if for no other reason than to leave my badass calling card. I moved all graceful and quiet around the rough-barked pine, low and controlled—just like the iconic superspy. Why weren't there more women espionage agents? I'd make a great one. I had stealth and freeze-frying power.

My daydream ceased when the bright beam of a flashlight hit my night-vi-sion goggles, blinding me. I screeched, landing hard on my less-than-bad ass and smacking my head into the bark of the tree. My ears rang from the new-est blow to my head as I clawed off the night-vision goggles.

"Dammit, Echo! Stop yelling."

My sense of sight was gone, probably forever, but my ears worked just fine. I heard every single annoying word Zeke whisper-shouted at me. I stood up, my back so ramrod straight, a drill sergeant would have been impressed. Maybe even taken lessons.

"Why are you here?" I asked. He smelled good. Like home. A couple of days ago, lavender and green chiles—my mother's unique fragrance—made me feel safest. But that was before spending hours wrapped around my heart-breaking *guerrero*. The last bit of my bravado drained from me, and I wilted faster than a crocus in the summer sun.

"Honani, we had a deal," I whisper-shouted.

The ghost warrior appeared next to me. At least I thought I saw the ghost. My eyes were watering, and I had big black blotches sliding across my vision. I clutched my head and moaned.

"You said he wasn't a problem."

I squealed in frustration as I stamped my foot. "I said he wasn't *my* problem."

"Then why raise a fuss if he's here?" Honani shot back.

"Stupid ghost logic. Of course Zeke being here matters! He *lied* to me."

I needed to be able to see again. The huge chunks of vision currently missing made it hard to exit the conversation, grandly or otherwise.

"You stole a motorcycle!" Zeke growled. "At knifepoint. If Shakola hadn't been with me, we wouldn't have been able to talk that dude out of pressing charges."

"She didn't stop him to help *me*. She has some agenda."

"Do you want to jeopardize the entire freaking world because you're in jail?" Zeke whispered again.

"No! I wanted away from you, you betraying ass!" I pushed against his chest.

Zeke ignored my shove and grabbed my hand, turning my palm up to study the bloody bandage I'd wrapped around it. The cut still oozed, telling me I should have gotten stitches. "What did you do to your hand?"

"I fell on a rock after I left the bar."

"Where else are you hurt? Did someone bother you? Hurt you?"

"No one else touched me. Nothing happened. I was doing great with my mission until you blinded and scared me. You need to leave so I can get on with Operation Magician. Honani and I totally got this."

"No, we really don't," Honani said. "There are lots of things on this ridge, and I don't think they're friendly. Bigger than those velvet ants."

I put my hands on my hips, my coat flapping open. I'd used the belt but hadn't used the buttons because I'd enjoyed the view of my cleavage. Feeling sexy imbued me with courage I wouldn't possess otherwise. "We do. Because I'm not working with Zeke anymore. He keeps bad company." I marched forward.

Zeke's hand shot out, stopping me just millimeters before I slammed my face into a tree I hadn't seen. I gritted my teeth.

"I'm sorry I didn't give you a heads-up about Shakola."

I grunted.

He continued. "I told you I had a plan."

"I call a massive bullshit on that."

"Echo's right. That goddess is the reason Echo's mom is dead."

I smiled at my spirit protector. "Thank you."

Honani's aura flared to an aggressive turquoise. "I told you not to hurt her," he growled.

"I didn't hurt her," Zeke said.

Honani and I both gasped in outrage.

"Fine." Zeke rubbed the back of his neck, a gesture that I found annoyingly endearing. "I maybe didn't tell her enough, but that's because her face telegraphs her every thought."

"I'm standing right here. And I don't need the cheating liar's help." I crossed my arms. I was petulant. And hurt. So screw Zeke.

"Echo, Shakola's given me updates about the gods before. We needed to know who's where and what they know. And we needed to know if the information she provided was valid."

"No, actually, *we* didn't. You wanted to snuggle close to your cloud goddess, whom I'm sure you've missed. I tried to give you what you wanted. That clearly wasn't me." I bit my lip, wishing I hadn't said that.

Whatever. I'd decided to get over him and move on. Or I would, once I saved Layla.

"You lack faith in me," Zeke said. "In us."

"I'll give you faith when you deserve it. And for the record, my mom was *very* important to me."

I lunged forward to grab Zeke's flashlight so he couldn't blind me with his light again, but he yanked the flashlight up and away just after my fingers closed around the metal shaft. I tumbled into his chest, grunting like a rhino giving birth.

"You're not touching me." I struggled, but Zeke wrapped his arm around my waist. He picked me up while I kicked my legs, hissing threats I couldn't possibly carry out.

He'd anticipated my reaction and dodged my flailing limbs while he skimmed his lips against mine, silencing me. The gentleness of the caress was unexpected. What I wanted. I stopped struggling and blinked up at him. His lashes shielded his eyes, and I didn't know what he was thinking. His lips brushed mine again, and I needed to melt into him.

No way. He'd intentionally met with my mother's killer. The woman who had offered me, trussed up, to Coyote, or, worse, Jaguar.

I tried to turn my head away. He pressed his lips harder to mine to the point of bruising. I growled as he walked backward so I was pinned against the thick tree trunk, his front pressed firmly to mine. I wanted this.

Except I really, really didn't. I struggled against my need and Zeke's body, bucking against his grip. I wasn't going to be carted around like a child. I was twenty-one years old. Everything in my life was so messed up, and Zeke loved another woman. A goddess.

I couldn't compete with a goddess.

"I wasn't done talking to you at the bar, and you're not moving now until I finish." He grunted when I managed to connect an elbow with his ribs. "Stop that! They're cracked already."

His breath panted out, wet and wheezy. I stilled, not wanting to hurt him further.

"Why didn't your *girlfriend* heal you?"

"She did the first time, but then I met up with a bunch of demons who were on their way up here. Good thing that bike was so fast. You outran everything."

He didn't deny she was his girlfriend. I bucked harder. I didn't care about his broken ribs. Well, I did. Very much. But my heart was breaking. Again.

Which should not be possible.

"Echo, stop it. She's not my girlfriend. She is just a friend."

"You're lying."

"If I was, why would I be here?"

"I don't know! To humiliate me some more? To rub my face in the fact that you know more about the gods and the situation than I do? That you can do whatever you want whenever and with whomever, and you expect me to just fall into line because I'm that pathetic?"

"You're really upset," Zeke said.

"You're just figuring this out?"

"She has a right to be," Honani said.

"Go away," Zeke said, not bothering to glance at Honani.

"I want him here. He doesn't try to betray me or manipulate me." I swung my arms in agitation. My jacket gapped open nearly to my waist. Zeke's eyes dropped. And stayed.

"Stop looking at me," I snapped. Thankfully, I was the only one who could feel others' emotions. Zeke couldn't know how his attention thrilled me. "You don't get to ogle me."

"Where'd you get this?"

"Honani went to Scottsdale and picked my clothes out," I huffed. "He also visited REI. I had him leave cash."

"Nice," Zeke murmured against my cheek.

This time I managed to turn my face away. "You hurt me tonight," I said, my voice low. "You're hurting me now. I don't want to play games."

"I've never played games with you, Echo."

All my muscles seized. I wanted to mold myself to him, hug him close and have him hold me. "I need to talk to the Magician."

"We can't just walk up to his tomb. Shakola said he doesn't do meet and greets anymore."

The night remained quiet. The stars were bright white beacons in the clear black sky. "Seems fine."

"Looks are deceiving. Like those velvet ants we ran into earlier. Like you.

You appear small and delicate, and you're an absolute hellion. Who doesn't listen."

I glared at him. At least he had the decency to look chagrined. I scowled harder. Zeke's cheeks suffused with a dull red.

"I'm sorry I didn't think more about your feelings," he said. "I've never had to think about anyone but me before."

I sucked in a breath but the fresh air didn't do anything to cleanse the hurt in my chest. "Not good enough."

He met my gaze, his full of sorrow. "You're right. It's not."

Oh, no, he wasn't going to take away my very righteous anger. "That—that goddess gave Coyote my location, Zeke. She's the one who told Jaguar where to find Layla."

Zeke stilled. As my words sunk in, his nostrils flared.

"Didn't know that one?" I added as much sarcasm to my words as I could. "Your friendly goddess doesn't like me. Which is fine. Because I hate her for what she's done. Not just for her part in getting my mom killed, but for Layla, too. I will not be near her again. Unless it's to kill her." I paused. "If that's even possible," I muttered.

Zeke set me on my feet. The color had leached from his face. Even his lips were white. "I didn't know that. About Jaguar."

"You also didn't give me a chance to talk to you about her first," I shot back. "Where's the trust in that?"

"I used her. For information. To see how she responded to you. I never meant to hurt you in the process."

"So you're really going to believe your cloud goddess about some stupid tests?"

"She isn't *my* goddess. It's not like that between us. Never has been."

"Uh, Echo. Something big is coming this way," Honani said from somewhere to my left. "Really big."

I pulled away from Zeke and tied the belt on my trench. I snapped my night-vision goggles into place. An enormous set of legs stalked through the forest. My mouth fell open with a choked sound. This wasn't your run-of-the-mill god-sized visitor. Those legs towered over us, as tall, if not taller than, the surrounding pine trees.

Honani drifted in front of me, once again causing my eyes to roll back in my head from the sudden glare.

"Tone it down! Can't you, I don't know, put a dimmer on your aura? That dude's using you as a spotlight."

He folded his arms over his chest. "I'm dead. Which means I get to choose who sees me. He's using his sense of smell."

I slipped my goggles back up onto my forehead and crossed my arms.

"Fine, Mr. Invisible. Is there some way around the behemoth? Be useful and figure that out."

Honani sighed dramatically. "You do not cope well with even the littlest of criticism. You need to work on that."

All three of us froze when we heard a loud thump just on the other side of the trees we'd come through. One of those tree-trunk-thick legs slammed into the woods a few hundred yards from where we stood. The thing spoke, his voice as loud and vicious as I feared he would be.

"I shall find you, *tiponis*. If you do not surrender yourselves, I will crush you before I eat you."

Zeke pulled his spear from its holster and shrugged his shoulders to adjust his armor. The giant stopped, waiting for our next move.

"If you come closer, the Magician's guardian says I can eat you. Unless you kill me." The giant chuckled at what he clearly thought was a joke. "I haven't chewed on holy children in quite some time. Come on, come closer. I'm starving!"

My scalp prickled. Great. Shakola had told the truth about the Magician's tomb. Zeke would take this as reason to continue to believe in her.

Zeke's stance widened, purposeful, but I saw the fear in his eyes and wondered if the same emotion was reflected in mine. Well, the way I saw it, we once again lacked choice. We had to talk to the Magician, our only lead to find Layla. I'd promised to find her and the cat, and nothing—not even a giant—would stop me.

"I'm not patient, little Halflings." The giant strode forward to the edge of the Magician's perimeter and picked up a huge boulder. The rock had to weigh more than a ton and was as big as my mother's old Toyota.

Zeke drew his sword. He winced a little at the motion. He tipped his head to the left just as the giant threw the boulder. I darted to the place Zeke indicated, feeling him close behind.

CHAPTER TWELVE

A hand bigger than a refrigerator shot through the trees, fingers as long as fence posts wiggling, feeling for one of us.

I backed away as I yanked out my knife, my damp fingers convulsing on the hilt. I held the blade in front of me, trying to emulate Zeke's hold on his weapon as I faced our newest test.

The giant wasn't just tall—way taller than Coyote—but also twice as wide. He held a large, curved stick, much like a shepherd's crook.

I gulped at the first glimpse of his body. A series of spikes fanned from the back of his neck. Where his face should have been sat a buffalo head, complete with ten-foot-long horns. His hair, long and straight, fell nearly to his waist and was matted with old bones and other things I refused to consider.

His chest transitioned from the short, curly buffalo fur to a humanoid form with thick, defined arm muscles that had to be both longer and wider than my entire body. His immense upper body tapered to a narrow waist. Dark leather breeches covered his hips and thighs; old style moccasins overlapped his pant legs.

With each step, the giant slammed the ground with his enormous feet, churning great chunks of the earth with the same capacity as one of those large, green John Deere tillers.

The lurching ground spat out a snake that tried to slither past the giant. He sniffed and grinned, his muzzle wet and dripping. He brought his foot down with precision and slammed his heal into the ground. The front half of the snake flew forward, toward us, its small eyes already sightless. The back half twitched, then stilled where the body stuck out from the side of the massive foot.

For the first time in days, I sympathized with a reptile's plight.

"Cheveyo," I gasped.

"The ogre," Zeke said. "Of course. It's May, the start of his normal hunting season."

"His?" I asked.

"Well, the only animals the rest of us can kill right now are bear or bison."

"You memorized the hunting calendar?" I asked.

"I hunt to eat," Zeke said. "Come on." He tugged me deeper into the trees, away from Cheveyo.

Honani's teal aura faded to sickly chartreuse as he kept pace beside me. "I thought Cheveyo was something parents told their kids about. You know, to scare us into behaving."

The ogre reached down and casually wrapped his hand around a thirty-foot-tall spruce. The tree lifted into the air, huge chunks of dirt and rocks falling on us.

"This is bad!" I gasped. I turned on my heel and ran.

Zeke stayed close behind me, shielding me with his body. He grappled to get hold of my hand. I let him snag my wrist, willing to set aside my anger and concern for the moment, because the alternative was certain death. That didn't mean I'd forgiven him for his part in Shakola's actions.

Zeke yanked at my wrist as he changed directions, and I followed him as we headed in a new downward route. The terrain flattened once we were out of the trees, except for the tree roots and an occasional small mound. I had no idea what those bumps in the ground would be for—maybe a burrowing animal? Seemed much too big for voles, but the mounds were too small to be graves.

Zeke halted, and I stepped up beside him, chest heaving. Running from demons and bigger, scarier monsters was the best cardio ever. If I lived another two weeks, I'd have the sexy bod all the women's health magazines shouted about on their covers.

The ruins, piled dark against the clear, twilit sky, sat a quarter mile from our current location. Maybe more. I glanced back to the vague security of the thinning line of trees. This arrangement had to be intentional. Anyone approaching the compound would be seen long before they reached it.

Zeke cursed, and I couldn't help but agree. I sucked in a great gulp of air and bounced onto the balls of my feet. For Layla, for my mother, I had to get to the ruins and…I didn't know what to expect after that, but it wasn't going to be the warm welcome I'd hoped for.

Cheveyo was only a couple of strides from us—his strides, not mine— thank the gods. Without so much as a word between Zeke and me, we started forward at a run. No way we'd outpace the ogre.

As soon as he stepped onto the flat field, the ground rumbled to life, rippling with frustration. The earthquake at Zeke's house and again at Coyote's den unnerved me, but this shaking pressed closer to the surface. My legs buckled and I grabbed Zeke's arm for support as the ground opened right along the edge of a set of burrows. Deep pockets of earth caved in, revealing dank hollows with all kinds of awful dead things. Animal skeletons crawled out of the pits toward us, their jawbones clacking an animated song that reminded me way too much of "Happy Birthday."

Cheveyo focused his dull eyes in our direction. They weren't the warm, chocolate color of Zeke's. Instead, Cheveyo's eyes reminded me of a dusty, dying brown of parched earth. Not that I spent a lot of time staring soulfully into his craggy, bovine face. One glance was enough.

Cheveyo whistled, an oddly beautiful sound. The skeletons slid back into the ground, burrowing about ten feet in front of us. Within seconds, the ground rose into a sheer, towering mass, blocking us from the buildings just ahead. The skeletal beasties poured out of the top, wiggling and grinding their way toward us, large mouths open to show off needle-sharp teeth.

Zeke managed to cut to the right and we spun around the initial mountain Cheveyo's creatures created. My breath came in short, hard pants as we sprinted around a second towering mass of dirt.

"Can you do something?" I asked.

"I'm running," Zeke snapped.

"With the earth. Can you—ah!"

The ground in front of us fell off quickly into a sheer cliff face. Zeke and I skittered to a halt mere feet from the edge. After a good hundred-foot drop was an empty twenty-foot ditch. The bottom of the moat wasn't filled with water—no liquid I could have used as a weapon or a barrier or something helpful. The ground below us writhed with hundreds more of the skeletal bodies.

Teeth sank into my sweet new spy pants and grazed the skin on my calf. I screamed and jumped forward, simultaneously trying to shake off the gnawing jaws.

The ground shook. Cheveyo was closing in on us.

My foot slid to the very edge. If I fell, those animated dead things would be on me faster than piranhas on their prey. I tried to throw my weight backward and to the left just as Zeke yanked me hard in the other direction. My wrist popped but I managed, barely, to stay along the edge of the mound and not fall into the moat. I swallowed down the nausea flaring in my gut as my wrist bones rubbed their broken edges together. Zeke bent and ripped the skeletal beast from my leg, its teeth shredding my pants.

I tried to run faster, gritting my teeth as my wrist jostled. I didn't want another one of those things biting me. My stomach churned harder from the pain combined with lack of air. I stepped on one of the skeletons, the shriek sounding from my lips even louder than the crunch of bones beneath my feet. Too gross.

I tapped the white-hot center in my mind to form a barrier around Zeke and me; anything that came close would be frozen. Ice piled around us. When my feet slid out from under me, Zeke picked me up, and threw me over his shoulder. He grunted as his ribs shifted under my weight, but he kept running. Cheveyo strode closer. Too close. One more step and he'd crush us.

Not happening.

My magical place blazed and a thick sheet of clear ice carpeted the ground behind Zeke. Cheveyo's foot skidded and he bawled. He'd already lifted his other foot to stomp us. The foot on ice slid out from under him and he slammed into the ground with an even greater earth shake than before.

Zeke grunted, staggering under my weight and the shifting ground. He righted quickly, shoring up the ground beneath us with his magic.

A huge tree groaned as its roots released from the soil. Cheveyo swung it, missing us by inches as Zeke leapt forward in a great burst of speed. We were almost to the buildings. Zeke must have used his Earth skills again because we'd run around or over the moat without getting chewed up by those skeletons. I didn't glance back to check. I was tiring, but I focused on the entrance to the ruins.

Another tree cracked, then another. Dirt clogged my nose as they hurtled toward us before crashing to the ground. My magic burst into high alert, slipping over me in a ripple of cold. Both Zeke and I were surrounded by white mist, not unlike the stuff that had pulled at me when I saw Layla last night.

"Helping. Keep doing that," Zeke panted.

"It just happened."

I groaned when my stomach slammed against Zeke's shoulder. I gripped my broken wrist with my other hand to minimize the horrible throb. Zeke skidded to a halt as a huge tree fell right in front of us.

"Set me down. We'll move faster without you carrying me." As my feet touched the ground, another tree landed behind me, nearly trapping us between the two. The earth shivered with its impact, rocking through my knees and up into my shoulders. I groaned. Zeke scanned me quickly to make sure I wasn't bleeding or trapped under the massive branches. His eyes darkened when he saw my wrist cradled against my chest.

"No apologies," I gasped. "I'm not dead, and that's really, really great."

"Broken?"

"Probably. Let's move."

Zeke's hand firmed on my elbow, ensuring I didn't run away. Again. My heart slid down in disappointment for both of us. I didn't want to leave him. I'd never wanted to leave him, but Shakola…She brought out my inner *loca*, sure. I didn't trust her—for very good reasons. More, I didn't trust Zeke when he was with Shakola. Zeke wouldn't hurt me, yet his emotions were so much more jumbled and angry when he was near the goddess.

We ran in the only direction we could, my icy bubble deflecting the trees now raining down on us.

I assumed Honani was right behind us, but I didn't bother to look back. He was dead already. Wasn't as though he could die again.

Wait. That's not true. My soul was ripped up by a demon this morning. I tried to turn around to see if Honani was there. I yanked my head away from another flying tree. This one might actually make contact.

A tree fell right in front of Zeke, halting our progress. Before we'd managed to change direction and sprint off again, my feet lifted from the ground.

"I got you, little girl." Cheveyo's mouth opened wide, his wet buffalo-snout dripping, his teeth white and razor sharp.

The chill from my body seeped into Cheveyo's hand, and he roared as the pain slid through his skin. Zeke yanked his spear from Cheveyo's foot. I made my skin even colder, my teeth chattering, trying to direct the chill down his arm and into his chest. Maybe if I reached his heart...

I didn't get the chance.

He dropped me.

#

Falling through the air was not my favorite pastime. I'd done this once before and the sensation wasn't any more pleasant this go-round. My stomach rolled with sickening certainty of the impending impact.

Zeke yelled my name. The ground was maybe thirty feet below and coming fast. I flailed my arms and kicked my feet, trying to slow my inevitable crash.

Zeke pulled his spear from Cheveyo's other foot as he slashed his sword across the back of the ogre's calf, just above his ankle. Twenty feet from the ground. I squeezed my eyes shut, my muscles clenching tight for the collision.

Honani gripped me in a firm embrace. My skin grew even colder thanks to his touch. I wasn't falling down so much as sliding sideways.

"Honani?"

"Busy saving you," the warrior grunted. "Call up the spirits."

"Please," I mumbled, gripping my pendant in my good hand. They wound around Honani and me, their chilliness so welcome.

"I'm not going to hit the ground?"

"You are," Honani said. "Soon. But not as fast. Shouldn't kill you now."

"When?"

"Tuck your head tight to your chest. Bring your knees up. We're rolling to break the momentum. Now."

I barely managed to get in position before I met the ground. The spirits' vaporous form took the brunt of the shock, but my shoulder slammed into something hard, and then I somersaulted over and over, rocks digging into my back, butt, and the top of my head.

I sprawled to a stop, holding my wrist to my chest. Honani flopped off me with a groan. I shivered as his frigid body peeled off mine. The rest of my spirits hung back. Some eyed the Ridge Ruin while others appeared dazed. Disappointment zinged against relief at being able to stand. My *abuelita* wasn't part of the group.

"Are you alright?" I asked Honani.

"I'm already dead. It's not like this can kill me."

"I'm glad. I was thinking along the same lines, but we need to discuss your sarcasm later. That's my thing. Ow," I muttered. I stood on trembling limbs and tried to orient myself. We were about a hundred yards from Cheveyo, who was still hounded by Zeke. My eyes widened as Zeke danced between the ogre's legs, slashing and stabbing.

"That's so impressive," I whispered.

"He's tiring," Honani responded. "Those cracked ribs are slowing him down."

"Why can't Cheveyo scent him? He plucked me off the ground without any trouble."

Zeke turned and sprinted toward us. "We need to find a place to hide," Zeke said, his voice raspy. "Regroup. We can't get into the ruins until we get rid of Cheveyo."

"Why?"

Cheveyo tipped his head back and sniffed at the air. He turned toward us, like a heat-seeking missile locked on its target. "He'll follow. He wants to eat you," Zeke said.

"Got that. He can't sense you," I replied. I snapped my fingers, frustration bubbling up under my exhaustion. "Gah! That's why. His name means spirit warrior. He can smell Honani and me because we're of that world. The spirit world. Me, thanks to my pendant and affiliation as the spirit seducer. You're not. You're Earth."

"Makes sense," Zeke said.

"Spirits, spread out. Let's see if we can buy time. And be careful."

They flitted across the plain, some toward Cheveyo, who stopped walking and sniffed the air again. He turned around, following the spirits back toward the copse at the edge of the plane.

Good gracious, the area was trashed. Massive tree trunks littered the flat area, their delicate roots were exposed, still covered in dirt. Holes pitted the ground.

We scurried back until we came to the cliff face.

"Give me a minute," Zeke said. His breathing had serrated into ragged pants. "We need to get around this, work our way down the ridge."

Cheveyo had turned back and was about one hundred yards from us, blood dripping from his many cuts, slowing his progress. He staggered and bellowed curses and threats. None of Cheveyo's skeletal animals moved on the field.

"I think I destroyed all the creepy-crawlies with that blast of cold," I said.

"You did."

"You stabbed Cheveyo in both feet," I said.

"A few times each, yeah. I hoped it'd slow him down, but he didn't pay me any attention. He's tracking you."

Zeke glanced upward at the sheer rock face, then back at the lumbering buffalo-giant snorting and snuffling toward us. He could barely hobble forward. A spark of hope ignited in my chest.

"Any ideas how to use that to our advantage?" I asked.

Zeke considered the terrain, then the rock face behind us.

"How did the tribes get rid of him before?" Zeke asked.

"They destroyed his physical body," I said. "One group drowned him, another buried him under rocks, like a cairn."

"That's our strategy," Zeke decided.

"What is?"

"You and Honani lure him over here. Toward the rock face. I'll do the rest."

I staggered forward, my limbs tired from the short sprint.

"Be careful," I said.

I took up my position.

"For what it's worth," Zeke said, his voice soft, "I trust you with my life."

I nodded, but warmth didn't fill me at his words. Because he didn't trust me with his secrets.

#

Zeke slid his spear back into its case, his sword into his scabbard. He pressed the thick leather bracelet on his wrist and his armor slid off him. The runes were archaic, a dead language. Perhaps Masau had given the armor-in-a-bracelet to Zeke. If the fighting gear was imbued with godly essence, that would explain why the leather and cotton protected him so well.

He turned back toward me one more time, his dark eyes filled with longing. He shook his head like a dog shaking off water from their fur.

"I need time to get to the top. Don't let him pick you up again. Get him as close to the cliff as possible, then run."

He sucked in a deep breath and ran back toward the cliff. Zeke pulled himself upward, the muscles in his arms and shoulders standing out in stark relief against his sweaty tee.

"Got it. Be careful."

He glanced down at me, his eyes softening. "You, too."

Cheveyo was twenty feet from us, about one of his strides. My spirits swarmed around his head, an irritation perhaps, but he'd caught my scent. Blood loss from Zeke's foot-stabs had slowed him down, finally, and he staggered to the right. He yanked himself upright and snorted. His wet nose trickled mucus. His long, pink tongue flicked out across his lips and nose.

I gagged. I *so* was not a bodily-fluids kind of girl.

"What do you think?" I asked Honani.

"I go right, you left? Make noise and try to distract him even as we get him closer."

I nodded. "Go."

I eased to the left, focusing on my task. I let my arm fall to my side, gritting my teeth against the pain.

"You should use a tissue!" I yelled.

Honani's signature cold disappeared. Heat licked its way back over my skin, and I shivered from the pleasure of being close to normal human temperature.

"Your feet are a mess. You should sit down and rest," Honani said.

"Maybe you should go home and clean them up," I hollered.

Cheveyo turned toward me, his dirt-brown eyes pinpointing me with scary accuracy. A quick glance told me Zeke had scaled the top of the cliff. His Earth capabilities made him fast and sure. Like a mountain goat.

I asked my spirits to group together around me. Once they were there, I moved back toward the right, closer to Honani. Cheveyo's head followed me, tracking me with those strange, dull eyes. The spirits hadn't fazed him at all.

Did my godliness give off a different odor? Still so much about my magic I didn't understand.

Ready? I whispered in my mind toward Zeke.

Not yet. He huffed back. *Don't die.*

I rolled my eyes. I tried to un-think my growing heat in case Cheveyo could sense that. Didn't work. I kept moving right, closer to Honani. Cheveyo waddled forward at an angle to intercept my path. Honani slid in closer to the ogre. For a second, Cheveyo seemed confused, his head turning toward Honani. He snuffled, mucus dripping from his nose into the short brown fur above his upper lip. He raised his hand and rubbed the snot into his fur.

"That has to be the worst hygiene ever," I said.

Cheveyo's head turned back toward me. Honani's aura flashed brighter in annoyance. Cheveyo ignored him; he stalked closer to me, less than ten of his paces. My spirits formed a wall in front of me, a solid mass of cold.

Run. Zeke's command exploded in my head.

You got it. My spirits dispersed, and I put my head down and ran toward

Cheveyo. He snorted and opened his hands as he moved forward to intercept me. I heard the crack and rumble of rocks tumbling behind me as I ducked down as small as I could while still sprinting. I darted to the right, closer to Honani and around Cheveyo's legs instead of through them.

"Stick with me," I begged them. The cold intensified, and my heart leapt. We might just survive this.

His hand missed me, deflected by the closest of the ghosts. Cheveyo bellowed. I darted forward. Honani stepped in front of me, and I pulled up so fast, I nearly fell. The spirits behind me caught me as I began to tumble, and Honani reached out his hands, steadying me under my elbows. My wrist throbbed and stomach turned over as I jolted to a stop.

"Zeke did it. Cheveyo's buried."

I turned, my chest heaving. A huge pile of rocks settled where I'd stood just moments before. Several more rocks toppled from the cliff face to land on top of the pile. I held my breath but the pile didn't move. I sank down into the grass.

"I can't believe we did that," I said. Glancing up at my spirits, I smiled. There she was, my *abuelita*.

"You, *mi amorcita*, are so brave."

I reached forward, but she stepped back, away from my touch. I let my hand fall. Sure, having dead relatives was better than none, but I couldn't initiate contact. I smiled at her, and she returned it, the same sadness filling her eyes that sat in mine.

"Thanks for the help. If you want to go home, I think I'm good for a while." My *abuelita* led the spirits back into my pendant.

I raised my eyebrows at Honani in silent question. He shook his head. "I'll stay here."

I nodded, grateful for his continued presence. Zeke clambered atop the rocks. I feared he'd jumped from the cliff face, which was lower, only about ten feet higher than the Cheveyo mound. Zeke examined each of the spaces between the rocks. He pulled his spear out and slammed the weapon into one of the larger holes. He did that another few times as I tried to catch my breath.

I cradled my wrist to my chest, wishing I could relieve the intense throbs.

Satisfied, Zeke hopped down the boulders. He stood in front of them for a long moment. Gah, if he called Shakola again, I was *done* with him. But he didn't drop into his prayer pose.

The rocks in the cairn shifted, fusing together. The roots from the nearby fallen trees grew, sliding over the huge mound of rock and dirt, encasing the cairn in a fine layer of interwoven tendrils. A loud crunching sound had me swiveling my head. The trees nearest the forest rolled back, realigning in the dirt. I gaped. Zeke's power was far greater than I'd realized. In the span of a few minutes, the grounds were tidied, all but two trees replanted.

Zeke walked over to us. He pulled me upward and dropped a kiss on my lips, careful to avoid my sore wrist.

"Impressive," I murmured. "But why'd you do it?"

"Part of fixing Earth is compulsive. Leaving the grounds as they were after our battle would mean the trees would die. My element, much like yours, seeks balance." He rubbed the back of his neck, a self-deprecating gesture. "And part is strategic: if the grounds look right, we won't call as much attention to ourselves. Might give us more time when people show in the morning. I can't believe I hurt your wrist," he said, frowning.

I wiggled my fingers, sighing in relief. "Just a sprain, I think."

"I'll put some ointment on it."

"Please tell me it's not from your girlfriend."

He kept his gaze steady on mine. "She's helped me when I needed it before, possibly out of guilt or, more likely, for her own gain. But she's a *goddess*, and not trustworthy because of it. But she's also a friend. That's all she's ever been."

"I don't treat my friends like she does," I replied, but I offered him my wrist. He spread my fingers with great care, watching my reactions. Once my fingers were opened, he touched the bones. I hissed, my body tightening. "She tried to kiss you. In front of me."

Zeke scowled, but his touch remained gentle. "I didn't kiss her. I need to set your wrist. It's broken. I'm really sorry I hurt you." He focused on my wrist, but his voice was soft with regret. For my broken bones or for the heartache he'd caused? "It's going to hurt worse before getting better."

"Do it."

He grasped my forearm, his other hand gripping my palm. I gritted my teeth but nothing prepared me for the agony that ripped straight up my arm and into my head as he aligned the bones. I must've blacked out.

I snuggled into Zeke's lap as his long, callused fingers gently rubbed yellow lotion on my wrist.

"Doesn't hurt as much," I croaked.

"Good. I'm going to splint it, then we need to keep moving." Zeke set me aside and picked up a couple of sticks next to him. At my questioning look, he said, "Honani found them." He laid my hand on his knee and pressed the smooth sticks on either side of my lower forearm. He picked up some gauze he'd pulled from his backpack and wrapped my wrist.

"What happened to Cheveyo?" I asked.

"The rockslide should be enough to send him back to the underworld. Just in case, I sealed the tomb. He can't get back out."

I nodded. "Let me do your ribs," I said.

Zeke considered me from under those incredible lashes. My breath caught before I glanced away, not wanting him to see my anger and hurt. And I had every right to continue to be angry and hurt.

"I put some of the salve on them earlier. They're getting better, and I need full range of motion. But thanks."

"Do we have time to eat anything?" I asked. If he wouldn't let me help him, I'd feign hunger to buy us a few precious moments of rest. My stomach rumbled, and I covered the expanse with my good hand. No need to fake anything.

Zeke's lips turned up a little. "You're like a little kid. You need to eat every two hours."

"Only since I started doing magic. The energy burn makes me so hungry."

"Yeah, I remember those days. Hella work until you can control it. Gets easier, just like any type of exercise. There's some jerky in my bag. Best I can do for now." He held my fingers in a firm grip when I tried to pull back. "She wanted to make you jealous, you know. So you would either lose control and bring a slew of demons into that bar, meaning we'd waste much of the night and be unable to get to the Magician here." He sucked in a deep breath and met my eyes. "Or you'd leave me."

"She got what she wanted," I swallowed. "I didn't like her touching you. The insinuation that she's your confidante hurt."

Zeke's lips pressed flat, his eyes drifting off as sadness filled his expression. "My mom abandoned me when I was six. I remember her telling me to wait there—at the entrance of Masau's village. That she'd be right back as soon as she could. She walked down the path, into the town. I never saw her again."

I squeezed his fingers—there was nothing to say.

"Masau found me late that night. I was cold, wet, blubbering; afraid of what would happen to me. Of what must have happened to my mom. She'd never disappeared before—it had always been the two of us. Masau brought me into the village. He took me to his house. I'd stayed with him for about a year, maybe more, when Shakola came to visit. She said my mother was killed by one of her storms. She stood in Masau's house and wept, saying she hadn't known my mother was there. That she was responsible and that as penance she'd help care for me. Masau agreed. But he didn't allow me to live with her—I stayed on with him because he said he'd already performed the fostering ceremony."

Concern and something more rolled off him. "He didn't perform the fostering ceremony until that night. The night after Shakola asked me to live with her."

"Because he didn't trust her either?" I raised my eyebrows then groaned, rubbing the ache from my eyes.

"Maybe. I don't know. I didn't ask."

"Why not?"

"I don't know. Look, I'm telling you this because I don't want you to shut me out." Zeke's voice was strained, like he'd been gutted. He sighed, his fists clenched on his thighs. His shame floated in the air, unwanted by us both. We were back to where we'd started the night; frustration and half-truths wedged into the space between us.

"I can't let you hurt me like that again."

He met my gaze, his eyes dark with sincerity. "There's nothing I wouldn't do for you, especially to keep you safe."

My eyes widened. Did that mean…Zeke cared about me, but I was still confused, I didn't understand what he was trying to tell me.

"Five minutes until midnight," Honani said.

His timing was awesome. I cleared my throat and stood, dusting off my dirt-encrusted black pants.

"How about that jerky?"

Zeke stood and handed me a piece of the dried meat.

I shoved the jerky into my mouth and turned back toward the ruins. "Wanna bet there's more waiting for us?"

"I'm not betting against a certainty."

CHAPTER THIRTEEN

Zeke flinched as he stood up. His ribs had to be killing him. We walked with slow, deliberate steps toward our goal.

The walls seemed to shimmer, flashing back and forth between the tumbled stones here now and what had been. I had to squint to see between the multistory pueblo great house that rose atop the volcanic outcrop, and the crumbling bits of rock and stucco that remained.

The area surrounding the large Chaco-style building was a series of terraces. These were as big as the Plaza in Santa Fe, each one flowing down to the flat expanse we currently traversed. Based on the low rock walls and the size, I assumed we were on a ball court, popular with the Hohokam tribe back around 1000 A.D. The game was imported from the tribes in Mexico and Central America, possibly the Aztec and Inca. Players moved a rubber ball around the large arena, never allowing the ball to touch the ground.

This particular site had once held two ball courts. We were on the one situated north-to-south. Beyond it lay another ball court that faced east and west. Between the two courts and the wall of the main building were multiple ceremonial kivas—any of which would house the protective spirits of the tribe who'd called this place home.

I'd planned a trip to visit this place a few years ago, right after I started college. One of my assignments required detailed information about the ceremonial customs of the people living in this community. The day before I planned to leave, my mom sat me down in the living room. "I found a lump in my breast," she said, her eyes dark.

Horror trickled across my skin, settling deep in my chest. The *tías* talked often of their fear of breast cancer after watching their mother fade and crumple from the disease. "When?"

"Last week. I'm seeing a specialist tomorrow."

I clutched mom's hands. They were cold, her fingers delicate. "I'll come with you."

"That will mess up your trip," Mom said.

"You're more important. My professor will understand."

Her eyes gleamed. I'd thought with disappointment, but perhaps she'd been triumphant, pleased to keep me from this place. "I'm sorry, Echo."

I'd gone to that appointment with my mother for her biopsy. Six days later, the letter came in the mail, telling us the tissue was benign.

She'd known she wasn't ill. She wasn't actually related to the *tias*, to the woman who'd died of breast cancer. No, I'd met her real mother yesterday when she told me to come here, to this hellish place.

Instead of asking me not to go or telling me the truth about my heritage, my mother willingly had her body cut open to ensure I didn't come this close to Sotuk's ancient lands. So much I didn't understand. Did she suspect Cheveyo lurked outside, ready to eat any Halfling dumb enough to walk up here? No. Somehow I didn't think that's why she'd kept me from this place. Fear for my safety, perhaps, kept her from telling me the truth about my father and my magic.

I squinted, trying to keep the ruins in their current form. No answers tumbled from the gleaming stucco walls.

"Welcome to the Ridge Ruin."

A man materialized in front of us. A ghost, not a man. His aura was strange—dampened like the black mountain cat's. His far eye was a gaping hole surrounded by rotted flesh. I fought and won the urge to step back. Zeke slid closer, perhaps sensing my need for his steadying presence.

The shaman's eyes narrowed and the non-eye pulsed a deep red for a moment before the space glowed aqua. I stared at it, wondering how a ghost got a glowing eye socket. That didn't seem possible either.

His voice was deep and rough like he drank too much *tiswin* and smoked too much tobacco. If he was as old as the Magician, he would have been familiar with the ancient fermented corn drink or maybe even saguaro wine.

"Thanks," I said. "We met your greeter. He wasn't very friendly. You should work on that."

"He wasn't meant to be," the ghost said.

"Then why are you welcoming us?" Zeke asked.

"You wish to see the Magician. First you must complete tasks to prove your worth."

With that, the ghost turned and disappeared into one of the kivas.

I sighed. Of course we had to go underground. My last experience there hadn't been positive. Layla and I nearly died in a cave after I broke one of Sotuk's tablets.

Honani faded out, returning a moment later. "He has no weapon, but he is powerful. More powerful than any spirit I have encountered, but there's something odd about his aura."

I nodded, aware of the blackness exuding from the shaman.

"Shakola said there are four tests. The first is to stand at the door."

I stiffened at her name but forced my body to relax before Zeke became aware of my displeasure. Rehashing our differing views on the goddess wouldn't solve the issue now.

"There are many rooms below. I don't trust him," Honani said.

"Both Raven and Echo's grandmother said to come here," Zeke said.

"I have to find Layla," I fretted. "At least this guy isn't trying to kill us."

"Yet," Honani murmured.

"Not helping," I said.

Zeke went down the ladder first. Always my protector, even with the jealousy and betrayal slicing our initial connection. I locked the hurt up tight and climbed down the ladder into the flickering darkness below. Sandwiched between Zeke's body and Honani's ghostly one above, the descent was more difficult because of my broken wrist and the guys' configuration, but we managed.

A rough-planked table covered much of the space, the wooden legs set deep into the earthen floor. Four swords in a leather container lay atop the table. The rest of the room was bare, not just of ornamentation but also furnishings.

Zeke hung back, eyes assessing, but I moved toward the swords, drawn to them with a compulsion I didn't understand.

"Call me Alo," the shaman said. He stood behind the table.

I dipped my head in acknowledgment. "And you may call me—"

"You were named for Palunhoya. I shan't call you such an exalted name. You have not proven your worth."

I forced my facial muscles to stay lax. This guy was dead and his opinion didn't matter. "Echo. My name's Echo."

He nostrils quivered in disapproval. "If you insist."

"Thank you, Alo."

"Your spirit guard has been invited to spend the rest of the night with the Magician," the shaman said.

Honani's temperature dropped well below the Alaskan winter norm.

"He stays with me," I said.

"Not if you wish to meet the Magician. That is one of the parameters for the meeting."

"What if we don't agree?" Zeke asked.

The ghost smiled but it was thin and ugly. "You may try to leave. Honani stays."

"No." I met the shaman's glare with my own.

"The Magician has already extended the invitation to the spirit warrior."

I glanced toward Honani only to realize he was gone. My head snapped back to the ghostly shaman in front of me. "I want him back."

"Then I suggest you complete your trials in a timely fashion." He tipped his head toward the blades on the table. "This is the next task."

I stepped forward and pulled out a sword. Not a European style sword. More of a wooden-handled club, lined with razor-sharp pieces of obsidian. Atop the club, at its end, eighteen inches of black rock had been chipped and honed to scissor-thin edge.

"The base is *maquahuitl*," Zeke said. "That's Aztec."

Alo dipped his head. "The base, yes. Not the blade. We borrowed their weapon-making genius. Improved upon it. These blades are kept sharp enough so the performer doesn't feel his death." The shaman's face split in a grin, his excitement palpable. "Few pass my door in human form."

"And how many tests do you plan to force us through?" Zeke asked.

The shaman dipped his head. Annoyance poured off him. I bit my lip not to blurt out the question hovering there. The shaman looked up, his one eye sharp, the hole glowing crimson with anger.

"Four. The sacred number."

I winced. Shakola had been right. "And we've passed the first," I replied. "Which leaves three until we can reclaim Honani. Who is *my* spirit guardian." I couldn't stop antagonizing Alo. Everything about him set me on edge.

"If you wish to ask your question of the Magician, you have but a few hours to accomplish the remaining tasks." Another reptilian smile slithered across those thin lips. "But if you fail, Honani remains here, with the Magician, forever."

"You've changed the rules," Zeke growled.

"If we pass, then the Magician must provide us not just answers but a boon," I said. Zeke stiffened beside me, but I gripped his fingers to keep him silent. For most people of that time period, wagering was one form of great excitement. The shaman narrowed his eyes at me, considering.

"I do not speak for the Magician," Alo snapped.

"Then we have no deal," I shot back. "Which means you must return Honani now."

Alo's eyehole flared blood red. I got the distinct impression he wished me covered in the color. And I don't mean by lights.

"Fine. But only if you pass all the tests," Alo said.

"Swear it," I countered.

Zeke tensed again, but before he could speak, Alo said, "Of this, I swear."

I dipped my head in acknowledgment, considering the blades in front of me.

"Echo, you can't really think—"

I cut Zeke off. My resolve would fail if he tried to talk me out of this. "I have to swallow each one without dying."

Alo's thin lips turned up in a cruel smile. "You are most mistaken. You must swallow all four *at once* to proceed."

My ancestors had some really bad ideas about what made a worthy warrior. A blade down the throat was nothing like avoiding a blade in battle.

I blew out a hard breath. "And the other challenges? You owe us, taking

Honani like that. We deserve to know what we're getting into."

"I owe you nothing, Halfling." Alo's nostrils flared and his eye socket ran a gamut of colors. "Because you've proven yourself more resourceful than any other, I will tell you the next tasks. Your lover's chance to show bravery will come." Alo pointed a knobby finger at Zeke. "The other test is to prove your power over the spirits as you claim. None enters the tomb of the one you seek but through those who sacrificed for him."

I turned to face Zeke, unsurprised by the flat set of his lips. His disapproval radiated off him in thick pulses. "What do you think?" I asked.

"You want to do this?"

"I *have* to do this. I can't leave Layla in that place. I can't leave Honani here, and the *brujo* knows it." I scowled, glaring into Alo's smug face. "I thought the Hisatsinom were the people of peace."

Zeke cupped my flushed cheek. "Calm down. They didn't sacrifice virgins and force wives to die with their husbands." He pursed his lips. "Well, not often."

"Time is waning, Halflings," Alo said. Man, the guy was pissy.

Do you think we can do this?

Zeke's face hardened. *You asked the wrong question. Is there another choice?*

"Let's get this done," I said, stepping back. "We're burning precious minutes."

Zeke stepped forward to take a sword from the leather container. Alo gripped his forearm, flinging it back.

"You mastered Cheveyo with your earthen cairn. Each face two. This is her test. She touched the blades first."

Zeke's back stiffened. "I don't think so."

Alo's smile turned vicious. "Then you forfeit before you begin."

The two of them faced off, Zeke angry, Alo still smug.

I smoothed my hand down Zeke's arm, trying to soothe the temper rising in Zeke's eyes. "I got this."

I swallowed, hoping this wouldn't be the last time I did so. I considered my options as I pulled another blade from the leather container. I held the sword out, studying the angles.

History was filled with stories of shaman swallowing swords, sticks, and even arrows to prove their mental and physical prowess, to show their ability to walk the line between the living and dead. Well, that was me. Cheveyo had proven our differences earlier when he sniffed me out and not Zeke.

I reached for another sword, shivering at the faint hiss as the blade slid from its protective sleeve.

Shouldn't you try one at a time? Zeke asked me. Concern tinted his words.

I tried not to let my hand shake as I pulled out the third blade. *I didn't think so. More likelihood I'll cut something important. Please. I need to concentrate.*

"No magic," Alo snapped as he grabbed my forearm. His skin was surprisingly warm. "This is to prove your ability, not the powers handed to you from a godly parent."

"Don't touch me again," I said with a pointed look at his grip. As if he had all the time in the world, he removed his fingers one at a time from my arm.

Inhaling sharply, I pulled out the fourth blade. With the hilts pressed tight together, they were nearly an inch-and-a-half wide. I stared at them, considering the bits of information I could remember about technique. Not much. Definitely not enough to survive swallowing four blades on my first attempt.

Alo leaned forward, his empty eye socket bright with interest. Zeal wafted from him. He considered me inferior, not just because I was female, but because I lacked training. A valid point. Zeke worried, which would have been sweet, if his emotions weren't making me so nervous.

I raised the swords over my head, the gleaming stone winking its deadly promise as I tipped my head back and opened my mouth.

The cool caress of concern rippled across my skin. Zeke lurched forward, intent to knock the blades from my hand.

Don't.

"You could die, Echo."

Before he had the opportunity to do anything else I opened my mouth as wide as I could and shoved the blades in. If Zeke touched them now, the movement would be enough to pierce my cheek or tongue. I paused, uncertainty turning my skin clammy.

I'd read about the gag reflex and how many sword swallowers died because they couldn't stop it. I willed my body to relax and breathed deep through my nose. The blades were at the back of my throat.

"*Tocha.*" Zeke whispered. A simple word, but Zeke imbued the endearment with fear and longing. Damn him. Now wasn't the time for our heart-to-heart.

Like I had when I left the bar, I switched off the part of my brain that connected us. Then, before I could think the action through, I pressed the blades deeper in. My body chilled, nearly as cold as a spirit hug.

Goose bumps broke out over my skin as I pushed until the hilts of the swords were to my lips. I inhaled slowly, carefully. At two-feet-long, the blades would be all the way into my stomach.

Alo grunted. "You pass. If you can pull them out without killing yourself." He turned away and stumped to the door across the room, the only exit except for the ladder that led up to the ground level.

"People spend years learning how to control their gag reflex and conditioning their bodies to accept a sword," Zeke said, his eyes wide.

My hand remained steady as I lifted the hilts from my mouth. The entire mass was encased in a thick layer of ice. Past the hilts, the blades looked like a massive icicle. I shuddered hard when one of the blades broke through the ice. The chunk slammed into the floor, breaking into tiny prismatic shards.

"Do I want to know?" Zeke asked.

"I'm Water. Which means I'm also Ice." I pressed a hand to my stomach. "Lowering my temperature that far really sucks."

Zeke smiled as he shook his head. I threw the swordsicle onto the table. Like I would've actually tried to swallow a blade without help. I couldn't walk a straight line without bumping into something.

"I told you no magic."

"I didn't use my magic. I used my body's innate response."

"That's—"

"Not against the ground rules you laid out," Zeke said.

Alo sneered. "I cannot refute your statement."

"That's right, bucko. What did you do when you were forced to swallow them? Burn the iron to ash? How'd that feel in your stomach?"

Alo gaped. "No."

"But you would have if you'd thought of it."

"Why would you think such a thing?" Alo asked. His eye socket flashed a rainbow of colors, his agitation clear when his hands clutched his tunic.

"Not so nice when people figure out your tricks, is it?" I said, pretending to study my nails. I kept my eyes on the *brujo*, rolled up on the balls of my feet, ready for the next attack.

"I do not claim governance over fire."

"You didn't claim to swallow the swords yourself at all."

Alo's lips peeled back in a sneer much like the hellhounds I'd faced outside of Zeke's house. I shivered, my thoughts returning again to Shakola and her desire to see me dead.

"We'll see if your young man has skill enough to survive your next test," Alo sniffed. He bowed, his arm out as we passed him into the next room. "Though, for all he projects such confidence, I doubt he has the ability when he truly needs it. Good luck, young Lakin. Time to face your fears."

The door from the chamber banged closed, the reverberations sliding through my body.

CHAPTER FOURTEEN

Alo disappeared, which was fine by me. The shaman bothered me. His nastiness, sure, but his aura, the ability to dampen it, smacked of power. Lots of power. I sidled closer to Zeke and pulled my weapon from the holster I'd had Honani pick up. I already missed my spirit warrior.

"The Magician won't hurt Honani. He's dead. That'd be stupid to hurt him. Don't you think?"

Zeke didn't answer. His face turned ashen as he stared ahead, his mouth gaping slightly. I followed his gaze but couldn't see anything.

"Zeke?" I gripped his fingers. They were cold. That sent my body into overdrive, warming my skin and his.

"No," he breathed. "He can't be here." Fear made his voice quiver. He yanked me behind him. "Stay back," he whispered.

Deep in my head, where my magic swirled, an ache built, much like the migraines that plagued me for years. Something was wrong. Magic filled this room. More than mine and Zeke's.

"What's wrong?" I asked.

"Stay back," he said again. His stance became more aggressive but his hand shook before he clenched his fists.

"Tell me what's going on," I begged. He needed to look at me, break eye contact with whatever he thought he saw. Whatever Zeke thought he saw was powerful.

Alo had said Zeke must fight this challenge. Even without Alo's snide voice confirming my fear, I was sure I'd break something inside Zeke if I tried to snap the connection to the magic that tortured him, but that didn't mean I wouldn't help him.

I stepped up next to him and touched his arm. The muscles there were bunched tighter than a magnet coil. "Zeke, please, I'm scared."

He wrapped both arms around me and buried his face in my hair. His shoulders shook. "I don't want you to know, Echo. You'll leave. I know you'll leave me."

I wrapped my arms around his waist, clutching him to me as tight as I could. I don't know what he saw when he looked across the room, but Zeke believed the shadows could hurt me, tell me tales he didn't want to share. Maybe he was reliving some of his more gruesome kills. I'm not sure why Zeke would worry about that, though. I'd watched him decimate entire armies of demons, and I'd been nothing but thankful.

Zeke shook. I forced down my jealousy when his snuggle-fest with Shakola popped into my mind. Sure, he'd said I was the only woman he wanted, but, really, how much did I know about Zeke?

I couldn't let him worry about my reaction on top of the images being projected at him. "I care about you, Ezekiel. I won't leave you. I want to be here with you."

"I can't tell you." His voice cracked. "It's bad."

I'd thought I hated Lissie Howard, that mean girl at the aikido place, when she said I didn't have a father who loved me. Nope, I'd just been getting good at hating. Prepping for Shakola. That goddess epitomized vindictiveness and spite—all the more reason to ensure she would never be remembered outside the Hisatsinom world.

"Let's move out." I unwound one arm from around Zeke and pushed the door. Didn't budge. Zeke backed away, into the corner, his gaze still locked on something across the room. He shuddered.

"No. No, not again."

Zeke's breathing escalated; mine sped up to match his. I followed his gaze. Nothing was there.

"We need to go forward, across the room."

"No! I don't want to be any closer to him. He'll hurt you," Zeke whimpered, his pupils dilated, his breathing too rapid.

I swallowed my panic and stepped forward, urging Zeke to come with me. His arms were a vise grip around me, but he didn't budge.

"Zeke, there's nothing there. You're fine. You're safe. I'll keep you safe." I had to bite back the hysteria bubbling up my chest. I didn't know what could do this to him. *He*, Zeke had said. Zeke's father? Shakola had hinted at his identity, but I'd been too upset to think more about his past.

Zeke's teeth chattered as he pulled me closer.

"Don't go near him, *tocha*. I did everything I could to make sure he didn't know about you."

"I know."

"I ran away as soon as my legs healed. I don't want to go back."

"You don't have to."

Zeke gripped my splinted wrist so hard I nearly passed out. "Don't leave me."

Screw the not touching. I reached up with my free hand and grabbed his face, turning his gaze down toward me. "I'm going to keep you safe. He isn't going to hurt you. He isn't going to kill me. You focus on me, on my face. Please, Zeke. Look at me. Let me help you. I'll always help you."

The grip on my wrist lessened, and I was able to calm my queasy stomach. I held Zeke's gaze and stepped forward. He followed hesitantly.

"Good. Again." I took another step, and Zeke did, too. His eyes flicked up to the far side of the room and he froze again, his breathing stopped.

His hands bit into the flesh on my arms. "You won't touch her," he snarled at the far wall. "I won't let you."

"There's no one there, Zeke."

"Get behind me now." Zeke pulled his sword from his scabbard as he picked me up with his other arm, thrusting me behind him. "Then you must kill me." He stepped forward and thrust his blade. Whoever Zeke thought was there was fighting him. I scooted along the wall just as Zeke grunted. He acted like he'd been hit. No, not acted. He had been. Blood dripped from his side. The gash was long, deep.

"No!" I cried. "Please stop," I breathed.

After another minute, Zeke fell to his knees. His head was up, his eyes blazing with hate and fear.

Ten feet. We needed ten feet and he wouldn't follow me. I nibbled on my lip, considering my options.

Sweat soaked Zeke's back as he staggered back upright, glancing toward me and pinning me with a determined stare. "I swear, Echo, I'll protect you."

"I know you will," I whispered.

"You stay away from her," Zeke snarled, lunging forward again.

I wished I could see whatever Zeke was seeing. Fear, anger, and even shame rolled off him in suffocating waves.

I have no self-control around you. He'd told me that at lunch. I'd thought he was being melodramatic, but it was the best option I could come up with right now. Zeke's phantom opponent could—and clearly wanted to—kill him.

When Zeke staggered back against the wall, blood dripping from another deep gash, this time on his cheek, I realized I had nothing to lose. More importantly, I didn't have any other ideas.

I dropped my trench coat to the floor. I sauntered in front of him in just my bustier and tight black pants. Knowing he liked my hair down, I unwound the braid.

"Zeke," I said in my most sensual voice. He leaned against the wall, eyes ablaze as they met someone's. I fisted my hands together.

"Help!" I screamed like someone ripped my limbs from my body. Zeke turned toward me, sword up, trying to assess the new threat. I stepped forward, so I filled his vision. His eyes dropped to my chest, over my hips, before coming back to my flowing hair.

I stepped forward and pressed myself against him, wrapping my arm around his neck, my hand twining in his hair. He jerked, clearly unprepared. I slammed my lips against his, letting my tongue drift across the seam of his closed mouth. Finally, his hand came up to my waist. He still held his spear but he held me, too, and his lips parted enough for me to slide my tongue between. I shifted back toward the far wall, tugging at him so he was forced to follow. He moved in, pressing his thighs against my lower belly.

What had he said? *I only ever wanted you.* That, at least, was something I understood. For years, I'd fixated on Zeke, the man in my dreams, and no one I'd seen in passing measured up.

I took another step back while I flicked my tongue against the sensitive center of his bottom lip. And then another step. He growled, and clutched me tight against him again. His desire, usually so carefully banked, exploded around us, pulling me under its spell.

"Zeke," I moaned as his hands drifted down my arms, then jerked my wrists upward. The pain jerked me back to the present. The room. The tasks. We had to move forward, open the far door.

"Stop."

Zeke raised his head and blinked. He glanced around the small, empty room, stunned.

"He's...he's gone. Did you see him?"

I cupped his cheek, my heart stuttering at his vulnerability. "I only saw you. Nothing else. But I hope you'll tell me, whatever it was."

He glanced away and swallowed, his face tensing, but he didn't take his hands from my hair.

"The door," I mumbled. Mere feet from where we stood.

"You seduced me," he said. He slammed the heels of his hands against his eyes.

"I beg to differ. Seduction means I tempted you, but I didn't. I held your attention through kissing." I wrapped my arms around my middle. He couldn't even look at me. My entire chest ached from the pain of his rejection.

Zeke inhaled like it was his last breath. His attention went back to the far corner. Whatever had been there before must still lurk in the shadows—if not of the room, then of Zeke's mind.

"Do you want me to kiss you again?" I snapped.

"What?" A sheen of sweat broke out across his brow, his eyes darting back to the corner. He stayed between me and the corner.

"Talk to me," he implored.

"Er..." Being put on the spot wasn't my strong suit.

"I don't want to be like him. Shakola said he had his demons, the Kachina, search for me."

"One of the gods controls the Kachina?" I asked.

Zeke stepped forward again, his body trembling with the effort to not fall back into the projected world he'd entered when we stepped into the room.

"Of course. They all have their dominion." He shoved me back into the wall, using his body to shield me. Blows I couldn't see rained down over him. He grunted as a massive weight slammed into his stomach. His head snapped back into the top of my head and blood poured from his nose.

"Run!"

I didn't need to be told twice. I darted out from behind him and sprinted the short distance to the door. I tried the handle but the knob didn't budge.

I turned and flattened my back against the door. I watched Zeke fight his way toward me. His footwork was graceful, lithe even, but his opponent was clearly larger and stronger. With each new blow, I winced in sympathy.

Watching was agony. Just as I gathered my courage to step between Zeke and his unseen opponent, Zeke lunged forward, his shoulder slamming into the wooden door. He gripped the handle and turned it with ease. He had to be the one to move us out of the space—to prove he'd completed the task. We stepped through.

"How badly are you hurt?" I asked.

"Not too bad," he wheezed. With a wince, he straightened. "Thank you for helping me through that."

I smiled even though I hated how stilted, how formal, he sounded. Melancholy filled my chest—Zeke's eyes were shut, the skin around his mouth pulled taut, as he relived whatever had been in that room. He wasn't going to tell me who he'd faced.

Zeke shut the door behind us with a satisfying thud.

"We make a good team."

"I see it's not swords that do you in. Emotion is a painful waste of energy." Alo appeared from the shadows. His voice, abrasive as usual, rippled across my skin.

"Less than five hours until sunrise," Alo said with a sly grin. "And yet another test to overcome."

"You seem way too happy about this, *brujo*," I said. "We've got a lot to do and no time to do it." I glowered. Bullying should not be magical. The Magician and I were going to chat about his henchman.

I walked forward. Much as I wanted to bury my face in Zeke's chest, I had to save Honani and Layla. And the black mountain cat. I hadn't forgotten him. The cat was important. Alo disappeared. No big surprise there. The shaman was good at mocking and disappearing.

"Just a minute, Echo," Zeke said, rustling through his pack. "I need to put some ointment on my wounds."

CHAPTER FIFTEEN

As I waited, the air rippled around us as it had when Raven visited. Through the murky white haze, an image materialized, slowly coalescing into a room I'd seen before. I hated that space.

A whimper ripped from my throat as she smirked back at me. I bit my lip hard, not wanting to let the anguished moan past my lips, not wanting to give her the satisfaction.

Shakola sat in the bar chair, her pale eyes gleaming the same unnatural white as the streak in the front of her dark hair. Layla's head rested on the chair next to her. Just her head.

Layla's beautiful gray eyes were sightless. The goddess dropped her hand to Layla's bright yellow hair and stroked it, like she would a pet.

My stomach heaved, choking off the next whimper. This couldn't be real. Zeke had seen things just moments before. I was imagining this.

People were on the dance floor. The music played, loud and twangy.

I rushed forward, my need to help Layla overriding everything else.

"Don't," Shakola said. Electricity crackled around her. "Not another step."

"You're not real," I said, and I stepped forward.

The pain was instantaneous. Not hot-cold like my ice—this was molten and consuming. Lightning. My legs gave, and I sank to the floor, unable to cry out.

"Echo!" I heard Zeke's voice from a great distance. The pain receded a little. My stomach revolted, and I vomited.

"Oh, I'm very real. You, however, shouldn't be."

"What do you want?" I asked, wiping the sick from my mouth with the back of my hand. I stood slowly. I refused to cower before this goddess. An arm wrapped around my waist again, but I slithered away. No one was going to hold me against my will. I narrowed my eyes at the conniving bitch who'd killed my mother and now, apparently, my best friend.

Shakola stood. Her lean body graceful under a silver dress. Her legs were bare, as were her feet.

"You were right to worry about me. I'll kill Zeke, too. As soon as I am presented the chance. And he won't even see what's coming." Her pale eyes gleamed and her smile was as cold as a January night. "He trusts me. As he should. I've worked for years to ensure he does. You won't undo my efforts."

Zeke. He turned me toward him, his face pale, his lips moving. He leaned in closer.

"The more passion you share, the more I'll hurt him." Shakola shook out her dark hair, the streak of white glinting in the dim light. "I'll enjoy drawing out his pain," she hissed.

She was jealous. Of me. I could use this against her. I stepped closer. "Because he didn't choose you?" I asked.

Another bolt of lightning ripped through me, forcing me from my feet. I landed on my bad wrist, the weight causing even more pain to slam into my bones from my shoulder and up into my jaw.

I rolled over onto my side, panting.

The scene had shifted. Shakola stood on a battlefield. She waved her hand and I saw the bodies. Hundreds of thousands of them. So many sightless eyes, just like Layla's.

"You've lost. Look at the destruction your mere existence caused."

I curled into myself, shuddering.

"You can't fight and win. We've waited a millennium for this chance." Shakola smiled—a closed-lipped smirk that felt more sinister for its tight control.

"You're nothing," Zeke said. He stood next to Shakola, looking at me with such disgust, my throat sealed shut. "Shivering on the ground. You can't even stand up."

"I told you he was mine," Shakola said, wrapping herself around him, sinuous as a cat.

Why was Zeke there, across the room, holding her in his arms?

He'd been next to me when we entered this space, sweat-stained and haggard. There, he looked perfect, except for the expression on his face. An expression I'd never seen on him before—disdainful, haughty. Like hers.

"Echo," I heard his voice. Next to me. He brushed the hair back from my clammy face. His thumb rubbed a tear from the corner of my eye. "Don't push me away again. Let me help you."

I shook my head, trying to understand. Zeke couldn't be in two places. But he was there, with her, pulling the goddess between his jeans-clad thighs. He leaned down and kissed her like he kissed me, his soft, wide lips trailing along the curve of her jaw, over the sensitive skin on her neck.

Pain exploded in my chest. I pushed myself upward. "This isn't real!" I screamed at the image. "This isn't real," I whispered. I pressed my head to my drawn up knees. "You aren't there." I squeezed my eyes closed. "This isn't happening."

"I need you to focus on me. I'm right here." Zeke's hands cupped my elbows, trying to draw me upward. I saw him, the same man I'd kissed moments before. His face appeared gaunt with fatigue and his eyes were dark, filled with concern and another emotion I didn't understand.

Across the room, Zeke was with Shakola—there, on that battlefield—his lips grazing hers. That caress, so like the one we'd shared, caused my chest to burn with shame. He'd turn his head next, and I guessed at the look he'd give her. The hurt deepened as he pushed her back against a wall so he could leverage her weight against his own.

Again the scene had changed—they were back in the honky-tonk and Zeke had her against the wall by the bathroom, where I'd run from him. His hands fisted in the top of Shakola's dress.

Oh, gods. I created this. Each negative thought, each fear, was thrown back at me, magnified. We were in an echo chamber of the worst sort.

The tip of Zeke's spear slid past Shakola's shoulder so fast the weapon was almost a blur. "Stop him," she hissed, her eyes wide. She edged away from his next strike.

"He's with you," I said.

And the echo chamber made the image a reality.

"Because he always wanted me," she said. She shook out her long hair and smiled. She looked like Alo—haughty and reptilian. Cruel. "I'm the only one he ever wanted. You are *nothing*. A mistake. You couldn't even save your friend from Coyote."

Shakola picked up Layla's head. Uncertainty slithered back through me. I didn't know where Layla was. She'd been tired, magically spent, when I'd seen her last night in my dream. Another full day of fighting demons may have been too much for her. She could be dead.

The spear thrust forward again and Shakola darted left. She slammed another bolt of lightning into me. I stood rooted to the spot, in agony, until the pain abated. She turned, so I turned with her, keeping her within a few feet of me, the wall at her back.

"I've killed Layla," Shakola snarled. "My weak-link half-sister is no longer part of your crew. And without her, the Prophecy of the Four means nothing."

She threw Layla's head toward me. I couldn't imagine that. I'd never imagine that.

I flinched, my hands pushed outward to ward off Layla's sightless eyes. "You did not. You don't know where she is. But you set the trap. At Coyote's. With the ants. You set all this up. Why?"

She stalked toward me, and I stumbled back. Zeke thrust his spear forward again, and Shakola writhed, pinned to the stone wall.

CHAPTER SIXTEEN

Zeke's spear pierced her throat. The point lodged in the center of her wind-pipe. His, aim, as usual, was spot on.

Shakola's eyes widened, her breath rattling and wet. She turned those pale eyes to me as she clawed at the weapon's wooden shaft.

"My death changes nothing," she rasped. "You still cannot win."

A raging tide of magic poured off her, licking over my skin, seeping into my mind. Much as I wanted to close my eyes to focus on warding off the on-slaught, I wouldn't. That place next to my heart—my mother's magic—beat in fierce rhythm with each of my breaths. The wave of magic receded as a thin trickle of blood slid from the corner of Shakola's mouth to her chin.

Focus on me. I'm right next to you. Zeke's words burned in my head. *Turn your head and look at me.*

I did without question. My Zeke crouched next to me. Dirty, sweaty, tired. His chocolate eyes filled with concern. Behind the worry was a pain too deep to ever completely overcome. I couldn't breathe. Too much.

"I'm here," Zeke said, wrapping his arms tight around me. How was he here, with me? He was there—with Shakola. "I've got you, *tocha.* Just hold on to me."

I clung to him. I wanted to glance behind me, but if I did, I feared I'd fall back into the image. I drew a deep breath. "Not real. Not real. Not real."

"No, Echo, it's real." But his breath hitched. He looked at the wall, so I did, too. Shakola was there, pinned upright by Zeke's spear. I clawed at his back, needing to be closer, to be safe. Unreasonable reaction but instinctive. Even when Coyote fought me, I wasn't this scared.

"I've got you," he whispered, the ache in his words swirling around us as his grief built.

"Layla's dead," I said. My teeth chattered. "She killed Layla." The rest of the words caught in my chest. I couldn't say it. I pressed my face harder into

Zeke's chest and shuddered. He picked me up and carried me. I tried to will the images from my mind, but they swirled there, mocking me.

Sadness whirled off Zeke. "Damn. I hope you're wrong."

He walked toward Shakola's inert form. She was empty, all her magic depleted. His emotions continued to pulse around us in dizzying waves: Relief that I was safe, grief, anger. Despair. Too many emotions licked across my raw nerve endings.

Much as I wanted Zeke to do something to stave off the blackness threatening to swallow me, I had to touch her. How else could I ascertain her dead? Zeke resettled me against one of his shoulders, his arm tight around my waist, and used his other arm to tug his spear free. His emotions veered from sadness to grief, but his hold on me remained firm.

He shuddered, once, hard, as Shakola's body slid, boneless and too pale, down the wall. I slammed my eyes closed and shoved my face back into his neck. He cradled me, his hold gentle.

Shakola would have killed Layla and me, maybe even Zeke as she'd said here, in this room, rather than let us reunite. The three of us, when we worked together, were powerful. Too powerful for her to attack outright.

She'd kept the three of us apart. I'd worked with Layla and I'd worked with Zeke, but we'd only worked together those few minutes at old Oraibi. When Coyote plotted his attack to separate us. The strategy to separate us was intentional—and effective. Necessary for her plans to continue on whatever course she'd set.

"I feel horrible," I whispered, shivering.

"Can you stand?" Zeke asked.

"Sure."

"I need to set you down. I'm going to get you some water from my pack."

"Okay."

He handed me the water and I gulped it, trying to rinse the foulness from my tongue.

Zeke pushed open the door. I tensed, expecting Alo's caustic words.

They didn't come.

Zeke motioned me toward the door. I glanced back into my torture room. A room of vision but also truth. Shakola's body still lay on the floor.

"Did you see her?" I asked.

Zeke shook his head. His eyes were still shadowed, the hurt burrowing deep. "Not until I stabbed her."

Oh. Maybe he wouldn't have. If he'd known Shakola tormented me…That explained the grief and anguish. He hadn't planned to kill the goddess.

Not even to save me. I gulped more water, which did nothing to refresh my dry mouth.

Zeke's emotions sank deeper into despair. But Shakola was a goddess.

"She's not really dead, though," I croaked. "Because she's a goddess."

Zeke's jaw clamped tight. His eyes dulled further, nothing like their normal rich chocolate color. He shuddered, a painful ripple from his soul.

"Remember what I told you when I gave you the knife? The blades are imbued with godly magic. All the diamonds are."

"I don't understand," I said.

"She's dead." His voice cracked. He inhaled sharply, exhaled in a long stream, giving himself time to master his emotions. "She can't come back."

I wanted to comfort him, but he might reject me. "I'm sorry, Zeke," I whispered. And I was. For feeling relief at her death. Not for her being dead. No matter what she had taken from me, no matter how much she'd hurt me, I hadn't wanted her dead. Except I had. Shakola killed my mother. Now she was dead. Justice was served—sort of. A hollow victory at best.

He shook his head again. Did he want me to stop talking or was that an effort to negate my concern?

"She's dead. That's the end of it." His voice was flat.

At a loss, I stared at him until he turned away.

"But why would the gods give you a weapon that can kill them?" I asked. "That seems stupid."

His head dropped forward, his neck muscles too tight. "They didn't."

"What?"

Slowly, he turned back toward me. The planes of his face were set in tired, anguished lines. "I told you the gods created the weapons."

Confusion built in my head, causing my temples to pound. "Right."

"But Sotuk didn't give them the power to kill other gods."

I frowned, glancing down at my blade. "Then who did?"

A snarl curled his top lip. "Pahana."

CHAPTER SEVENTEEN

"Pahana. As in, the one we don't want to meet, ever?" I asked.

Zeke nodded, his lips compressed so tightly they were almost gone.

"Why would he do that?"

"He had his reasons," Zeke said. Bitterness dripped from his words.

"Like what? Why do you hate him so?"

Zeke shook his head, a mutinous expression settling over his features even as shame once again wafted from him. "We need to talk about what *you* saw," he said.

I slammed my lips together in a tight, hard line. Once again, he was hiding something. "I don't want to change the subject."

"I need to know," he said, urgency driving him. "Shakola was there, in that room. Like really there."

"Got that," I snapped.

"Which means she wanted you—and by extension me—to fail. Because I wouldn't have left you, *tocha*. Never alone. Never scared."

My lids fluttered closed as my need to lean into him blossomed along with the image of him wrapped around Shakola. Sure, those moments had been an illusion, but just the idea of him with her sliced my heart.

"That's what you did in the bar," I said. "Not physically, but emotionally." I didn't want to rehash that argument. Not here, when we had so little time. "So let's go back to why you hate Pahana so much."

Zeke's shoulders drooped, his lips pressed together in firm denial of my request. His gaze slid from mine.

I barked a short, unhappy laugh. "That's what I thought."

I straightened my shoulders and shoved through the door he'd opened. As soon as I placed one foot into the room, trepidation fluttered through me, like birds' wings battling a strong wind.

Zeke stepped through behind me, and the door slammed shut behind us.

As with each of the previous doors, there was a finality to the sound. I pressed back into him to keep my balance. There was no floor beyond the small landing about two-feet wide and three feet deep.

Blackness swept out from the landing. The hole was so deep, I couldn't see the bottom. A cold, bitter breeze drifted upward, voices rising on each puff of air. My pendant heated and the voices strengthened, questioning. Why hadn't the clay worked in the last room? Why hadn't I thought of it?

We were supposed to be done. Cheveyo, the swords, the two hellish rooms—that made four tests. I leaned forward, needing to see who was there. Zeke gripped the waistband of my pants. "Careful. You lost your coat."

"I'm going to pretend we've been too busy fighting for our sanity, and that's why you're just commenting on how all my hotness is exposed."

"I noticed in the last room, but you were busy."

Trying for nonchalance doesn't cut it, guerrero. But I had other, more pressing issues to deal with.

"Those voices aren't human," I murmured. Shocked, I gripped my pendant as heat flooded the cool clay. "My pendant's warm."

"What do you think they are?" Zeke peered around me, trying to see something in the deep pit. "And what happened to your coat?"

"Left it on the floor of your vision room."

"Why?"

"A failed attempt at seduction," I muttered.

"I wouldn't say you failed. Kissing you is the highlight of the night."

Not going there. I couldn't think about that and also concentrate on the task at hand. Whatever that was. "I was worried about you," I said. I sifted through the lore about this area. "I think that's a doorway to Kuskurza."

"The Third World?"

Zeke pulled me back until we were pressed against the thick wooden door. No accessible doorknob on this room, and the door itself remained shut. No real surprise there. Alo would ensure our only option was forward. Or down. He was an ass.

Maybe those rooms, the two chambers of distortion and fear, were one test and this was the fourth. Seemed sneaky to break the tests into two parts, but Alo seemed the sort to try such a hair-splitting of rules in order to break the person attempting the gamut.

That's what they were all designed to do—break the people who attempted to meet the Magician. If the person was lucky enough not to be eaten by the ogre guarding the Magician's theoretical gates.

Concern built, pushing through my chest. Why hadn't we seen Alo here, in this room? He'd announced all the previous tasks, and his lack of appearance was more chilling somehow. Like we'd severed a connection.

I shuddered. Much as I didn't want to fall, I really, really didn't want to go back into the room of visions.

"The Third World, Echo?" Zeke repeated.

"I could be wrong."

"But you're pretty sure," Zeke said.

I shifted my jaw as I considered his question. Each time I thought the name, my pendant heated. I understood the magic in the clay better now. The pendant helped me channel some of my father's past magic. "Yeah."

"We have to cross to the other side," he said. "Are you cold?"

I was, but not as cold as I'd been earlier when I near-froze myself to swallow those swords.

"I'll be alright."

He pulled me behind him and balanced carefully on the narrow ledge, pulling out a hoody from his backpack. He yanked the soft fleece over my head and zipped it to my chin. He nodded.

"Now I can focus. You half-dressed was killing me."

"Thanks." The material shifted and Zeke's scent drifted upward, calming me. For better or worse—probably worse—his scent immediately brought a brush of calm, safety. I cleared my throat. "How are we going to cross the gap?"

Our options weren't ideal. This room, the largest we'd been in yet, was circular, the walls smooth with adjoining stones. There was only the narrow landing on which Zeke and I stood, then nothing for about twenty feet but the abyss with the sighing voices far, far below.

I stepped forward to the very edge of the small wooden shelf, hoping I'd see a rope or something hanging from it.

Nothing down there.

The ledge groaned and lurched downward.

I stumbled back into Zeke. He pressed against the doorframe, trying to stabilize his feet on the narrow jamb. The ledge shuddered under us. Cursing, Zeke stopped moving. His heart slammed into his chest, pulsing in a rapid tattoo against my back.

"I don't think this'll hold us much longer," Zeke said. The wood buckled. The support braces screamed in protest.

"Any ideas?" I asked, trying not to sound panicked. "Can you transport us to the other side?" I asked.

Zeke shook his head. "No, I can transport us out of the building, but not into the next room. There are too many magical protections on the place. Plus, that kind of magic is dangerous right now."

He didn't say it, but my breaking Sotuk's tablet was the reason. Right as I wanted to ask how using magic could be more dangerous than plummeting into a netherworld, the right side of the platform collapsed. The boards we were standing on slid out from under us with a sickening finality.

Thank all the gods for Zeke's quick reactions. His arm clamped around my waist as we began to fall. He caught the remaining support post with his other hand.

We looked up at the two-by-four—all that remained of the ledge we'd been standing on. The wood had been cut deep at the base of the slat. There was no way to grip the uncut side; the cut was too close to the wall.

The wood groaned in protest, the slice in the wood pulling open and splintering under the strain.

"Wrap your legs around my waist. I need to pull out my spear."

I did as Zeke asked, locking my legs tight around his middle. I gripped my hands into the wide leather bands on the front of his armor. When had he put that on? Oh, like that was the most important problem I faced.

I refused to fall into that hole.

My pendant heated more. Something slithered from it, but whatever it was was gone, swallowed by the black below, before I managed to look.

Zeke let go of me, and I barely swallowed my scream of protest. He reached up and yanked his spear free, slamming the tip into the hole left by the other bracket just as the one he still gripped broke from the wall. He grunted as the wood gave, swinging his arm over in a monkey-bar maneuver to grip the shaft of his spear with both hands.

"Got a good grip?" he asked.

I nodded, too frightened to speak. I watched the board fall. The pale piece of wood faded, swallowed by the inky darkness.

Spirits stirred below, their curiosity pulling them upward, closer to us.

We were quiet for a second, absorbing our predicament. I didn't see anything we could use to our advantage. My eyes sped across the space; there wasn't a chink in the smooth walls, no dangling rope—why couldn't this be an Indiana Jones movie?—nothing to aid our cause.

"Any ideas?" I asked.

Fine tremors shivered up Zeke's arms. My added weight made holding on even more difficult.

"Your spirits?"

I shook my head with regret. "Honani's the intermediary. I need him to communicate to the others."

"Not even your grandmother?" Zeke asked.

I concentrated as hard as I could, trying to force a message through, but the pendant seemed locked somehow. Like Honani was the key and without him, I wasn't tuning in with a clear signal to the spirits on the other side.

"Nothing," I admitted.

"There aren't any cracks in the walls near enough for me to use my spear to work us around the edge, even if I could figure out how to pull it out of this one."

The spirits moved closer, whispering and clucking. I looked at them—long, dark hair, skin smoothed over bone, even the clothes they'd died in. Lips peeled back in grimaces and grins. Like Alo, they lacked eyes. Both their eyes. The effect of the gaping black holes, skeletal in an otherwise normal face, was jarring.

"Know any magic that'll build a bridge or a provide a rope?" I asked.

"Not my area," Zeke grunted. "I'm not sure that it's possible to create something from nothing."

I quickly discarded the idea of borrowing a bridge from somewhere else because I wasn't sure where we'd find the right sized bridge to fit the space. Plus, there were the logistics of the people on the bridge. So, bad idea.

"Maybe shift rope here from a store somewhere?"

"Nothing to tie the rope to. There's no knob on the door."

"We could tie the rope to your spear."

"I can't move objects like that, Echo. I need to be in close proximity, preferably physical contact with them."

Another dead end.

"How about if I built a bridge? Out of ice." I started to concentrate, my body shaking with the effort to pull water from the air, the surrounding area—anywhere.

"You can't," Zeke's voice was gentle. "The span is too great. And, I told you, putting that much into your magic will kill you."

"We may die anyway," I said. I huffed, pressing my nose tighter against Zeke, breathing him in. I didn't want this to be the end, but of everything we'd faced, this moment scared me the most. My mother's magic beat harsh inside my ribs—a warning, perhaps. My magic, even the magic she'd provided, was drained. One of the spirits touched me, its voice questioning. I couldn't understand the words. I shuddered. Zeke's heart sped up under the strain.

The rest of the ghosts moved under us, so close their spectral hair brushed against Zeke's boots. Men and women looked up at us, their pale skin shockingly bright against the surrounding gloom.

Much as I wanted to claw my way up his chest, I forced myself to stay still. My muscles quivered under the strain. Sweat dripped down Zeke's taut cheeks into my hair.

Zeke's effort was valiant, but even he couldn't hold on indefinitely. His sweat dripped in a steady cadence. Plunk. Plunk. His arms quivered. He'd scaled a mountain earlier and fought an ogre. We hadn't slept in over twenty-four hours. After the emotions of the last rooms, he'd held out longer than I'd imagined possible.

His joints strained as he tried to breathe through the pain. We were going to fall.

"I'm sorry," I whispered.

"Nothing for you to apologize for," he gritted. His breath came out in puffs. "We'll hang out with your buddies down there, I guess."

"Not mine," I said with regret, but I'd try anyway. I gripped my pendant tight. "Can you help us?" I asked the spirits circling below us.

Nothing. They weren't locked away from my request like the spirits in my pendant, but I didn't know how to communicate with the gray ethereal beings swirling below us. Their chatter grew more insistent, their eyes filling with color. Orange—for caution? Because I should fear them or because they were worried about me? I didn't know.

"There's something I need to tell you, Echo." Zeke's voice filled with strain, his emotions churning wildly. Shame bubbled up past his other emotions again. This feeling, more than any of the others, was consistent.

I eased back so that I could grip my pendant in my hand. Zeke grunted, his heart pumping louder and faster under my cheek.

"In a minute. I have an idea. *Abuelita*. Father. Sotuk, I need you to show me how to talk to these spirits."

My pendant flashed red as heat seeped into my hand, up my arm, and into that magic place in my head. The spirits looked up, their empty, black eyes focusing on me.

Fear shivered over my skin, burrowing deep in my mind, even as I heaved a sigh. *Thank you, Father.*

"We need help," I said.

The spirits drifted closer, their eyes flashing to yellow. I hoped that meant they were curious. They wrapped around Zeke's legs but were careful not to touch me.

That's right. They had to want to touch me for this to work.

"My dad's Sotuk. Zeke here fostered with Masau. Skeleton Man, the god of spirits."

One of Zeke's hands slid from the spear. He groaned as he tried to bring his arm back up. His other arm trembled harder as he strained to right us.

"And we need to cross this chamber," I said in a rush.

Zeke's far hand started to slide off the spear.

"My understanding is that you can help us with that," I shouted. Adrenaline spiked through me as I held my breath. I couldn't help Zeke.

Finally, I heard one of them speak. His voice was lyrical, soft and completely devoid of emotion.

"What will you do for us, daughter of Almira?"

"Almira? I'd thought you'd care my dad was Sotuk."

"Oh, we do. Your grandmother sought us. She told us of Almira, how she broke certain protocol. Led to your existence."

"My grandmother?" The sensation of something leaking from the pendant. "Where is she?"

"Gone."

What the hell did that mean?

"Hurry," Zeke gritted.

"What do you want?" I asked.

Another spirit moved closer, her eye sockets lavender. The shape of her face was like my mom's, the chin pointier. "We want peace. Some say you endanger that."

"I like peace. Love it. Want more of it."

"Enough to destroy the gods who seek war?"

Zeke groaned. "I can't hold on much longer. Can you speed up your negotiations?"

"I don't know which gods want war."

"Your lover knows," she said.

"He's not my lover." I was quiet for a moment, trying to logic out an argument. "If I kill the gods of war, then I'm not peaceful."

"We can discuss that. After we're on the other side," Zeke gritted.

"I want peace," I repeated to the spirits. "I sent Coyote to the underworld because he used his chaos magic to kill people."

"We know this. That's why we've chosen to speak. That and because your grandmother asked it of me."

Honani knew things, too. The dead's gossip grapevine must be fast and really advanced, what with the dead not really heeding space and time like live people did.

"I didn't kill Coyote."

"You alone cannot kill a god. Each piece forms the kaleidoscope of the whole."

"I don't know what you're talking about, but apparently I can kill some gods with our weapons. Zeke killed Shakola, the cloud goddess."

The murmuring increased, the spirits more agitated. "I'd be happy to discuss once my feet were on a solid surface."

"We know what may come to pass if you lose focus. How do we know So-tuk won't use you to flood our world again?"

"I can't make promises for the gods. I'm not one, and they don't even like me." Frustration bubbled into my throat. Zeke's face was gray with exhaustion. "Can't you just take my word that we want to help you and the people in the Fourth World?"

The spirits spoke around us.

"The Fourth World doesn't concern us," the lady murmured. "We will never live there again. We fear for our eternal souls."

"You can be reborn," I said. "Into the Fourth World."

"Only if the confluence of events is exact. But that solves nothing. Your death or the death of the other gods—that's the question we must ask. The outcome of which affects us all."

Zeke groaned as his fingers slid from the spear. He tried to grab the shaft with the other hand and managed to wrap his fingers around the very end. That pulled the spear point free from the wall.

I wrapped my legs more firmly around him as we began our descent.

CHAPTER EIGHTEEN

"Ah, *tocha*, I failed," Zeke whispered into my hair. His remorse swirled around us and merged with my own.

"No, I didn't do my job. I didn't convince the spirits to help."

The wind picked up around us.

He cupped my chin and tilted my head up, pressing a soft kiss to my lips.

I smiled past the tears filling my eyes.

"Are you finished?"

I startled, a scream ripping from my throat. I flailed, my arms unraveling from Zeke's torso as I tried to ward off the spirit who was just inches from my face. Zeke wrapped his arm around me, pulling me flush against his chest. His other hand still held the spear.

"She's flighty," the male spirit said. "Maybe we should let her fall."

"You scared me." I focused on the woman; she looked like my mom, more like my grandmother. "We're related," I decided.

The spirit tipped her head. "I'm one of your ancestresses."

"We stopped falling," Zeke said. He sounded as shocked as I was. I wrapped one fist into the leather straps in his armor and used the other to shove my long hair out of my face.

"Does that mean you'll help us?" I asked the spirit.

"We're deciding."

"Well, you're in a great bargaining position." I raised my eyebrows. "As you intended all along."

She smiled, her face lighting up with the same inner beauty my mom had. She had eyes in her sockets, thank Masau and Sotuk and all the other gods. They were brown, a couple shades lighter than Zeke's. About the color my mother's had turned when her magic faded from her body.

"Let me guess. You can project certain images to mortals."

The spirit nodded. "I'm called Sacnite."

"White Flower. Lovely name. It's a pleasure. Thanks for stopping our fall."

Sacnite glanced down. "We haven't decided to save you yet. We wanted more time to talk. And consider what Adeline has told us."

"Where is she?" I asked again.

Sacnite frowned. "Gone."

Frustration bubbled through my fear. Sacnite's answer wasn't much of one.

"What would you like to discuss?" Zeke asked before I could question Sacnite further.

I'd been through many surreal experiences since I'd learned I was a Halfling, but this might be the most difficult to wrap my mind around. Dead people held us aloft in a deep pit, and we were exchanging pleasantries.

Sacnite barely glanced at Zeke. Her eyes remained trained on my face. "Can you do it?"

"What?"

"Return our worlds to peace."

"As I told you before, I want peace."

"You don't know yet what sacrifices you must make."

"You're right, I don't. You could tell me."

Sacnite shook her head with reluctance. "I cannot. Then something else would happen because you'd changed the possible outcome."

"If there are multiple outcomes, then maybe peace is inevitable."

"There's only one path to peace," Sacnite fretted.

Zeke and I had talked of this before. My response was instantaneous. "If there are infinite options, there can't be just one path to anything."

Sacnite smiled again, this time with relief. "Your wisdom is greater than your years." She spoke to the spirits circling below us, holding us aloft. I couldn't understand the conversation; the dialect was more ancient than the ones I'd managed to grasp before. I'd never heard these syllables. Some of the sounds were clicks, others grunts. None seemed to join well with the others.

"We've agreed. We place our faith in you, Echo Ruiz, daughter of Almira, keeper of balance."

"I thought you said my mom undid the balance."

"She went against protocol. But as Adeline states, the balance unraveled faster before her breach. She slowed time and a need for action for twenty-one years. She is part of why we grant you your chance."

"Thank you," I said.

"She spoke to you of the need for finding ways to right the equation back to harmony," Sacnite said. My heart pounded fitfully in my chest. Something important lurked in our discussion. But I couldn't quite grasp it, the elusive tendril faded before I glimpsed it. "Forget not her lessons, daughter."

"So you'll help us to the door?"

Sacnite shook her head, her thick white hair floating around her shoulders and down the back of her simple buckskin frock. "We cannot. But if you look hard, a secret will be revealed. You don't have much time left. Hurry."

The spirits below us fell away one at a time. "No, stop," I cried. "We'll fall."

Sacnite pursed her lips. "Look for the secret, Echo. I cannot say more. Good luck, daughter of Almira, granddaughter of Adeline."

Sacnite dove downward. The blackness swallowed her like a hungry mouth. We were close to the far wall—the one we needed to reach. The wall remained smooth, free of handholds.

"Echo, they're leaving," Zeke said.

We jerked downward before the spirits still there caught us. They didn't look happy.

"What's the secret?" Zeke asked. Panic poured off him.

"If I knew what it was, it wouldn't be a damn secret." I glanced down as another spirit drifted away. Nothing but endless black.

"You can do this," he said as we jerked down again.

"The air feels weird here."

"Because we're way, way underground."

"How far? What's the earth telling you?" I asked.

"Really far. I'd say a couple of miles."

"Far enough down to—I don't know—be through a *sipapu*?"

Zeke tightened his arm around me. I wasn't sure if the gesture constituted a hug or if terror had overcome his normal calm. "Maybe. I've never tried to travel down."

"Not down so much," I said. Something shimmered to my left. I inhaled as much air as possible before I turned my head. Nothing there. We jerked lower.

"What do you mean?" Zeke gritted.

"Could we be in Kuskurza?" We jerked to a stop. The spirits below us babbled with approval.

"You mean, we're in the Third World?" Zeke gulped.

We fell again. Faster. The wind burned, as if we were nearing the molten center.

"This is where Layla is," I said. "It feels the same. The black mountain cat came back here to help Layla. Which means it's time to get off this train." I reached out with my good hand, which slammed into something solid. I gripped the smooth wood with both hands.

"Help me," I gritted.

"What are you holding on to?"

"I don't know, but it's solid. I can't do this alone. You weigh too much."

"I don't see anything," Zeke said.

"Put your hand between mine." My shoulders wrenched as another spirit deserted us. I cried out as the pain burst into my wrist. Zeke reached his arm over mine and gripped between my hands.

"Holy—that feels like a ladder." Zeke twisted and tried to find a foothold. "Can't feel anything below."

"Maybe I have to touch it? Let me put my feet down." I unwrapped my legs from Zeke's waist. He re-sheathed his spear and wrapped an arm around my waist as I twisted. I scrambled for a moment before my foot found the rung. I leaned into the dubious support, shaking and gasping.

"Can you put your foot where mine is?" I asked. My wrist throbbed once again, this time from supporting so much of Zeke's weight.

He shifted and managed to rest his feet next to mine.

"Okay. Time to climb." I reached up and found the next rung. Our speed was hampered by my need to find the rungs before Zeke could grasp them, but we hauled ourselves upward. The climb was long, tortuous.

"I think we fell too far. The heat was intense," I said.

"Meaning we were close to the center? Could be. Like I said, we're miles down. So keep climbing."

I puffed up another few rungs. "It's molten there, right?"

"That's what I was taught in school," Zeke agreed.

"Where was that?"

"North of Flagstaff. Masau steered clear of Kachina Village."

He gripped the spot between my hands, his body pressed tight against my back. I shuffled upward, Zeke keeping pace.

"Because there's Kachina there?"

"I've never gone. Didn't see the need to." Zeke's foot slipped off the rung, and he muttered a few curses as he righted himself. "The only choice is to keep going, Echo."

"And we must reach the Magician before dawn."

"Let's hope Kuskurza doesn't run on Fourth World time."

My arms and legs shook with fatigue. I gritted my teeth against the pain in my wrist and heaved myself up another rung. Then another.

"Why?" I gasped. Much as I wanted to stop, I forced my arm up again. Zeke moved in tandem. We worked together smoothly, almost effortlessly, now.

"Because we've been down here for ages."

I missed the next rung and slammed back into Zeke. He grunted as his foot slipped from the rung. Pain exploded in my wrist and I sucked in air, trying to stay conscious.

"You're okay, Echo. I got you."

"Give me a second," I whimpered.

"I don't think we have time. Come on, you can do this. You've got to do this for Honani and Layla. I'm with you. I'll be right here."

With my good hand, I grasped the ladder tighter. Planting my feet, I hissed out my breath. I'd come too far. I refused to stop now. Honani depended on me. Layla needed me—if she was still alive. I'd promised that black mountain cat, and I wanted to fulfill that vow.

"I see the door," Zeke said, relief sweeping off his body. I grasped another rung and pulled myself upward slowly. Zeke had to time his movements in tandem with mine because the rungs disappeared when I no longer touched them.

"Is that light coming from underneath?" I asked.

"Hurry. Dawn must be soon."

I grappled my way up another couple of rungs, Zeke staying with me.

Because he was taller, he pushed open the door before I could even reach it.

"You're here." The voice was brusque and rough, but nothing like Alo's. We hadn't seen the shaman since we entered the chamber where Shakola attacked me.

I pulled up another rung and spotted moccasin-clad feet. I bit my lip against the pain in my wrist as I pulled up again. Long, tanned legs stepped back.

"Come in. I'm so glad you made it. Thank you, thank you for releasing me from her spell."

I scrambled up from my kneeling position on the floor, my eyes seeking the Magician. He was tall, taller even than Zeke. His dark hair was brushed back, the two long braids on either side of his temples decorated with shells, turquoise, and feathers. His brown eyes were lighter than Zeke's, his cheekbones sharp, his nose bulbous in the middle but long and straight. His jaw was square, his mouth thin and wide. His lips curved upward in a smile.

"Er, you're welcome," I said, disconcerted by the effusive greeting.

"We've much to discuss and little time left."

CHAPTER NINETEEN

Zeke crawled into the room, turned in a crouch, and hauled me in by the armpits of his hoodie. I was thankful for the added layer of cloth because my bustier was soaked through—the climb had been sweaty work.

"Echo!"

A cold weight wrapped around me, instantly freezing the sweat in all my pores. I didn't care. I hugged back, relaxing a little for the first time in hours.

"Honani," I whispered, my face buried in the spirit's cold chest. "I worried about you."

"I wasn't happy about being taken by that witch."

"What?" I asked.

"But the Magician has been great," Honani said. His aura sparkled a bright turquoise. "He gave me many details of our history."

The Magician inclined his head. "I enjoyed the company, warrior." He turned to peruse Zeke and me. I stared back, not hiding any of my frustration or anger.

"I'm so pleased you worked through the tests."

"We almost didn't," Zeke said.

The Magician's eyes dipped down to the ground, his expression contrite. "The vision chambers were not part of the gamut. Reaching me, getting information was to be the fourth and final task."

"You instituted those grand trials after the archaeologists raided your tomb?" I guessed. Zeke helped me to my feet. My legs still quivered from over exertion.

The Magician inclined his head. "No, I was not the implementer of the tasks you were forced to endure last night."

"What?" Zeke asked. The early morning light shone off the hard planes of his face, highlighting the dark circles around his eyes. His cheeks were ashen with exhaustion and smudged with dirt and blood. I couldn't look any better.

The Magician kept his focus on me. "To answer Echo's question, the pale ones took my most sacred artifacts. Thankfully, some have been returned to their resting place, but achieving this small victory took many years. I cared not for the years of limbo. I was offered an opportunity to spare me further indignity."

"Shakola," I decided. "She's the witch Honani mentioned."

Zeke hissed out a curse. What? Did he think I liked blaming the cloud goddess for more mayhem? I let my arms fall back to my sides once I realized I'd crossed them. No way I wanted to appear even more defensive.

"Shakola had many facets and many opportunities to work her magic."

"Hold up!" I exclaimed. "She was the projection—the shaman we saw at the entrance. Alo. That's why he—she—didn't show up to announce the spirit room. Because Zeke killed her."

Zeke flinched hard.

The Magician smiled, his eyes shining with approval. "You figured that out. Yes, I've been her prisoner in my house since my return."

"Why?" Zeke asked.

I blinked back the images from that room. "Power," I said.

The Magician's face fell into grave lines, sorrow etched in the grooves around his eyes. "She'd faded to one of the forgotten ones."

Much as I wished on her not long ago. But perhaps she'd been unable to live as she slowly disintegrated from the minds and hearts of her people. That couldn't be much of a life.

"Without remembrance, she, too, began to fade. Until she made her alliance with Pahana and began to turn negative energy into bad magic."

"This whole time?" Zeke asked. "From your death onward?" His eyes continued to dart around the room, expecting another attack, no doubt. Or maybe just unsure how to process this other side of the goddess he'd obviously cared for.

"Relax. No additional tests await you this night." The Magician turned to look at the window. "Or day, as it has become. And no, not from the time of my death."

"Do you know about Layla?" I asked. "She's the reason we came here. Shakola held her head…"

The Magician pulled on his lip between his thumb and forefinger. "The black mountain cat you met and sent back protects Layla. Shakola hasn't killed her as she projected."

I sagged against Zeke's side in relief.

"You requested a boon of Shakola when you thought her Alo. Since Zeke eliminated Shakola, my captor, I shall fulfill your favor with the remnants of her magic."

"You can do that? Give us back Layla?"

The Magician pursed his lips. "Alone I would not have the ability. But my followers have offered their help. They harnessed much of Shakola's magic as her powers left her body. With their help and Shakola's magic, I am able to draw Layla from her place deeper in the world I have spent a millennia protecting."

"You protect?" Zeke asked.

The Magician dipped his head. "You know this from your time in the kiva."

I bounced around. "When can I see her?"

"Soon. My spirits lead her toward the *sipapu*."

"So she is in Kuskurza?" Zeke asked. "The plane you protect."

"Yes, as Echo reasoned. Layla needs time to traverse that land, and I have not the power to bring her here any faster." He clapped his hands. "While I may offer the hospitality, to nourish your bellies and magic, I will do so with pleasure."

Zeke mumbled his thanks, but his tone was decidedly frosty. I elbowed his ribs. He winced. Right. They were cracked.

"How are you feeling?" I asked.

Zeke tucked a strand of hair behind my ear. "Better, knowing you're alive."

He looked so sincere, like he truly cared about me. I pressed my cheek into his chest, needing to give us both a moment to recoup from last night's ordeal. He leaned down and pressed his nose into my hair. Concern and something more complex wafted from him.

I pulled back. We still needed to work through the Shakola incident. I wouldn't give that…that goddess the satisfaction of calling her by her name ever again. She'd be CG, short for cloud goddess. Or Cruel Girl. Or…No, that name was too dirty to consider.

Zeke let me settle back into a wood-and-leather chair near a big fireplace. The fire within crackled with merry abandon. Was it real? I didn't care, because the flames were warm and comforting. Honani settled into the corner nearest me, his eyes avid, his aura still bright turquoise.

"I'd like to speak with my brethren," he said, nodding toward my pendant. "I'll speak to your *abuelita*, ask her to come visit."

"Sacnite said she is gone," I said, my brow furrowing. What did that mean?

"I'll check on her then."

"I'd like that," I said, holding the clay in the palm of my hand. Honani drifted closer, sliding into the clay disk. I clutched it tight, glad Honani once again stood nearby. I'd missed him.

A thin man dressed in a traditional loincloth brought in a big wooden platter loaded with tortillas, guacamole, and thin strips of meat.

"This is Chaa'. He has served here, working to free me his entire adult life," the Magician said. "He does what I cannot—provides for the living. Thank you, my friend." The Magician dipped his head to the servant, and I scampered to the tray, remembering at the last second to let the servant past. I thanked him, and he bowed to me, eyes dancing with pleasure.

I scooped up a tortilla and filled the warm bread past the danger point. I'd never grow accustomed to the sensation of near-starvation. I bit into the wrap, the spiciness bursting across my tongue. So good.

Zeke followed me, chuckling at my exuberance. "Like a puppy. I swear you almost tripped over your tail." He picked up one of the tortillas, filled it with meat, and took a bite.

"How about a veggie to go with those carbs and hunks of protein?" I suggested. Zeke took another bite, ignoring me. I sighed as I slowly made myself another, smaller fajita, much heavier on the guac this time.

The Magician waited, eyeing the gathering light.

"When your tomb was raided, you were forced to stay here?" I asked.

The Magician frowned, considering the question. "No and also yes. I've been tied to this great house from my birth. Mine to protect. My death was an honorable one, for I forced back the northern invaders. But our people's decline had begun." He shook his head. "I tied myself to the land, hoping to keep this place sacred for our people. But their memories are much shorter than I'd believed."

"You were stuck here until that archaeologist dug you up?"

He made a face. "That man did not value our ways. I drifted between worlds for many years, unable to latch on to any plane."

I nodded. This was a common frustration with the native tribes. Disturbing graves was the worst kind of disrespect. "But now you're free."

"Yes." The Magician beamed at me. "You've broken the spells holding me here."

"Spells you implemented," Zeke pointed out.

"As I said, not I. While I planned for many eventualities, those dirt-digging thieves broke my magic and the barrier we'd built. The kivas here serve as gateways to and from the underworld. Your foster father sought to repair the damage. He was unsuccessful."

"Masau came here and he failed to seal the *sipapu*?" Shock radiated through me.

"Failed is incorrect. He passed through this *sipapu* to check on Pahana, to ascertain a truth he only just learned," the Magician said. "Cheveyo arrived after Masau passed down into Kuskurza."

"He never came back," Zeke murmured. He built another fajita. "But someone gave Cheveyo the pass to come back to this plane."

"Working through who knew about his plans, young Lakin?" the Magician smiled, approval radiating from him in jovial ripples. His happiness grated across my nerve endings. "You're finally reaching the heart of the matter."

The Magician's focus remained on Zeke. Zeke's breathing escalated. Shame surged off him. What in their exchange had caused such a reaction?

"The vision," Zeke said, his voice raw. "It's happening?"

"The vision—*your* vision?" I asked. For a few minutes, here in the rosy hints of dawn, I hadn't been out of my head with fear. Guess that was over.

The Magician shook his head. "You misunderstand. Visions can be altered. Consider what Shakola showed Echo. Layla is not dead, but Shakola projected it to injure Echo, weaken her ability to fight back."

"Makes sense," I said. "That was the part of the vision I couldn't wrap my head around."

The Magician inclined his head. "There are many possibilities and decisions that must be made for a specific future to exist. Shakola showed you the future *she* wished."

Zeke's eyes settled on me. He didn't want to discuss those terrible moments in the first closed chamber. Whatever Zeke had seen, the images unnerved him still.

I bit down on the hurt bubbling up my throat. Zeke didn't plan to tell me, ever. One of his secrets might very well be the extent of his relationship with the CG. He'd said she'd helped raise him, but maybe that'd been to gain my cooperation for the night.

Wow. That hurt.

"When Zeke killed Shakola, and with her, the illusion of Alo, she could not force you through the many more tasks she had planned for you," the Magician said. Once again, Zeke flinched.

"To keep us too busy to get to the end of the gamut?" Zeke asked.

"Exactly," the Magician said. "For then you could not free me and I couldn't share your true mission. The one Lord Raven mentioned."

"What is our true mission?" I asked.

Silence dragged out. I waited. The Magician raised a thick eyebrow. "Zeke knows. He's always known."

Each word pummeled on my shoulders, weighing down my heart. "Which is what the cloud goddess said at the bar. What you saw in that vision chamber. What you don't want to tell me now."

The guilt radiating from Zeke didn't surprise me, but it did confirm the Magician's words. My gazed locked on to Zeke's. I begged him to tell me he wasn't intentionally hiding details from me. He raised his hand to cup my cheek.

"I don't want you involved in that, with him."

I'd taken comfort in his gesture before, assuming he offered the caress out of his feelings for me. I inched back, glaring first at him then at his hand. He dropped his arm back to his side, his shoulders drooping.

I mashed my lips together and faced the Magician, who pulled one of his braids, clearly uncomfortable with the emotions swirling through the room.

"Tell me," I demanded of either of them. I didn't recognize my voice. I sounded…broken. Maybe I was. I'd lost my mom, Layla, the only life I'd known. Zeke's feelings for me seemed genuine, and I'd latched on to them, him, in an effort to stop the slow unraveling of my sanity.

Zeke's shame built, a noxious taste in my mouth even as it flayed my nerve endings. I gritted my teeth. Zeke met my eyes, his so tortured. "You'll hate me."

I bit the inside of my lip, instituting my mother's favorite tactic: silence.

"I'm the reason Sotuk's missing," Zeke whispered. "I led him to Pahana."

"By mistake?" I breathed. "It was a mistake. You didn't mean to cause me to lose my father, for us to be here."

Zeke slammed his eyes shut and pressed the heels of his hands to his sockets—as if looking at me was a new level of pain. "No. I did what Pahana asked of me. He imbued the blades I have with more power, like I told you. In exchange…for Sotuk."

"But," I spluttered. "But why?"

Zeke still didn't remove his hands, still refused to look at me. "He's my father, Echo. Pahana is my father."

CHAPTER TWENTY

Holy *frijoles*. My mouth fell open, too wide for comfort. My vocal cords froze.

"You'll not heed my warning against returning to his prison," the Magician said. "You will need protections to walk that plane. Those, unfortunately, I lack the power to offer you."

Whose prison? Pahana's or Sotuk's? Masaus? All of them? Were they held together?

The Magician placed a quiver on the table next to the empty food platter. The opening of the quiver was barely wider than a bud vase, but the length from top to bottom was nearly three feet. A soft buckskin strap attached to a harder case. Next to the quiver, the Magician left a long bow at least four feet tall, made of some thin, supple wood I didn't recognize.

"Instead, I offer you these gifts. Use them well. You'll know when. These arrows were buried with me; they will return here after one use."

The Magician tilted his head toward the small leather-wrapped bundle on the other side of the quiver. "History is a useful tool. Your friend has all the weapons he needs."

My stomach clenched at the words. "Thank you," I said, but even I heard the frustration and fear in my voice. I *needed* Zeke to speak. To tell me more.

"Do not thank me for the gift, Echo. These aren't given out of generosity. But for you, the cloud goddess would still hover over me, forcing me to her bidding."

Up until a few moments ago, I'd thought Shakola—er—the CG was the worst of my problems. Once again, I understood nothing.

Zeke betrayed my father. Zeke had *lied* to me this whole time, helping me to assuage the guilt weighing on him thanks to his decision to imprison my father. While my heart had ached before, when I thought Zeke played with my emotions with the CG, now the organ blew apart, tattered and useless.

"I appreciate the chance to explore my better nature, and now I shall," the Magician said.

Like I cared. But he was waiting for me to answer him. Zeke was no help, still covering his eyes, still unwilling to look at me. The shame encased him now, pressing ever harder against me as well. I shifted, trying to ease the myriad aches.

"I don't really understand."

"You will, Echo. You've earned these weapons, as a true warrior."

Zeke tensed, and I pulled further into myself.

The Magician shot us an annoyed glance. "You two must work together. As Shakola told Echo, she's set much in place that you must undo if there's a chance to salvage this world."

How was I going to work with Zeke? I shook my head. Not happening. *So not happening.*

"Is Shakola really dead?" I asked. "Did Zeke tell me the truth about that?"

He flinched again. Too god-freaking-bad! My trust was as shattered as my heart.

"Since her magic leaked from her, her death seems most likely," the Magician said. "Raven asked me to give you as much truth as time allowed."

He turned away from us, his eyes distant as he focused on the fire. What did he find so mesmerizing?

Zeke dropped his hands from his eyes, his face even more gaunt than before, his gaze pinned to the Magician's back. The ghost raised his staff, moving the long shaft of wood in a slow, wide arc across the opening. The flames dulled a bit so that we could see several misty figures.

I gasped. The smaller figure was Shakola.

The Magician grasped his staff more tightly and seemed to pull the figures from the fire, using his staff to fling the image onto the tabletop. Unfortunately, I wasn't prepared for this move and yelped, backpedaling to the couch before I realized he wasn't trying to kill me with phantom coals.

My heart slowly fell back into its appropriate cavity as I slid down onto my butt.

Zeke stared at the image the Magician had magnified with his staff. Shakola was indistinct, as if she'd made herself fuzzy because she didn't want to be seen. Zeke's fingers curled into a fist as he glanced between Shakola and the second figure. Not the Magician. But he was big, his aura powerful even in the smoke. A god?

He was large, pale. Paler even than she was, like he had albinism. But his eyes weren't red. They were a deep, electric blue. Next to the god stood a spider woman, six of her spiked arachnid legs drumming the ground. My eyes roved upward to see that the spider's legs fuse to form a furry abdomen littered with gleaming eyes. Her chest sprouted human arms, and a neck that held up a haughty face framed in braids. Her forehead was lined with more numerous dark eyes. All were trained on Shakola; none blinked.

"Who is that?" I asked as I rose from the seat, intending to move closer to the couple. I wanted to see what the goddess held in her left hand.

Zeke pulled me back down next to him, a reflexive gesture, because his gaze remained fixated on the deities. Shock built in my chest when his hand sought mine. I didn't know exactly what he wanted. Was he looking for comfort, trying to ensure I was still here, next to him, or was he comforting me?

"The spider woman is Sussitanako," Zeke said. He turned his face toward me, then toward the Magician, seeking the confirmation I couldn't give. Zeke's fingers trembled in my grip. "Layla's mother and Shakola's too."

"And him?" I asked.

"Pahana," Zeke spat.

"Shakola gave Pahana valuable information years ago," the Magician murmured, looking like he'd just smelled a decomposing corpse. "Not long after your birth, Zeke, which led to the killing of a guardian and the theft of one of Sotuk's tablets. But that wasn't the worst of her treachery."

"There's more?" Zeke rasped.

"Yes, and that is what you must unlock."

"Why?" I asked.

"Because the Fourth has broken free of his prison, only to be rejailed. You and Layla became close, and you and Zeke formed a connection despite even your mother's desire to keep you apart. One you'll need to restrengthen."

The Magician dipped his head toward me. So my mom hadn't wanted me near Zeke because of his part in Sotuk's disappearance? Grief swelled in my chest, like a balloon too large for its confines.

"Do you know why she wanted us apart?" I asked.

"Not because of the prophecy. For that you *must* work together. "'From the broken tablet, the Four of ancient power and bloodline pure, must work as elemental life to repiece that which was broken.'"

"I've heard that bit before. Is that all of it?"

"No," Zeke said.

"What else is there?" I demanded.

"Later," the Magician said. He seemed more transparent now. "Your mother worried most about Zeke's heritage."

Zeke stood quickly, the couch we sat on shooting backward. Just as I'd thought. My mother knew of Zeke's treachery. But why, then, have him protect me? His guilt wasn't a strong enough bond to hold him true to me—to have him actually protect me. None of this made sense. I gripped the arm of the couch, feeling slightly seasick.

"The father who wasn't one," I murmured. "Pahana."

"The history I know best," Zeke said, his voice harsh. "I learned treachery, pain, and lies at his knee."

The Magician eyed Zeke as he shuffled toward the far wall. He kept his back to us.

"Shakola believed it too late to fix the Fourth World. At least to her benefit," the Magician said.

And since there wasn't a Fifth World, we ended when this world did. Lovely.

Zeke raised his eyes to mine; they were full of anguish. "She's the reason we can't close the gates between the worlds."

"Which you said started when the guardian of Sotuk's tablet was killed and the tablet went missing," I said.

"When the Fourth disappeared," Zeke said, spitting a curse.

The Magician nodded, his face grave. "This was her most terrible betrayal.

She set the entire world on its current path. Without the Four, this world's destruction may be impossible to avoid."

Zeke's body snapped taut, like a bow pulled too tightly. Instead of anger shoring me up, giving me strength, disappointment drained me of the tiny bit of energy I still possessed.

"So we go, break out Masau to man the portals between worlds," I said. "Sotuk, too, if we can find him."

"No." The word was emphatic, harsh. "I will *not* involve you in this. Pahana's cruelty is immeasurable, Echo."

"You will need Echo there with you," the Magician said. "With Layla and the Fourth. This is the crux of the prophecy. As well you know."

"I don't want you near him, *tocha*." Zeke's hands came up. I flinched when his palms cupped my cheeks. "He'll hurt you. I saw what he would do to you in that chamber."

"No, you saw what *Shakola* wanted to do to me."

"I did not act when she tricked Masau into the kiva, for I had no strategy," the Magician said. His voice was quiet, a strange juxtaposition to Zeke's near hysterical rant. "But when she approached me, suggesting I kill Echo, I had a chance to do some research."

The Magician leaned oh-so-casually against the table. Like he spoke of the weather and not the loss of my mortal body. "Thanks for not killing me," I said, my voice dry. "I rather like being alive."

"And alive you must stay. Together, as well."

The table disappeared. So did the walls. I sat on the floor. "Is your house collapsing?"

"Ah. No. Not again anyway. It's in ruins. Time and the elements are nearly as bad for my masterpiece as abandonment," the Magician scowled. "With each new day, I must face what my home has become, not what I made it or wish this place still to be."

"Visitors will be here soon, won't they?" Zeke asked.

"Soon. Yes. Know this: Here, I protect the only *sipapu* to Kuskurza. That is why I built my compound here, why I stay here still. To protect the gates to the Third World from those who would misuse it."

That comment was cryptic, as was the long, hard stare the Magician gave Zeke. I turned to look at him, too, but Zeke's lashes shaded his eyes.

When I turned back, the Magician was gone—just a long, thin stream of sunlight where he'd been standing.

CHAPTER TWENTY-ONE

"Echo, you're going to fall down," Honani said. I didn't recall his return.

"I'm already sitting."

"Yes, but you must rest properly. You've been awake for much too long."

"I need to find Layla. When will I see her? And the cat. He's important. Not a demon." Perhaps more. My *abuelita* suggested as much. I needed to see the black mountain cat again.

Honani's chill slid over my skin as his spectral arm slid across my shoulders, waking me up.

"When did you come back?" I mumbled. "Did you find her?"

"Just now." His aura faded to an avocado green. "I could not find your grandmother, Echo."

"But, why? Sacnite said she was gone. So she must come back. I want her back."

Tears stung my eyes but, I blinked them away. I was tired, emotional, but I refused to let the tears go. Not so much because I wanted to be tough anymore—I was too exhausted to fight my emotions, and if I started crying, I might never stop.

Nothing—*nothing*—was as it seemed. Nothing was easy.

"Perhaps she will reappear."

"She went into Kuskurza. She came out of my pendant and spoke with the spirits in the pit. That's the only thing I can think of."

Honani's face slid into solemn lines, his eyes dark pools of sadness. "She did what she thought best."

"When do I get a say in what's best for me?" I cried and tugged at my hair. I needed to regain control, find some way to ground myself in my new reality.

Hoani slid his palms up my arms. If he weren't colder than an industrial freezer, the caress would have been soothing.

"You need some sleep. Layla makes her way toward the *sipapu*. You should rest before she comes."

"I don't want—"

"We both need to rest," Zeke cut in. "Honani, will you direct Layla toward us?"

"Of course. I do better with her cat protector than with Layla. She struggles to see me," Honani said. "Much as you do."

Agitation flitted across Zeke's face. "Thank you, spirit."

He began to walk out of the ruins, but I leaned against a low wall. "You promised me honesty," I reminded. Swallowing, I forced my gaze to his tortured one. "Did you believe in her—the cloud goddess—at the bar?" I asked.

He grasped my hand, and I immediately pulled away. No more touching or kissing or anything until he told me the truth.

"Would you believe me if I said no? That I was testing her? Waiting to see how she'd try to hamstring us?"

I didn't know what to believe. Zeke had stabbed Shakola—unwittingly, sure—to save me. We'd have to talk about that, just as I'd need to discuss the anger and desolation I'd felt since my mother's death. With a rough, anguish-laden sigh, I let Zeke lead me from the bits of ruined wall and foundation—all that was left of the building.

I stumbled, nearly landing on my nose. Zeke righted me, lacing his fingers through mine this time, squeezing my hand with gentle pressure when I tried to extricate myself again. He kept his face forward and continued walking. "Where are we going?" I mumbled.

"To the other side of the ridge," Zeke said. "There are more trees there and a stream. Honani, will you find a good place for us before you leave to help Layla? Echo can't travel far."

My spirit warrior disappeared as we stepped from the outer ring of the ruins.

"I can, too," I said, indignant. I stumbled again. My legs were shaking harder, my feet turned to cement blocks too difficult to lift. "Layla has to be able to find us," I said.

"Honani will make sure of it," Zeke said.

I stopped to watch the sun cast its golden light over the eastern peak. I smiled, thankful for this morning. Zeke's chest expanded, filling with the clean, early morning mountain air.

"You have every right to hate me," he said, his voice soft.

Because I wasn't sure what I was feeling or how to express it, I snuggled deeper in Zeke's hoodie, wishing for more of his warmth. I wouldn't offer him even more of me to gut or punish. Not until he told me why he would betray my father—betray me.

"I should have trusted your instincts from the beginning, *tocha*."

I yawned so wide, my jaw cracked. "True. I know things. What instincts are we talking about, specifically?"

His lips flipped up a little. "You are so tired. We need to work on that stamina."

"My stamina is amazing. I can go forever." He steadied me when I tripped over another rock. "Crap. That hurt."

"You can't see straight." He used his free hand to rub the back of his neck. "I wanted to tell you more. The reasons why I…" He shook his head. "When I started drawing demon attention, Masau decided I should train in various forms of combat. He brought in all kinds of teachers—some more interested in working with a moody teenager than others." The words poured from him faster and faster, as if he'd held them in too long and they couldn't wait to tumble out.

I blinked, trying to fight off the bleariness. Much as I didn't want to talk, I forced myself to engage. "Moody, huh? That's code for troublemaker."

"I'd become angry at the world. For being what I was and for being abandoned by my mother."

"I don't think you were," I murmured. "For what it's worth, I think she loved you. Wanted you. Tried to protect you."

Zeke shook his head.

"You said there was a storm nearby the night your mom left."

Zeke shoved past some low branches, holding them out of the way for me. "Yeah. There were flash floods that night. I nearly drowned before Masau found me up on a rock."

"Your mom didn't abandon you," I said. "CG killed her."

"Who?" Zeke asked.

"Shakola."

Zeke flinched.

I sighed. "You flinch every time I say her name, so I'm calling her CG. You know, for cloud goddess."

Zeke inhaled deep, then even deeper. I squeezed his fingers, trying to ease the shaking there. Unable to stop myself even now, I leaned into him, offering what comfort I could. He wrapped his arm around my shoulder, rested his chin on the top of my head. After a few minutes, he pulled back. Some of my hair caught in his days-old stubble. Our bodies tried to stay connected even though my mind screamed against any further intimacies.

"You're probably right. I think Masau didn't trust her."

"So you remained with Masau?" So much I needed to know. This seemed a relatively safe topic.

Zeke nodded. "Mostly. But I saw Shakola often. Masau seemed to like me even though I was difficult to raise," Zeke said.

I sighed. "You know I toed every line my mom laid down. I worried she'd leave, too, if I misbehaved. Like the dad I never met."

He flinched, but his arm tightened around me. "No one said being a Halfling was easy."

"Good thing. Because growing up not knowing sucked."

"Growing up knowing wasn't much better," Zeke averred.

I gnawed on my lip.

"Why didn't you kiss me in that chamber like I kissed you?" A stupid question, but one that I couldn't let go.

Zeke's eyes darkened, the corners lined with concern. His Adam's apple bobbed. "I thought you saw Jaguar. I assumed he was trying to rape you. You were crying and kept fighting me when I tried to hold you."

I sucked my upper lip into my mouth. "Just so you know, I didn't understand this connection between us. Not until I stepped into that room. And I'm not sure how I feel about us now. You hurt me sometimes without even trying."

He tightened his fingers around mine. "I don't want to. I've never wanted to do anything but to protect you." He blew out a breath. "Masau suggested I take the post as your protector, but I would have even if I didn't garner his approval. I would have because you deserved safety. And because I feel guilty for my part in Sotuk's disappearance."

I released a shaky breath. "Your actions took my father from me, Zeke. That's big. And guilt isn't a strong foundation for a relationship. I need you to like me. Want to be with *me*. Like I do—did—with you." I shook my head, sighed.

Zeke's fist clenched into the fabric of the hoodie at my neck. His eyes darkened to black, obliterating his pupils. I had to look away. "That's—"

"I found a place," Honani said.

"Where is it?" Zeke asked.

Honani pointed behind him. "Just through there. I think it'll work well."

"Thank you," I said.

Zeke helped me navigate the boulders and loose shale. Within ten minutes, we were in the small clearing Honani had found.

"This is perfect," Zeke said. "Good job."

"You shouldn't make Echo so upset," Honani said. "I'm going to check on Layla and her cat." He faded. I sat down on a large rock and leaned my head against a tree.

I studied Zeke, wondering again, with heart-breaking stillness, if I could and should believe him. The longer I stared, the more shame rolled off him, thickening until once again, an oppressive weight held me down. Zeke pulled a thin blanket from his pack. How he'd managed to keep it and hold me up over the abyss amazed me. He scooped up handfuls of last season's dried pine needles and formed a thick wedge on the ground. He flicked the blanket over the top.

"We need to talk," I said. "You have to tell me everything. And I mean every little stinking detail."

The soft, rhythmic beat of wings filled the air. Glancing up, a familiar shape approached.

"Raven," I said.

"We meet again, younglings," the god said.

I turned to face him. I owed Raven much for helping save Layla. Well, if that truly happened.

"She comes," he said before I managed to open my mouth. "Have patience."

Um, no I wasn't going to be patient. I wasn't going to just accept that the gods were on Team Echo and that Zeke was good and that my life—my world—would ever again be safe and just.

Raven tapped the tip of my nose. "Have faith, Echo Ruiz. Is that not what your mother told you?"

My teeth sank into my bottom lip and I waited until my chin no longer trembled.

"She meant that more than anything else she said," Raven crooned.

I wasn't sure how to return to a place of faith. More, I wasn't sure I wanted to.

"You never asked Zeke how old he was when his father gave that command," Raven said.

"Don't." Zeke stepped back, his shame between us a physical barrier I didn't know how to break.

"Or why he would step between the monsters and you. Over and over," Raven whispered, bending closer to my ear.

"She has every right to be angry, to be betrayed," Zeke said.

Raven's whispers grew persistent, and as Zeke's shame continued to wash over me, images of his past flooded my mind. I heard the threat coming from Pahana's snarled lips. Heard the hard crack of a bone breaking, the whimper of a boy.

"Did you not hear him? Pahana broke his legs."

More visions flashed before me, and I saw the fear in Zeke's eyes when he'd faced down the unseen assailant. *I ran away as soon as my legs healed. I don't want to go back.* His mother abandoned him when he was six. Oh, gods. He was young, so very, very young.

"But he lied," I cried. "He lied to me!" I was too tired to try to stem the emotions in my chest. They grew, and I struggled to breathe through the turmoil.

"What's wrong, Echo?" Honani asked.

"She is tired," Raven said. He brushed my hair back from my brow, the gesture disturbing instead of tender. I didn't want the god to touch me. Didn't trust his magic or his reasons for being here. "Sleep, little Halfling, and think on what I've said. I shall return again."

I spun away from him, but my eyes were too heavy to stay open. Another wave of exhaustion hit me harder than before. With it, the emotion grew, like soda shook in a can. I clenched my jaw tight, unwilling to let the tears leak out.

I didn't want Zeke to see how much he'd upset me. He had enough guilt for me to understand his choices hurt him, too. Tears slid from the corners of my eyes, silent and sullied by the words I hadn't said. I hadn't told him about how deep the connection was between us already. How, like Zeke, I'd do anything—*anything*—to keep him alive. That realization, more than the others last night and this morning, scared me the most.

Zeke pulled me to him, saying nothing. From the sadness wafting from him, he was aware of my weeping.

Was Raven really so obvious as to tell me Zeke's history shaped him? Much as mine did me. Duh. My mother's love molded me, gave me courage at times like tonight when I didn't want to go on. I persevered for her, in her memory, refusing to let her vision for a balanced world to die.

Zeke's mother figure, Shakola, was a power-hungry witch. Masau, whom Zeke cared for, had abandoned him in his time of need. And Pahana...*I ran away as soon as I my legs healed. I don't want to go back.*

Right. He'd spoken with a child's fear. A child's need for security. Something Pahana took from him at a tender age.

What did his history make Zeke? How stupid was I to trust him? I kept my eyes shut tight, feigning sleep, too tired to tease apart the intricacies of Zeke's relationship with the gods, let alone my relationship with him.

"Now that she sleeps, listen well, young Lakin," Raven said. His tone was stern. "Sussitanako seeks you. She will avenge Shakola's death. You've brought more trouble upon yourself and Echo. You must leave, and soon. Free Masau. He can help you locate Sotuk. That's your best course of action."

"I didn't mean to kill her," Zeke said. He clutched me tight enough to leave bruises. "And the Magician wanted me to go to Pahana's prison with the rest of the Four."

"You'd risk Echo's life? Sussitanako will kill you on sight. Echo, too. And yet, you'd travel with this woman you claim to care for?"

I shifted closer. I wanted to comfort Zeke, I wanted to open my eyes. I could do neither. The weight of Raven's magic was oppressive, but the place in my head refused to succumb.

"What do you suggest?"

Raven cackled, sounding just like the large black bird. "Oh, Ezekiel. I'm so glad you asked."

This time, sleep slammed its fist into my skull.

CHAPTER TWENTY-TWO

I woke, sweating. I gasped, trying to force the remnants of the nightmare from my mind. Raven. His words, words I couldn't quite remember, rippled across my mind. Chilling me.

I reached for Zeke. The place beside me was empty, cold. Sitting up, I shoved my tangled hair from my face, cringing when strands stuck to my tear-streaked cheeks.

Zeke's pack was gone. The space beside me looked untouched. A couple of pine needles lay on top of the blanket.

I jumped up and looked around, my heart pounding.

"He left about an hour ago."

"Honani." I pressed my palm to my heart, massaging the pain there. "Why didn't you wake me?"

"Zeke wouldn't let me," Honani said, annoyance flaring through his aura, turning it into a mini supernova. I backed away, falling down on the pine needle bed Zeke had made for me. "I pointed out you'd be upset, but he said you wouldn't understand. He made me promise to tell you he cares about you." The spirit crossed his arms over his chest and huffed. "I told him he should tell you himself."

"Thanks for watching out for me while I slept." I cleared my throat. Best I could do now was pretend I didn't hurt as much as I did. "What time is it?"

"Still before noon. He left you the jerky and he said to make sure you saw that."

Honani tipped his head toward the base of a tree. Turning, my gaze landed on the four arrows the Magician had given me last night, nestled in their leather quiver. The long bow rested next to the bundle. Zeke must have brought them with us this morning.

He'd made me a bed and held me while I cried.

He'd saved my life last night, and the day before, and the day before that.

He'd kissed me senseless. He continued to keep secrets. I didn't know what to do, how to push forward.

"Was Raven here?" I asked. I tugged at my heart. I needed that memory to push forward. "I remember him. He forced me to sleep."

"I returned when I felt your magic stir," Honani said. "When I saw Raven, I stayed within the trees. He and Zeke spoke at length before Zeke left. Not with him. The god moved in the other direction." Honani pointed back over the ridge. The way we'd come.

My eyes fell to the small package next to my new weapons. I recoiled. The Magician's gift to Zeke. *"History is important,"* the ghost had said as he looked at Zeke. Then something about honor.

My legs wobbled as I made my way to the parcel. My breath puffed out in gasps as I picked up the small leather bundle. My life splintered around me, all because of this thing that weighed less than a pound.

"Open it."

"I don't think I can."

"He told me you'd say that. He said you must."

"He?"

"Zeke. Surely you know Raven has his own agenda. One you mesh with, otherwise he wouldn't help you."

"Do you know what's in it?"

Honani shook his head. "No. Zeke struggled to hold it and he didn't wish to leave it. I don't understand what was going on inside his head. He seemed preoccupied."

If he'd acted here as he had in the chamber, Honani had every right to be upset. My fingers shook so hard I could barely peel back the soft edges of the leather.

A small piece of clay fell from the wrappings, landing at my feet. I scooped up the pottery in my cold hands. The image etched there wasn't new, but one I'd seen many times in my textbooks.

My stomach plummeted. Not what I expected, but now that I held it, the certainty built in my chest, lodging next to the pain of his disappearance.

"He went back toward the Ridge Ruin," Honani said. Not that I hadn't already figured that out.

"To the *sipapu*. Dammit, Zeke," I whispered. "Why do you think you have to do this alone?" I tried to grasp Zeke's leaving.

I held out the piece of clay, unsurprised by how unsteady my hand was. "He went to find Masau. As Raven suggested."

Honani's aura faded to a sickly puce. "He won't be easy to find. Not if Shakola imprisoned him."

"Shakola doesn't have the power to imprison Masau," I said, meditative. "He's the god of death but also god of the Fourth World."

"Then how?"

I chewed on my lip. "Pahana."

Honani faded further. "Is he really Zeke's father?"

"Zeke thinks so."

Raven's words, the story Zeke told me of Masau finding him in the night, Shakola causing the flash flood that killed his mother. The missing tablet...I didn't believe these were coincidences. Those pieces fit together, formed something larger I couldn't quite make out. Not with so many pieces still missing.

Whatever Zeke lived through in his fear chamber wasn't the first time. *I ran away as soon as I my legs healed. I don't want to go back.*

"How old was Zeke when Pahana broke his legs?" I asked.

"That's not my story to tell," he said.

"Young," I said on a sigh. "He said he was six when his mother went to Masau. Because of the abuse?"

"He planned to answer your questions. Whatever Raven told him spurred him on."

"And you didn't hear any of that conversation?" I asked, incredulous.

"Gods have ways to keep conversations private," Honani responded, both his aura and voice dour. "But Zeke mentioned righting his wrong."

I rolled the piece of clay in my palms. My father or Shakola? Perhaps it was best to let him go.

No! He owed me answers. I turned the piece of clay over. The other side was smooth as if something had been rubbed away.

"Do the spirits like Masau?" I asked.

Honani shrugged. "I see where you're going with this question. Some do, many do not. Their hatred is strong."

The spirits there wouldn't like Zeke, not with his connection to Masau. And Zeke carried magical weapons as dangerous as the demon's, with the ability to destroy a soul. At least I could talk to the spirits he'd pass.

What had Raven told Zeke? My mind emptied of thought. I couldn't remember anything beyond Raven telling Zeke Sussitanako would kill him on sight. What was I missing?

"Masau and Pahana are brothers, are they not?"

"Once, at least," Honani said.

I slipped the piece of clay into my pocket next to the remainder of my mother's necklace. Fitting that they'd sit next to each other—relics from the two most important people in my life. The only one missing from the shrine was Layla.

When would I see her again?

"He said not to allow you to follow. He worried the journey would be too dangerous."

"More so now that he isn't with me."

Honani sighed and his aura flared bright turquoise before fading to a sedate lime. "When do we leave?"

I glanced around at the bright spring sunshine.

I pulled a piece of jerky from the pack tied to the top of my bow.

"After we find Layla. And as soon as I figure out how to shoot this bow."

"You with a bow?" A soft, light voice said from the edge of the trees. "This I've got to see."

"Layla!" I flung myself into her arms, squeezing her. Until this moment, I'd refused to believe the Magician's promise. She clung to me, the two of us shaking in relief and happiness. "I've been so worried," I managed to choke out.

Layla's face was wan, her eyes surrounded by dark circles. Like me, she'd lost weight. But her eyes were bright and alert. Cautious even as her gaze drifted around the clearing.

"How'd you end up here?"

Layla swallowed hard, the long line of her throat working hard. "The cat," she pointed her thumb over her shoulder at the same sleek black cat I'd saved days earlier. His tawny eyes had faded a bit, but were still unnaturally bright, not unlike mine. "He forced me into the *sipapu*. You know how I feel about going underground."

"But you did it," I said.

Her mouth twisted in displeasure. "We came up through the Ridge Ruin and he shoved me this way."

I touched her hair, her shoulder. "I'm glad you're here. You, too," I said to the cat.

He bowed his head. Honani snorted out something that sounded like, "Wonderful."

"Why did he know to bring me here?" Layla asked. Her posture remained stiff, as if she anticipated another attack.

"We met with the Magician after Zeke killed Shakola. He said he'd sent spirits down to guide you."

"She's really dead?" Layla asked, surprise lacing her tone. At my nod, she smiled. "No loss there. Can't say I'm going to miss that relative. But I am surprised Zeke managed to do it."

"The Magician promised to abide by her promise for a boon." I hurried on, not wanting to explain Zeke hadn't meant to kill Shakola. "I wanted to rescue you. And here you are."

I hugged her again, hard.

"It's really good to see you, E." Layla's voice was choked. "I missed you. Gods, I did. I've been worried since I sent your *coyopa* back."

"I worried about you, too. But you did it. You survived."

She blinked her eyes, opening them wider than usual. I gripped her hand, despairing at what more my friend had gone through. Her eyes never rested, even as they began to slide shut. "I'm tired."

I gestured toward the thin blanket covering the needles. "Rest. Honani and

I will watch over you. I need to practice with this thing." I hefted the bow, careful to keep the arrows in the quiver. The Magician had said I got one shot with those.

The cat demon laid down next to Layla, his head on the edge of the pallet. She rested her hand on his head. Within moments, they were both asleep.

"Why didn't you tell her about Zeke?" Honani asked. "Or your belief that the cat is more than a demon? More important to all of you?"

"I will. Once she wakes up. She's dealt with enough right now."

"And you didn't want to tell her you must go back down into the *sipapu*."

I faced my ghost warrior, my jaw set with determination. "I need Zeke to fulfill the prophecy. He's the only one of us who knows the whole of it."

Honani's aura blazed teal. "I agree that you need Zeke."

"So you'll come?" I asked.

He caught the tremor in my voice. Honani didn't touch me often. Now, he raised his hand and cupped the back of my neck. I shivered as his chill settled into my skin. "For you, Echo María Ruiz, Spirit Seducer and Halfling, I would lose my very soul."

I prayed fervently whatever we faced wouldn't require that.

ACKNOWLEDGMENTS

First and always, thank you to my family, especially Chris, for your support and love. Hugs, kisses, and yes, I'll make you scones again soon.

To my fellow LERA members, you keep me motivated, looking for light even in the darkest tunnels. Thank you.

Shane, our calls keep me focused on the end goal. You've made me reconsider what telling a story—my stories—mean to me. Thank you for that. And thank you for the bimonthly levity. I love talking to you!

Jeffe, well, there's lots I could say. Some I shouldn't. So I'll keep it succinct: You are a wonderful friend and one hell of a writer. I'm blessed to have you in my life.

Nancy, I so appreciate your continued ability to call me out when my descriptions are muddled. Thank you for your hard work and editing skills.

Nicole, as I've told you before, I love working with you. You make me try harder—with a smile. Thank you.

Clarissa, this cover, like the others, is beautiful. You're a kick-ass designer, and I'm so grateful to work with you.

To my readers, y'all are the best. Truly. Writing for myself is loads of fun. Writing stories you enjoy is so much better. Thank you.

ABOUT THE AUTHOR

With a degree in international marketing and a varied career path as a content manager for a web firm, marketing director for a high-profile sports agency and a two-year stint with a renowned literary agency, Alexa Padgett has returned to her first love: writing fiction.

Alexa spent a good part of her youth traveling. From Budapest to Belize, Calgary to Coober Pedy, Alexa soaked in the myriad smells, sounds, and feels of these gorgeous places, wishing she could live in them all—at least for a while. And she does in her books.

She lives in New Mexico with her husband, children, and ginormous, piano-hating Anatolian Shepherd, Mozart. When not writing, schlepping, or volunteering, she can be found in her tiny kitchen, channeling her inner Barefoot Contessa.

Read on for a sneak peek of THE CURSE OF KURSKURZA,
Book Three in the Echo Series

CHAPTER ONE

The mountain cat lay with eerie stillness next to Layla, its aura dark and damaged. His sides expanded enough for the next breath, imperceptible against his obsidian coat. Even asleep, pain filtered not only from the animal's joints but from his soul. The longer I prodded at the animal's mind, trying to keep my touch light enough not to wake the cat, the more human his thoughts and emotions flowed. It was then that I realized: his eyes were human. Even when I first saw him, I'd known there was more to this being than his dark, dangerous demon aura that spliced with tiny breaks of bright gold.

I sucked in a breath, dropping my new bow to the ground as I pressed further, trying to get a handle on his emotions, to read his desires. Desire for Layla to love him.

His eyes, brighter than new gold, popped open, and he snarled, lunging toward me. Pulling back, he managed not to rip into the skin at my throat with his long, pearly teeth.

"Sorry!" I fell back, landing hard on my hands. "Do you understand what I'm trying to do? You're not a demon."

The cat lowered onto his sleek black paws but his eyes never left mine. He flashed an image of a boy—five, six, maybe—with dark hair and tawny eyes approaching a huge being. I gasped. A god. This boy approached a god. Unfortunately, I couldn't sense his emotions in that flash. Was it a memory? The cat's ear twitched, his golden gaze still pinning me to his mind. Another memory boiled up, slowly coalescing.

"What are you doing, Echo?" Layla asked.

She sat up from the pallet, confusion filling her bright silver eyes. She *would* wake up right at that moment as I sprawled across the ground, a ridiculous heap of magical potential.

"You okay?" I asked.

"Better than you," Layla said. Her cheeks were gaunt, covered in grime. Small nicks covered her neck, jaw, hands, and arms. Teeth marks. Her matted hair faded from its former golden cap to a grayish-blond.

"You look terrible," I grumbled.

"Yeah, well, you're almost dead based on your appearance."

"Being almost dead comes with the territory."

Layla rolled her eyes. "Where's Zeke?"

Embarrassment lashed through me, nearly drowning out the pain of his defection. Sneaking off in the midmorning sun was still sneaking off. And he'd promised me more of an explanation—of his past, his role in my father's disappearance. "He left this morning," I said. "Before you showed up." Right after admitting Pahana was his father. A god who broke his legs as a child. A god who worked to imprison creator god Sotuk—my father.

Whoever said relationships were hard work was an *idiota*. Relationships sucked balls, and if I wasn't so damn compelled by my feelings for Zeke I'd leave him to rot in Kuskurza for being a lying, cheating ass. Who saved my life hundreds of times this week. Who told me I was the only woman he'd ever wanted. Who killed his friend, the cloud goddess Shakola, to save my life.

Still, he was a lying, cheating ass. And I'd stay mad at him long enough to tell him so. Again.

"Hmm." Layla's stomach rumbled louder than a jet engine. She gripped her T-shirt with her left hand, a grimace crossing her face. "Tell me why in a minute. Do you have anything to eat?"

"Some jerky."

"Where?"

"In my pack."

Layla dove at the bag, her fingers clawing at the plastic wrapper surrounding the dried meat. She moaned as she bit into the strip. "So good." She bit off another large piece, her jaw working hard to chew up the desiccated meat. The cat nuzzled her hand. Layla offered him a piece, and he purred his pleasure. Layla's free hand stayed on his head, just above his eyes, which he closed, contentment mixing with the constant pain.

"Do you have any of that salve?" I asked.

Leaning on her hip and oversetting the cat, Layla pulled a small stainless steel container from her pocket and shoved it in my hand. The cat huffed before standing, shaking his thick black pelt as though readjusting all two-hundred-plus pounds of his body. He lay back down as I dabbed the cream onto her neck while she ate. I recapped the container, handing it back to Layla. When I held out my hand, she grudgingly relinquished a piece of jerky.

Layla shoved the last bite into her mouth and stood. She leaned her shoulder against the six-inch-thick wood shaft that stood a foot taller than she. She slung my pack over her shoulder. "Thank the gods I found you. I'm near starvation."

"We'll send Honani for some more supplies before we head back over the ridge."

Honani scowled, and I raised my eyebrows. Sure, he didn't want to leave me with the huge, black mountain cat. I got that. But eating was necessary—at least for Layla's and my continued survival. Our stare-off broke when Layla asked, "Where'd you get the bow and arrows?"

"The Magician gave them to me," I said.

"You had to fight your way to the Magician?" Layla gasped. "The challenges were designed to break a person's soul."

"Yeah. I know." The shuddered ripped through me as I recalled the chamber with Shakola, holding Layla's head by her beautiful blond hair, staring into one set of dead eyes then to another. "The Magician's a cool dude."

Layla shook her head. "Don't talk in slang. You can't pull it off."

"Honani, would you please find us some supplies?" I asked. I handed him a wad of bills. "Easy food to carry with us. And water. Lots of water."

"You expect me to go into a store during prime shopping hours and purchase items, like through a checkout?"

"No need to take that tone, *fantasmo*. You not up to the task just because you're a ghost?"

Honani snorted, his aura flaming bright teal. "Of course I can do this. Just making sure you're cool with freaking out all the people in the store."

"He's right, E. Not being able to see him could cause a mass panic."

I sucked on my bottom lip. Honani continued to smirk at me, but I didn't care.

"When Shakola died, did you feel it?" I asked.

Honani nodded. "The Magician and I commented on the magic rippling from the room. It was like . . . a thick wave rolling over us."

"Right," I said. "And I was the closest one. When her magic rolled over me, it did something."

Layla touched my arm. "She hurt you, E? How?"

"More like woke something up from my mother's magic—the magic she gave me when she died. Not the ability to feel emotions but to . . . for lack of a better phrase . . . project my thoughts onto others."

"Like she did when she insinuated you into the Ruiz family," Layla said, her voice filled with awe.

I swallowed down the grief and resentment that seemed married to thoughts of my mother. She should have told me about my heritage—she should have helped me learn how to fight the demons and gods who wanted me dead. "Probably," I croaked.

Honani's face twisted into a grimace, and both he and Layla offered silent sympathy, but I ignored their emotions and chose to focus on my magic center. Narrowing my eyes, I imagined what I wanted. Honani squawked, unprepared for the hot slice of energy slithering down from the top of his head to his feet.

"Nice," Layla laughed. "Digging the leather pants."

Honani tugged at the tight black pants as he frowned, trying to make out the logo on his white baseball shirt. He shoved up the blue sleeves. "Def Leppard? They were popular when I died."

"Your favorite band," I smirked. "That's why you got the shirt. Can't hide your deepest desires from me." I blew him a kiss. "You're welcome. You'll be as corporeal as you need to be. For a few hours, I think." I rubbed my thumb over my lip. "I hope," I sighed. "You wanting to be seen by people will probably help. Remember, it's just a mirage, an image I'm projecting."

"Got it. Thanks, Echo. This is so cool." Honani's aura flared again when the black cat came over to sniff him.

The cat's long, sharp teeth made a small appearance—a smile?—before he settled onto his haunches, wrapping his three-foot-long tail around his front feet.

"Glad I amuse you, kitty," Honani said.

I shoved the money into Honani's hand. "Meet you back here in an hour. 'Kay?"

He saluted me with a jaunty tug at his dark shoulder-length hair before he disappeared into the forest.

I turned back to face the cat, staring into his eyes. "Now to do something about you while we wait."

"What do you mean?" Layla asked. "He's been helpful."

"I'm not going to hurt him, Layla. I want to help him. You know that, right?"

The cat's lips twitched back, a deep growl rumbling through his body. Layla petted his head and he pressed into her hand, his eyes shutting for a brief moment before flashing back open to meet mine.

The image he delivered was brief but the pain took my breath away. Pahana's magic pummeled him, forcing him into the body of the dead demon-cat. Pahana lifting him from the ground, ignoring his screams, the thrashing fingers as they became claws, slamming his cat-body to Kuskurza, where he'd lived for many years. Time didn't flow the same for demons, and he'd lost the ability to mark days, busy destroying demons rather than being destroyed. Each day, sides heaving from the exertion of the battles, body aching from the wounds, and bruises incurred caused another shred in his soul.

"That was the point. To hide you. Destroy your humanity." My throat tightened and my chest ached for the child he'd been, the scarred man he'd become. He hissed, his midnight fur ridging across his back in a ripple before my hand made contact with his muzzle.

"I won't touch you," I said, yanking my hand back. "I didn't mean…I'm sorry." My breath broke. "I'm so sorry you had to deal with that."

"What are you talking about?" Layla was indignant, stepping back between the cat and me.

"The cat speaks to me. Rather, shows me images."

Her brow furrowed. "Why to you? You don't even know each other."

"I can communicate with all spirits."

"But he's not a spirit," Layla said. "He's a cat."

Demon possession never made my study list. If I'd known I was *the* spirit seducer, all-things-demons would have been number one (followed by how to make people tell me their deepest darkest secrets). But all my mom told me about my background was that my dad left years ago not long after my birth—not because he wanted to but because he had to—and that I inherited her strawberry allergy.

Mom owed me a lot of answers. Too bad she was dead and couldn't give them. I kept my eyes on the cat's. His shoulders flinched but his eyes remained steady, somewhere between angry, resentful, and pleading.

"He's more than that," I said. "But his body is that of a demon."

Layla yanked her hand from his fur as she gasped. Horror wafted from her. I didn't need to feel her emotions or even see her eyes to know she was reliving the night that Jaguar—a Kachina that was part man but created with the head of a demon—raped her.

This black cat lowered his head, his shoulders falling forward in defeat. "But…But…" She stumbled back a step, then another. Her eyes were too wide and her breathing choppy. "But…"

"He's not a Kachina. He's not even a demon. He's in a demon body. He's proven he won't hurt you," I snapped. The cat hunched further, turning his head away from her. Could Layla's rejection hurt him? "He hasn't hurt me either, though it's programmed into his demon DNA to do so."

She sucked in a broken gasp and shook her head once more. "No. No no no."

I stepped up to her and gripped her biceps. With one shake, she quit repeating the word. "He's not Jaguar, Layla. He's as much a victim as you. From what he's been able to show me, Pahana forced him into the demon when he was quite young." Holding her gaze, I waited for her pupils to contract back to normal size.

Her breathing slowed. "Can you...can you fix him?" Her voice was raspy, painful.

"First of all he doesn't need to be *fixed*. He needs to be rescued." I dropped her arms and tugged at the ends of my hair.

She twisted her hands into her dirty T-shirt. "So he's the Fourth?"

"Best guess."

We both focused on the cat; his paws quivered, and his claws dug deep into the soil.

"So that's how he disappeared," Layla murmured. "That's why I felt him near-by—when I called you. Remember? I said I hadn't seen the Fourth, just felt him. Fool I was, I never considered the man I was looking for was a demon."

"He's more than a demon, Layla."

"You said Pahana did this?"

I pulled her hand from my arm, grimacing at the sharpness of her nails. "That's what he showed me. I don't know how to extract a human from a demon, Layla. They've been together a long time. Close to twenty years."

Layla's emotions wavered from anxious to sympathetic. "Can't you dissolve the demon?"

"How? They're linked. He has to want to come out. I think." I rubbed my temple. "And there has to be enough of him separate from the demon to be extracted."

The cat's head rose and he tilted it, studying me. With tentative steps, he positioned himself in front of me. All the while, he kept those golden eyes trained on me as he lowered himself to the ground. Layla stumbled back, her fear overtaking the sympathy. Slowly, each of his muscles and joints protesting his mind's will, he turned over, exposing his belly. But more important, he trusted me with his heart.

Layla's breath hissed out but she didn't return to my side. The cat's eyes filled with sadness. I dropped to my knees, uncaring as the rocks dug into my jeans and cut my skin below. Slowly, even more cautiously than before, I reached out. My hand shook but I kept moving forward. The cat's eyes squeezed shut and his jaw locked. His breathing huffed out in harsh pants. His claws shot from his paws but he made no move to lift his arm and swipe me. The pain radiating from his body intensified.

I placed my hand on his ribs, right over his heart. The man inside huddled deep in the beast, ragged, unkempt, desperate for release.

"Do you remember your name?" I asked.

The pain wafting off the cat made him groan and pant. Even more slowly than the others, a memory floated forward. Distorted, too hazy to be anything less than his earliest consciousness.

"Oh," I whispered, my heart stuttering. "Your mother."

She was beautiful. Bright, shiny as a new day. Her eyes were a rich indigo blue, and her hair glinted with ginger, copper, and even rose-gold. Pink lips pulled back in a bright smile, illuminating a heart-shaped face. She reached down, brushed light brown hair from his lashes. "I'll always love you, Zerah."

"Zerah?" I whispered. "That's your name?"

The cat dipped his head, chuffing into the dirt. I folded my hands into my lap and let his emotions wash over me. His whiskers twitched as the memory slid back into the deep bank of his mind, behind the more recent violence and death Zerah lived through. Wind rustled through the pine needles.

"Not unlike your rape, Layla," I murmured. She made a garbled, pained sound.

"What do you mean?" She stepped forward once. The next footfall was as tentative. I didn't look away, even as she moved to the cat's other side. In fits and starts, she managed to again lay her hand on his head above his ear. The cat sighed, his breathing easing a little.

He needed her close. Her touch soothed the worst of his insecurities. Not unlike my desire for Zeke. Interesting.

"He's been forced to do unimaginable things living in Kuskurza with the demons," I murmured. "Those acts were meant to break his spirit, destroy his humanity. To let the demon take over."

I met her shocked gaze. Her eyes flared an even brighter silver. She swallowed hard and dipped her head in a small nod. This wasn't something to sugarcoat or a reality I could even empathize with, not completely. After another deep, cleansing breath, she dipped her head and placed her other hand on the cat's muzzle. He whimpered. The deep thud of his heart escalating.

"Find a way to get him out," Layla breathed. Her eyes hardened to near gunmetal.

Damned if I knew how. I sucked in a breath, steadying the white-hot center in my head. I sliced at the bonds holding the man within the demon—the links deep in their joint mind—with delicate strokes. The cat whimpered and I paused. "Hurt?"

He opened his eyes and the cloudiness there answered the question.

"Now, E." Layla's voice was clipped, harsh. Her fingers sank deep into the fur around his throat, soothing.

I gripped my pendant, eyes focused deep on the cat's aura. Small fissures broke through, a deep golden hue reminiscent of dawn. I pressed harder at the black, trying to crack its shell. The cat's claws slid out and his head thrashed. Sweat streamed down my back. I broke off, both of us panting.

"I don't know how," I wheezed. "Not without causing too much damage."

The cat rolled over, displacing both Layla and me as he surged to his feet. His head dropped low between his shoulders, and I sensed his need to kill. Destroy.

Before I could scamper back, we were surrounded by five demons. They'd slid from the shadows, probably drawn by my use of magic. Stupid to use it here—anywhere, really. This round of death-beasts was a cross between an emu and a tiger. Their feathered heads featured large, dark eyes and sharp beaks; their front feet had three long claws. Large wings spread from the backs, which turned to short, striped fur at their muscular rumps. The one in front of me flicked its tail in a sinuous beat. Probably telling its friend how to maul me. The emu-tiger opened its beak and squawked.

I giggled. I couldn't help it. The creature wasn't scary, not when making that weird breathy noise that sounded more like a wounded goose. Another one of the beasts honk-wheezed, and I guffawed.

"Get it together, E!" Layla scolded.

"But they're so ridiculous," I managed to gasp, wiping tears from my eyes.

The front demon lunged at Layla, raising its long front leg, planning to slash her with those vicious claws, but Layla sidestepped. Another one lunged, grazing my cheek.

The cat's growl was the only indication of his attack. In a flurry of black, he whipped around us, the first bird-tiger dissolving under his teeth and claws.

"If you go home now, I won't kill you," I said to the demon closest to me. The beast tilted its long neck so that I stared directly into its black bird eye. So dark. I fell forward, slipping down, way down, deep into the Tokpella abyss.

Layla grabbed my waist, pulling me backward, screaming at me to look away. I'd figured that out already, but I couldn't rip my gaze from his.

"Drop your eyes, Echo! Dammit, drop your eyes now!" Layla yelled directly into my ear.

The volume made me flinch, and my eyes drifted away enough for my body to settle back into itself just as the beast roared. This time the demon sounded like a tiger, a really angry one. Its friends answered in kind.

No, they weren't funny.

One of the beasts launched itself toward Lalya, that beak opening wider than a python's mouth. Layla rammed her staff into its mouth and the beast paused, blinking. The cat launched itself at the demon and it, too, disintegrated into a pile of dust.

The three remaining monsters honked and growled. Dizzy and unprepared, my mind still wasn't fully inside my head, but I sought my center and drew out large whips of water.

The water was a natural extension of my hands. Just days ago, I'd feared the substance, nearly drowned in it. My smile was feral as I wrapped the lashes around one of the beasts with an easy flick of my wrist, watching with a morbid fascination as the water-whip rippled and tightened around the long, feathered neck. My mother's death destroyed the magical charms she'd forced on me. One was fear of water. But the Element was me and I was the

Element. With a sharp tug, the liquid chain tightened, and the beast shriveled before my eyes.

Layla palmed a stone, which shown with cold, glittery light. As one of the demons snapped its beak, she slammed the stone onto its head, and the thing shattered into billions of demon particles.

The last beast feinted with its beak and front claws, trying to find an opening with the cat. The cat raked its claws around the demon just behind its wing, where it's tiger pelt met the feathers, as I whipped my watery ropes free from the first beast and lashed them, whip-style onto the last demon. The final beast yowled in anguish as it dissolved back into the dirt.

I slid to the ground, breathing hard as I shook from the adrenaline dump.

"Unhinged jaws. That was a pretty cool trick. I want to start a trophy collection of badass demons I've killed," I said. I sucked in a huge lungful of air, trying to calm my racing heart.

Layla made a disgusted sound while the cat prowled around us, growling long and low. "They came out of nowhere," she said.

"More will come. Until we can close the *sipapus*." I rested my palms on my knees, lightheaded from my raging heart. "There will be more. Soon."

THE SPIRIT SEDUCER, Book One in the Echo Series

A god undone by prophecy. A warrior strong as the earth. And the woman who will decide their fate...

The dream comes every night: A warrior clad in leather and wielding a spear, fighting off demons with the heads of jackrabbits and pumas. Defending her.

Echo Ruiz knows it's ridiculous. There's no one in Santa Fe less likely to need defending. Thanks to the migraines, she's confined to her mother's house. Her Native American Studies classes are online, and she hasn't made a new friend in a decade.

Until her twenty-first birthday party, when trickster Coyote himself shows up. An hour later, Echo is on the run from the power-hungry god. Her headaches are gone. Her mother is a hostage, and she's been thrust into a mirror-world of deadly loveliness to fight or die.

Her dream warrior? He's as real as the sweat on her skin. His name is Zeke, and he remembers a lot more about Echo than she does about him. So does her best friend, Layla, who has secrets Echo's never guessed.

But if Echo wants to defeat Coyote—if she wants to survive—she'll have to discover the way herself. Because that's one ending the legends have never told...

SWEET SOLACE, Book One in The Seattle Sound Series

She Knew Him When

When they first met, she was far too young—seventeen, and already in love with the man who would break her heart. Asher Smith was an up-and-coming songwriter, but he knew better than to show his fascination. He wrote a song for Dahlia. And then he moved on. His whiskey-rough voice made him a star, even as fame extracted its price.

He Never Forgot Her

When she sees Asher next, Dahlia Dorsey is the widowed mother of a teen-ager, a reclusive writer. She's given up on happy endings—she can't even script them for her characters. But a moonlit beach and the touch of an old friend turn loose her pain and her desires, whether she's ready or not.

They're Risking It All

Dahlia's career is on the rocks. Asher's family is falling apart. Neither can chase a passing attraction. But for two souls wounded worse than they can admit, the connection between them is a balm too precious to refuse—and a thrill too exhilarating to resist...

BETWEEN BREATHS, Book Two in The Seattle Sound Series

Grief Brought Them Together

A hospice center is no place to fall in lust. But with his world cracking during his estranged mother's last days, Hayden Crewe needs something sweet to focus on. It doesn't matter that he's the backbone of Australia's hottest international rock group—here, watching his mother die, he's more alone than ever. So when he meets long-legged, clear-minded Briar Moore, he suddenly knows exactly what will fill the hole inside.

Fortune Will Drag Them Apart

Briar has just escaped a job and relationship that nearly crushed her. Crawling out of the wreckage of her previous life, she's done playing it safe. Sexy, vibrant Hayden is what she wants, and Briar is going to take him. For as long as she can…

Out of Heartbreak Comes Hope

With their time short and the ghosts of their pasts haunting every moment, Briar and Hayden know they've fallen too deep. While those few, intense days changed them both forever, everyone knows a connection this intense should burn out as fast as it ignited…